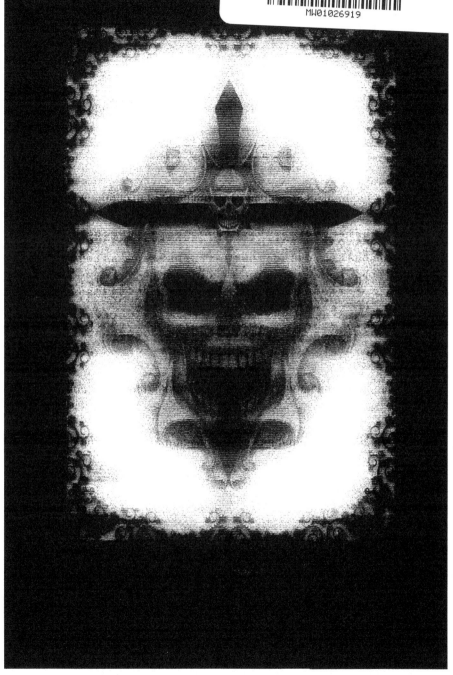

# OPAQUE MIRRORS

courtney lane

Opaque Mirrors

ISBN-13: 978-1530900701
ISBN-10: 1530900700

Cover Artist: Courtney Lane
Skull Illustration: Jiewsurreal, via Shutterstock
Edited by: K. Swiss and Silla Webb

# WARNING

This work of fiction contains themes that many may find offensive. If you are not a fan of erotic, dark, twisted, dimensional love stories, this story may not appeal to you. It also contains mental manipulation, sadomasochism, murder, and extreme sexual violence.

Please note that this book is a work of fiction and is only meant for entertainment purposes. It is not meant to be a manual for relationships, condone the activities portrayed, nor serve as inspirational literature for any of the topics listed here, or contained within.

Thank you for reading.

# DEDICATION

*Dedicated to everyone who has been judged for what they like, what they read, what they watch, and what they do.*

# PROLOGUE

THE SWISH OF MY thigh-highs and the quiet whirl of my overcoat followed my steps as I made my way to the hotel suite. The gorgeous Rocco decor soothed me. Cream carpet with brocade designs lined my steps; walls adorned in gold textured wallpaper with matching fixtures greeted my view.

My heart thumped out of rhythm with the steady pace of my stride, beating rapidly to an erratic rhythm. A sense of foreboding implanted itself inside my core. The signals of pending danger resounded.

I ignored everything that plagued me and held a tighter grasp on my mother's words: "Just one more time, Whit. I promise. It'll be like all the other times. No sex. Take his money, do your thing, and leave."

The tale of how my mother became my employer began in a strange way— much stranger than the fact that my mother was my madame. Many of the country's top CEOs had licked my mother's stiletto heel while supplicating to her and begging for her approval by way of pain. On one fated day, my mother came down with the flu. She asked—told—me to tend to one of her appointments for her. To most people who led a life similar to what I watched on television, this would've been unusual, possibly disgusting. Normalcy has always been an elusive entity to me, and I'd never bared witness to what a normal family did. Having grown up with a retired porn-star for a mother, stage name Mistress Sin, who treated sex and pain like a trading commodity since before I was born, I had no reference for normal.

Sex was apparent and often presented due in part to my mother's associations. I tended to avoid it or disconnect from it completely in the rare event I shared my bed with someone else. I fumbled through my very first client. Somehow, it mattered little to the man. The following month, he requested a date with me. Eventually, I learned to become comfortable in what was asked of me; it was never sex, and it was never what my mother did with the men she saw as clients. For a short time, my newly adopted kink was liquid gold, filling a cup I didn't know was empty.

The dates became second nature, and eventually, bordered on predictable and boring. Maybe it was my growing envy over my client's experiences and not my boredom. I supposed it would be something I'd ponder until I found the answer.

This appointment fell out of the norm from the very beginning. The client had meticulous directions for my appearance: a menswear-inspired black on black skirt suit, a leather tie, hair tied in a bun, and red lipstick had to be worn.

The hotel and the time of day were also listed in his directions. The time impeded on my sleep cycle, falling at three o'clock in the morning.

I'd never met a client as particular as he was, and the ones who slightly matched him were unusually difficult. They haggled for sex or more than I would provide. Their requests were met with a less gentle adventure during the time I fulfilled their fetish fantasies. It was intimate in its own way. It was wrong but felt right. After suppressing myself for a long time, and indulging my clients, I experienced an indescribable freedom. Somehow, I had begun to leisurely retreat back into my prison; the instant gratification had eluded me.

I knocked on the door with two short hard knocks. Silence filled the halls so fiercely when I heard the lock unhinge, I startled.

A man greeted me on the other side of the newly opened door. The catch in my throat, closing the soft inner walls, made it impossible to speak momentarily. "Nick?" I asked, clearing away the catch in my throat.

His grin widened, deep dimples created indentations in his gorgeous and flawless tanned skin. "Sumi?" He raised a brow over his dark—almost black—brown eyes with question over the name I chose to use with clients. In a strange sense of irony, the name was ill-fitted.

There was something contradictory in Nick's gaze. It was as though he had the ability to be a cold and calculating killer, or the capability to be the most charming man I had ever met. Underneath the surface rested a coded emotion. Whatever it could've been, it completely disarmed me.

I darted out my hand to shake his. Thinking better of it, I played off the act by reaching up to rub the back of my neck.

A black blur down the hall caught my eye. When I turned my head to discern what it was, it disappeared.

I strolled inside the room, brushing past him. My shoulder grazed against his tall and fit form. White furnishings and gold accent pieces added to the lushness of the suite.

"Would you like a drink?" His stride led him toward the wet bar in the corner of the living area.

Shaking my head to decline his offer, I unbuttoned my suit jacket.

He held up his hand to halt me. "Not yet."

My hands froze, pinching the single button of my jacket. "The more we talk, the less time we'll have for what you really want. Do you want what you paid for or not?"

"The money doesn't mean shit." Appearing offended, his charm made way for a stony expression.

Turning from the wet bar, he rounded the coffee table wedged between the loveseat and the flat screen mounted on the wall. He gestured toward the metal case atop the dark wood table and settled into the couch.

I freed a breath of annoyance and marched toward the table. Unhinging the latch, I opened the case and turned it toward me. He had brought far too much cash. I could only assume he wanted more than an hour of my time. "My rate is one thousand per hour, and I don't do weekends away."

A dramatic slant of his head failed to move a strand of his dark hair, molded back in a pristine fashion. The track lighting overhead shimmered across the glossy strands and doused him in an attractive glow. "I only want the night, *Sumi*." My name whirled around his tongue like a foreign language. When my dark brown eyes latched onto his even darker brown hues, I caught on to his knowledge of my obvious fake name.

"I know it's odd for me to go by a name like that. My mother was obsessed with Japan when one of her clients—friends—took her there for a month. There's a reason I picked that name, but I can't share it with you."

"You mistake me." He pinched his cufflinks and removed them from his shirt. Working methodically, he pulled the tails of his dress shirt from underneath his pants and unbuttoned it. His posture remained rod straight as he planted his feet on the dark wood floor. The starkly white material of his shirt separated across his chest, revealing the flesh underneath. From the neck down, he was covered in a daunting and intricate skull tattoo, which extended from his shoulder blades down to a place hidden by his pants. When he slid his shirt from his body, allowing it to pool to the floor, I gasped.

There was beauty in the darkness swirling around the theme of his tattoos covering every inch in his skin. Illustrations symbolizing death and destruction rang familiar for a reason I didn't want to reveal.

"Do you recognize these?" He extended his defined arms, tensing the muscles; the illustrations danced across his skin.

"I don't recognize them." My denial was as fast as my urge to escape.

He rushed past me and blocked my path to the door. His posture curved, turning unassuming. "I have no ill intentions toward you. If it'll make you feel better, you can tie me to the bed."

I never saw his face or heard his true voice in his many movies. His features were obscured by a part of his uniform, and his voice was always modulated. I would never have known who stood before me if it hadn't been for the tattoos.

The man I watched degrade, demean, violate, and stage the beating deaths of other men had somehow found his most enthusiastic fan.

"Tying you to the bed would make your erotic asphyxiation fantasy pretty hard to accomplish." Inhaling to steady my panting breaths, I reminded him of my rules, "I won't touch you. The only thing I'll touch is the belt around your neck."

"I'm not much for rules, and I know you aren't, either."

To stave off my trembling hands, I crossed them in front of my chest and hid them underneath my arms. The last thing I wanted to reveal was how much he had shaken me. "You don't know me at all."

"Let's not play *that* game, Whitney."

The unshared knowledge he held threatened parts of me that were left vulnerable. I circled around him in an attempt to leave. Brawny hands gripped my shoulders and secured me against the wall.

"Let me go, or I'll hurt you." The cutting words passed through my teeth.

Showing no signs of backing down, he lurched forward, pressing his hard and towering frame against mine. With prickling light movements, his fingertips glided down, finding their way to my wrists, encaging them in his grip.

"You can't keep me here. After I receive the money, I'm supposed to send a text to man waiting in the lobby. If that doesn't happen, he will come upstairs and give you a very bad day." Courage, courtesy of my mother providing me with a bodyguard at all times, carried me through.

"The money is yours. All of it if you do what I ask of you." He cast a passing glance to the case full of an obscene amount of money. "Stay. Let me tell you exactly what I want from you."

"Well…" I yanked my wrists out of his hold and left them to hang limply at my sides. "Get on with it."

"I want you to make it stop, Whitney—"

"Stop calling me that. To you, I am *Sumi.*"

The tension in his face deepened the hard lines in his features. The dark mass moving over his eyes sent a ghost sensation through me. He wanted to hurt me. A visible battle was waged, and he intercepted his unclear compulsions to harm me.

I couldn't make sense of why he would hold back when I knew his secrets.

My small tinges of disappointment were also beyond my comprehension.

"I want you to tie me to the bed, fuck me, and when I come, I want you to hold the belt and never let go. If you're worried about a murder implication, there's no need. I have precautions in place to make sure I'm found. My death will be deemed an accident."

My ample lips parted, desperate for more air. My mask, holding steadily in place, prevented him from bearing witness to the torrential thoughts brewing inside me. "What if I don't want to do this? What if I don't believe the fallout won't affect me?"

Soft fingertips brushed against my lips. His gaze was trained to my mouth as he dipped his front teeth into his own. "I have no plans to make you pay in the after for my death."

"Why?"

"Why you? Or why do I want this?"

"Both...I guess."

"I have a poisonous compulsion." He receded, taking a few steps away from me. "I think you can tell from the ink on my skin, can't you? It tells my story. I can't stop. I won't stop hurting, killing, and violating. I want...silence."

My suddenly parched and slightly obstructed throat made swallowing impossible. "But...none of it was real. You didn't hurt anyone." My voice was a whisper, quaked by abject fear toward his blatant and emotionless admission.

A dour smile presented itself along with a halfhearted laugh. "You're inviting the monster who wants to defile you. Don't wake him. Make the right choice. Whether or not you decide if you can do this, I won't allow you to leave this room if there's still life in my body. It's either your life or my death."

Leaning forward, he brushed his lips against my mouth. "I'll make what I know to be your fantasy reality if you don't kill me. We'll make our own movie, without the cameras. The pain I elicit from every piece of your flesh will be genuine. The blood I evoke from your body will be real. Your death will be real." The scent of his cologne lingered on my senses as did his firm and warm touch. "Silence me. Stop me, and you'll never have to resort to doing this to pay your bills again."

Words forming complete and coherent sentences eluded me. The fire pit in my belly, threatening to burn me to dark embers from the inside out, defied my self-preservation. His offer was tempting and seductive. He turned my fantastical idea of death into an alluring reality.

"Did the woman you spoke to—the one who arranged this—know what you planned to ask me?"

"I'm sure that's not really what you want to know." His eyes darkened as they perused over my body. A heated exhale burst from his mouth and was so forceful it tingled against my face. "Ask. I know you want to."

"It's not my business."

"I want you to make it your business."

"Okay…" I drew out the word slowly, buying time to formulate my thoughts. "How did you find me?"

"Two years ago, you went digging around in a place not many know about —a place deep in the dark—and asked for something that didn't exist. Do you remember what you wanted?"

I fumbled with my fingers as I recalled. The dark space on the web. An IP address that changed daily. An embarrassment I couldn't admit to verbally. Nick's movies were unique and they titillated me in depraved ways. I had become desensitized, and I wanted more—something so disgusting and devoid of any mark of humanity it made me question my morality.

"I-I was told it didn't exist," I confessed.

"You were lied to. No one would be inane enough to record criminal activity and place it where it could be discovered unless they were terrorist or maniacal individuals who crave the media attention. The smart ones leave it where it should be—as a well-secured secret. The people responsible for keeping it in existence are powerful enough to make the world think it's an urban myth. I want to give you what you were looking for in a different way. We don't need a camera. We'll make that movie and we'll both be the stars. But…I'm sensing your torment over who will play the victim and who will be the perpetrator. Don't. Let me be the victim."

A pained squeak of air escaped my lungs and robbed me of the ability to continue the involuntary action.

"I could've selected anyone to do this." He reached out for me. A cold hand clasped the side of my face. If it was meant for comfort, it did the opposite. "I think we share so much in common. I want you, but I know if I have you, I'll destroy you like I have all the others—the ones you didn't see."

A lie nearly slipped out: I didn't enter a specific IP address in search of something very depraved to fill the holes that the staged version of my desires didn't. The need to experience someone's torture and eventual death in the most brutal and horrific of ways debilitated my grip on the sane.

At the time I sought it out, my request was met with proclamations that true snuff films didn't exist. One man had uploaded a video of him torturing and killing a woman, but he was quickly found and apprehended. The video was erased from the web immediately. More had to have existed. I wasn't in an elite and secretive club, and as a result, it wasn't within my reach.

"How did you...how did you find out who I was to stalk me like a crazy person?" I questioned.

"Someone brought your very bold request, in a place you weren't supposed to be, to my attention. Had you not mentioned my name and my... work, I'm sure I would've never known. I researched who you were and had you followed. Imagine my shock when your secret stash of films that shouldn't be legal in porn, but are, were found. I sent a few clients to you with explicit directions to catalogue their experiences with you. You couldn't be more perfect; your talents are rare."

I lifted an incredulous brow. "I don't have any talents. I have a deficiency. A sick, debased deficiency."

"A deficiency? Is that what you'd call it?"

"What else would you call something that pushed me into therapy and something short of a room with padded walls?"

"You're allowing the world to label you with ideas of what you should be. I need you to be who you are. Nothing more. Nothing less."

I stared at him for a while, unsure if I'd regret or relish in what he had planned.

"Don't worry. I promise you'll enjoy it." Studying me, he rubbed his mouth as it curled into a smile, although conversely, his eyes were weighted with a look that sent a cold, shocking chill up my spine. "Are you ready? Because I'm anxious to get to what we came here for."

The burn of acid flooded my throat. A bottomless well, siphoned away at my comfort, creating an aching pit inside my gut. Anticipation enfolded me in its unfamiliar territory.

I shouldn't have wanted it as badly as I did. Rules had been drilled into me, forcing me to adapt to a moral compass in order to appear as normal to public society.

In Nick's eyes, I saw the years I waged a war with my personal enemies and pretended to come away as the victor. In the fight against myself, I was always on the losing side.

My heart fluttered with a greedy need for a thrill. "I'm ready."

His hand found its way to my torso and slid up to my ribcage. "I can tell you're very excited for this." His breath splayed across my ear. "Tonight, be who you really are with me, Whitney. Make me experience the final orgasm—my death."

# ONE

THE FILTH STAINED MY dreams and marred my life with a mark so encompassing and dark, it changed me instantly. Committing an act of murder had repercussions, inscribing indistinguishable sentiments underneath my skin. I was unable to dig out any of the emotions and dissect them. All I knew was I had to escape my life—to run away from the increasingly darker visions of death, murder, and mayhem manifesting into a ghost haunting over my bare bones.

Attempts were made to carry on with my life after Nick's death. For three months I tried, and for an additional three weeks, I lost myself in a new town, a new place, and a new personality.

It has been three weeks since I first came to Bible-town, as it's affectionately known by the locals. Most of the businesses' and inhabitants' lives centered around the church. For me, the town was an exit from my previous life and a place where I could start anew.

The crushing edge of oppression inside the town reinforced my act to pretend I was normal. I blended in, fading into the background by becoming active in the community while maintaining the exterior of a shy and quiet woman. By doing so, I was deemed invisible, or simply a person with no thoughts or feelings of her own. I was a neutral-colored fixture in a neutral-hued town, and it hindered the lightless shades from coloring me in their malevolence and controlling me.

The local church was bigger than most homes with the exception of a few; one was rumored to belong to an athlete. No one had ever laid eyes on the inhabitants of the second home in order to state who they were. The third belonged to the owner of the world famous Wingettes—a popular tourist destination. Travelers wandering along the east coast stopped by while on their way to somewhere better. Summer months were the busiest due to its location in close proximity with a major route for the Northerners to utilize while fleeing south to vacation. Outside of the restaurant, that had received much attention and accolades, there wasn't much else to keep anyone entertained outside of the activities provided by the church.

Unfortunately for the natives, if they were unable to leave when given the chance, they were stuck inside the little town without means for a different life somewhere new. Employment opportunities were scarce, especially with my lack of experience in things that would've mattered to most employers. Luck was my friend and allowed me to obtain three jobs in a short period of time.

The money I received from Nick remained untouched on my end. After my failed attempt at going on with my life in Manhattan for three months, I handed the case of cash to my mother and asked her to never contact me again. Distracted by the money, she hardly questioned me—much less stopped me—when I left her for good.

"Housekeeping!" my co-worker, Kylie, knocked on the door of the motel with urgency. Owned by a singular unknown person who purchased squalid properties and lost interest in their ideas for renovations, it wasn't well maintained. The exterior was in dire need of a new paint job and the interiors were permeated with a particular pungent scent I could only describe as rank curry intermingled with body odor. The dark carpet had probably been a pale shade once. It was saturated with stains and permanently darkened. The only inhabitants were those passing through for a quick night's rest, or the more unsavory types who were later kicked out by the, oftentimes, belligerent manager.

Forgoing the delay for a response, Kylie used the master key to open the door, and I followed behind her, shuffling my feet to trail her steps.

She pursed her crinkled lips, painted in a bright red, shiny gloss, at the condition of the room. "People are such slobs."

Kylie was an older woman, maybe mid-forties. Her style of dress and choices in makeup painted her as someone in denial of her movement out of the teenage years. The men I'd see her with out in town were usually in their early to late twenties. "I bet those stupid meth-heads did this."

Keeping my eyes downcast, I placed the generic bleach-based spray cleanser on the dresser. I turned my attention to the bed with the intention of removing the linens for laundering.

Kylie wrestled the bundled up dirty sheets from my arms and nodded toward the bathroom. "Get the bathroom. I'll handle what's out here."

The bathroom was left in a such a disgusting state, I fought the urge to wretch. The disgusting smell emanating from the shower worsened the air quality. The dark cloth shower curtain hid away the disaster that might lay in wait there. I took my time, making sure I tended to what might've been the strongest offender to the putrid air: the clogged toilet.

"Do you take classes at the community college in Jefferson County?" Kylie shouted to me from the bedroom. "I've been thinking about doing it. I always thought you were super smart. Super smart people barely speak, because they know what many don't. They don't need to speak to show how smart they are. You're like them. You only speak when you have something important to say." She filled the doorway with her presence, observing me as I cleaned the toilet.

"I wonder about you sometimes, Whitney. I don't know why anyone would

12

choose to live in this big ol' dump. As soon as I save up enough, I'm gone. Tired of those old bats always judging me and calling me a whore because I didn't let some jerk put a ring on my finger and keep me barefoot and pregnant."

My chin and my eyes were always downward when interacting with people. It worked to activate my cloak of invisibility, or made me a wall whom townies spoke at but never with. I remained quiet and didn't put forth an effort to make friends. Friends meant attachments. Attachments resulted in sources of my private anguish.

Despite never having a conversation outside of a few sentences with anyone, I was made privy to quite a few secrets. People would often come to me and unload on me as though I were their therapist. I supposed they trusted that my silence indicated I was a safe source for confessions.

Kylie stepped inside the bathroom to primp her bleached blond mane in the mirror, worn down in body curls. A stray strand of her hair floated down and rested on the sink I had recently scrubbed down. She flexed the skin around her green eyes, pulling at the wrinkles on her skin with her fingertips. Holding contempt over the sight of her reflection, she ceased the manipulation of her face to watch me through the mirror. "Don't you work with my daughter, Penny, at your other job? Maybe I'll talk her into hanging out with you. Doesn't seem like you have any friends around here. Every young girl should have at least one best girlfriend…"

As she allowed a cloud of verbiage to fill the air, I scrubbed at the porcelain bowl with a new purpose, wishing to drown out the sound of her voice.

The seconds in which my eyelids shuttered my eyes, horrid visions I hadn't experienced since I left my mother stole my breath.

*Kylie screams as my hands envelop her throat. She fights to fend me off by scratching at the skin on my arms. I slam her down in the tile floor. Blood spurts out of her mouth and…*

I opened my eyes and focused on the stains in the toilet, punishing my daymares, luring me into doing something sinister. I focused on sunnier thoughts: ocean, beach, seagulls singing to the shore—peace.

Kylie gave up and returned to vacuuming the room.

Minutes of peace powered my speed with completing my task of cleaning. With the porcelain and cheap fixtures sparkling clean, the putrid scent lingered in the air. Finished with the toilet and ready to clean the last piece in the bathroom, I pulled back the curtain.

The oxygen was robbed from the immediate air. I couldn't scream. I could barely gasp. Frozen in place, I became glued to the horrific scene in front of me.

I had only seen him in passing a few times. He was a drug addict who constantly spoke to himself and squatted in the vacant rooms to get high. He'd been chased out a few times, and he'd always return. The last interaction I had with him, I paid for it with a bite mark on my arm and a tetanus shot.

Today he met a bitter end, hanging by his belt tied to the shower sprocket. His legs were bent at the knees and tucked underneath him. Grungy cargo pants pooled around his ankles, leaving his genitals exposed. His head was swollen and a bluish tint. Ashen lips were gaped open with a darkened engorged tongue falling limply out of the side of his mouth. Swollen eyelids presented a small peek into his eyes, marred by a dark red horizontal line. From the state of the mess beneath him and the rigid state of his body, he'd been there for presumably longer than a few hours.

The sound of the vacuum cleaner stopped. The smell of smoke announced her arrival before her mouth could. Her feet shuffled toward the doorway and halted. An ear-piercing scream shocked me out of my walking catatonic state.

I WAS NEVER MORE nervous when the cops arrived. An older man, a cop, barked questions at me and seemed to grow more and more impatient with my lack of answers. When he began to yell, a younger cop waltzed over to us.

"I've got this." His smooth baritone voice floated underneath the loud protestations of the cop who had questioned me.

# Opaque Mirrors

"Waste of time," the older cop said and spat at the ground near my feet.

My nail beds were torn to shreds underneath the violence of my teeth. I glanced back to Kylie unsure whether she was recounting what she had seen or flirting with the man in the blue uniform.

"Miss Tyler." M. Reid, from the name etched in gold nameplate, caught my notice. He was a bit too baby-faced to have been a beat cop. His smooth light fawn skin and chiseled features probably garnered him a difficult time with people taking him seriously. I'd seen him around here and there since I moved to Bebletown a few weeks ago, but lately, his presence became more frequent. It could've been I noticed him more, or it could've been a complete coincidence.

He brushed his hand over his parted and pomade-laden dark blond hair. Deep set brandy-hued eyes, planted between lashes that nearly reached his upward slanted brows, glimmered as they shot toward whom I assumed could've been a superior officer. "I apologize for that. He can be an impatient ass. You're probably scared shitless having never seen a dead body before."

"I have...I mean, I haven't."

A hand reached out to pull my hand from my mouth and intertwined with my fingers as some sort of gesture I could only assume was consolation. "I understand you're nervous, so take your time."

Prickly little ants worked around inside the nerves of my hands. I pulled my hand away and wiped the embarrassing amount of perspiration from my skin onto my apron. "I told the other cop everything I know."

"Is there a number we can reach you at in case we have more questions?"

"Yes, but I don't know why you'd need it." I jammed my trembling hand inside my apron. "There's nothing else I can add."

His broad and angular jaw clenched in either aggravation or impatience—the muscle ticked with a spasm. I believed he assumed I had more to say and was far from satisfied with what I was willing to state.

"C-can I go? I have another job to get to." I shielded my eyes against the dawning sun poking through my eyelashes.

"I'll need your home number," he reiterated, hoarseness swathed his calm tone, deepening the octave.

I gave him a series of digits that could've been someone else's phone number but wasn't mine, accompanied by an apology for needing to leave and went on my way.

The metal handle of my rusted and beat up twenty-year-old car was in my grasp when Kylie called out to me.

"Whitney!" She stopped what she was doing and trotted over to me. "Are you okay? You kind of went into shock back there." She rubbed her shoulders as she shivered. "That man…" She shook her head, her lips twitching with the onslaught of tears. "It's a thing that's surely going to give me the heebie-jeebies every time I come to work."

"I'll be okay," I assured her, eyeing the time on my cell phone. "I'm sorry, but I'm late for my other job."

She quickly blotted her tears away with her fingertips. "Go on. I'll fill the manager in when he gets back to his office—*if* he shows up today."

Giving her a slighted nod, I entered my car.

I shoved my key in the ignition and swung my head around to check for a clear way to pull into reverse. I caught sight of M. Reid fiddling with his phone.

He aimed an accusatory look at my car. Mouthing the words, "What the fuck?" he lifted a hand to flag me down. His steps hurried forward, but he was too late and too far away to catch up to me.

# TWO

AFTER MY OVERNIGHT SHIFT at the motel, I traveled to my third job—a call center on the edge of town for a car insurance company. I planned it perfectly in order to eliminate any opportunity for a social life, and for that matter, more than a few hours of sleep at night.

"It's been slow, but it's really starting to pick up." Penny slipped her behind on my desk and moved her earpiece down, allowing it dangle down the side of her neck. Her bottle-dyed red hair grazed her shoulders. Emerald green eyes glanced around the immediate area. "I can't wait until I make enough money with Avon to stop working here."

Seeking attention from anyone in her immediate vicinity, Penny turned her attention to me. "You should really let me do your face one day." She circled her finger around my face. "You would be so much prettier with some makeup."

Camera-ready makeup was a signature look in my previous life. During the day it was slightly toned down. I wouldn't have been caught dead without at least foundation. I had my mother to thank for worrying about things that shouldn't have mattered. She had an image she wanted to project and required her two daughters to follow suit.

Penny leaned closer, imposing on my personal space with her body heat. "I heard you were the one who found the dead homeless guy. Are you okay? Had to be a pretty gruesome thing to see."

The only downfall of the small town: the grapevine was efficient. The transportation of information, whether false or true, spread like wildfire in an arid land.

"I'm okay," I assured her, flashing a smile.

She fluttered her spider lashes, examining me. Rolling her shoulders, she slunk away, giving me room to breathe and approached the woman in the cubicle across the small pathway.

Pointing to the area behind my chair, she nudged the woman seated in the cubicle. "You see the new hire over there?" She nodded to the cubicle opposite my desk.

I glanced over my shoulder for a brief moment and only caught the back of a thick head of dark brown hair cut in a graduated taper and swimmer's shoulders dressed in a crisp dark blue collar shirt.

"No," the woman across the isle from me replied, exhaling exhaustively. "You know I don't date."

"I know. I know." Penny dismissed her with a wave of her hand. "But you won't believe who he is."

Watching them interact, I couldn't deny how much I missed my sister, Sloane, who had become my only friend. Growing up, when I attempted to make friends, it ended badly. The identity of my mother was uncovered along with her exploits and became a fracture point in our relationship. Either they judged her too harshly, wanted to condemn her constantly, or become enamored with her infamy.

I wouldn't consider Penny my friend. I wanted her to be, but what few conversations we did engage in were mostly one-sided, ensuring I kept her at a distance. I couldn't get invested in anyone in the event I had to move again and shun the life I cultivated.

"I think he's the son of the owner of Alloy Insurance," Penny said, her mouth widening into a surreal grin.

"What's he doing here?" the woman wondered on the cusp of me putting my earbuds in and pretending I had a stack of data entries to complete. I turned on my music and tuned out their conversation.


Two hours left until the end of the work day, and I couldn't keep my eyes open. I poked my head up over the cubicles and scanned the path leading to the break-room on the far side of the open landscape of the office. It appeared to be unoccupied and the pathway leading there was clear.

Acting swiftly, I grabbed my mug, matcha powder, and my bamboo whisk.

Taking the least noticeable path toward it, I flittered around the cubicles, heading to the small kitchenette.

Blake, my asshole manager, and a man I couldn't place were conversing with one another and standing in front of the coffee machine. I turned on my heels to leave, but something about the scene drew my curiosity. The unnamed man appeared cornered by an intrusive conversation, perpetrated by Blake. As Blake spoke to him, the new employee's annoyance grew stronger, yet he remained silent about his irritation.

Blake never kowtowed to anyone, but it was clear he was kissing up to the newcomer for an unknown reason. Upon closer scrutiny, I recognized the dark blue shirt as that of the man who was new to my working area.

His glassy eyes fell equally under the light brown and earthy green shade, and wandered until they eventually came to rest on me.

Aware of my staring, I whirled around to leave.

"Hey!" Blake's familiar voice intoned.

Unsure if he was actually speaking to me, I peeked back at the two men.

"Can we get some fucking help over here?" Blake waved me over as though I was an errant lapdog who refused to heel.

"With what?" Behaving and speaking in a demure tone, I kept my eyes to the dark gray Berber cut pile carpet and my chin against my chest.

Silence passed between us for too long, provoking my glance to level up at him. The man next to Blake caught my eye once more. His stare sank into unnerving territory.

"You know Penny, right?" Blake snapped his fingers and he plodded toward me, demanding my undivided attention.

"Sort of," I answered him. "Why?"

Hayden arched his thick jet brows, a cocky curl of his lips began to lighten his face. "What's your name?" He nodded to me and stepped closer, bypassing the man who annoyed him earlier to stand closer to me than Blake did.

In response, I stepped backward. "Whitney."

Blake nudged Hayden and shook his head in chastising manner. "Don't get involved with her. She's weird. And didn't you say she's a four?"

*They were rating me and the women here based on her looks? Pigs.*

"I can help you if you're looking for lipstick or foundation, Blake," Penny said, waltzing into the area to stand beside me in the doorway. "Maybe you want some guy-liner? The brand I sell also has a men's line with aftershave balm and facial washes. I'm told the blemish control wash works wonders, maybe you can check it out? My mistake; with all the pits in your face, it's too late for you."

Blake's hand instinctively went to his jaw, covering the cratered skin he had there.

Penny turned a furtive glance in Hayden's direction, but he didn't seem to notice since he was too busy dissecting me in silence.

"I'm Hayden," he introduced himself to me. "I work right across from you." His lips flexed into a smile.

"I have to get back to work." Silently excusing myself, I began to head back toward my cubicle to give them privacy.

On my heels I could hear Penny introduce herself to Hayden.

I planted myself back at my desk and stared at my empty mug with a frown. Promising to get a cup later, I distracted myself with the mundane task of data entry.

For whatever reason, an invisible lure attracted my gaze toward the kitchenette. Penny continued to try to engage a less than interested Hayden. I recognized the look on his face, he wished he could disappear like I had worked hard to do every day.

"Hey." Blake slammed his hand on my desk, startling me with the rude introduction to his sudden presence. His tanned skin turned ruddy at the sight of Penny visibly flirting with Hayden. "As I said, I'm having a get together for Hayden, and I want you to come."

I must've somehow missed a part of the conversation. I shook my head no at him and continued to type up a random data entry. "If I'm a four, and Penny is a ten from the way you can't stop looking at her, why are you bothering to invite me?"

Having garnered his direct attention, he began to scowl at me. "I want you to come, and I want you to bring that hot little red-headed number, Penny, along."

I added, "With all due respect, Mr. Grant," in the most sardonic tone I could muster. The man was otherwise married, but he couldn't help himself from flirting or arranging meets with the women in town when his wife was away on one of her many missionary trips. It was no secret the town often forgave the sins of the men and doubled up their social punishments toward the women for similar crimes.

Blake whistled too loudly and too closely to my ear.

"Can you please get off my desk, Mr. Grant?" I brushed my hand across a piece of paper and lightly shoved at his thigh with the flat of my palm. "I don't want to waste the company's time when I have things to do."

He scrutinized me in a way that yanked my small blanket of comfort away from me. I tilted my chin down again, staring at the flat screen monitor through my dense black eyelashes, hoping I would become invisible again. "Put in a good word for me, and make sure Penny comes with you to the house this weekend."

"Comes with me where?" I continued to have problems engaging in eye contact.

"To the thing I'm throwing at Hayden's temporary place. It's the house behind the big knoll on Hellen Avenue." A tinge of bitterness seeped into his voice as though I should've known it was an invite.

I regarded him with a small hint of panic. "And again, I ask why're you inviting me to a party, when you're interested in Penny?"

"You speak English, right?"

Baffled, I fluttered my eyelashes over my dark brown eyes repeatedly. I was seconds away from rolling my eyes and allowing my mouth to expose the truth about what I really thought of my boss. "Yes, English is my first language."

"Are you trying to smart off to me?" He searched the black blazer I had worn over an unassuming white button up shirt, fastened up to the collar, for the gold name tag we're forced to wear for no immediate reason. Customers never visited. I assumed the purpose was to ensure the manager could remain personable even if he'd forgotten our names. "Whitney?"

"I don't think it's a good idea to attend the party. Thanks for the invitation."

He shot up off my desk, throwing his incredulity and a modicum of disgust at me. "You'll come. Because it's probably the most fun you've had in years."

"How would you know that?"

"What?"

"How would you know it's the most fun I've had in years? You don't know me."

He threw on a smile, switching gears. "Come on, cutie." He balled his fist and gently brushed it against my chin. "You'll have fun. I'll hook you up with one of my friends." Leaning down, far too close to me, he ran his finger up my arm.

I recoiled from his touch, and the painful burn worked its way up my arm. "You mean you want me to come, somehow distract Hayden, and give you a chance with Penny?" I pushed through to his agenda in an effort to quickly end the interaction.

"Distract Hayden from what?" Hayden made his presence known, his gaze darting from me to Blake.

22

"Nothing, man." Blake playfully punched Hayden in the arm and flashed me a smile. Blake pointed an accusatory finger at me while walking backward. "Just come to the fucking party and bring her. Since you're into girls, I can arrange something."

Ignoring him, I put the ear buds in my ears and began to busy myself with my data entry. A sharp pop in my ear brought my hand up to soothe the burning sensation.

I thought he had left, but it seemed today wasn't my day. Blake stood beside me, spinning the wire to my earbuds around his finger counter clockwise and unwinding it by spinning it clockwise. His lips tightened deeply, making his lips appear nonexistent. "How much do you make an hour?"

I reached for my earbuds and he moved his arm out of my reach. "What kind of question is that to ask someone?"

"I'm your manager, did you forget that? Seems you did. So how about his, if you want to be a bitch, I can be an asshole."

"Isn't it too late? This can't be a nice version of you."

People around us, privy to the conversation, began to gasp or chuckle quietly.

"Get back to fucking work," Blake barked at them.

Guiding himself on my desk with one arm, he placed his face mere inches from mine. "Fuck with me again and you'll no longer have a salary."

I rolled my neck to relax myself and casually turned back to Blake. "Eleven-fifty an hour."

He pulled out a roll of bills and threw them at me, one by one. They fell on top of the desk and onto the floor. "That's three hours of pay for the three hours you'll spend at the house with Penny. So we're good, right?"

I bobbed my head, as I stared down at the money. There was more than three hours' worth of work there. It was over eleven hours' worth of work.

Gazing at his neck, I imagined what he would look like with a belt around it while he was tied to my bed. The thought made me smile—despite the knowledge of darker thoughts slowly making a return—and I kept up my act to remain pleasant.

"We're good?" He cast an unfriendly smile in my direction and didn't delay for an answer prior to his exit.

"He's an ignoramus," Hayden said from his desk, his chair angled toward me. His dark and heavy brows shadowed over his eyes. The moment I met his eye contact, he gave me a friendly grin. Had it not been for the light dusting of hair extending from his sideburns along his jawline and above his lips, he could've easily passed for someone barely legal. His high cheekbones and the gaunt space below it showed no semblance of the ability to produce hair.

I turned back to my computer, hoping to become inconspicuous again.

The message was received. From over my shoulder, I observed him sigh with his eyes cast to the ceiling, then he returned to his task on the computer.

Penny snarled after Blake's exit path and loitered by my area. "Does he think you're my pimp? I wouldn't piss on that man if he was on fire. Not that I would—you know—piss on him. It would be a waste of pee."

I stared at the money scattered on the ground, delaying the urge to pick it up. Sliding my chair out from underneath me, I got on my hands and knees. I balled the twenties into my fists and shoved them inside the pocket of my gabardine slacks.

Penny continued to stare at me, expectantly lifting her perfectly arched dark auburn eyebrows. "You should go to HR about his behavior." It became clear she wouldn't leave until she received a reply.

"He's the manager, no matter how much of an asshole he is, and I need the money." I returned to my chair and retreated into the cubby. "Does Blake's family really have a connection with the Alloys? How?" I pressed my lips together. My pesky need to do something dangerous and connect with someone had begun to act on its own accord.

She held up her finger with her eyes cast toward Hayden. On his own accord, he suddenly decided he had business elsewhere and left his cubicle. "From what I could get from the hottie who just left, Hayden's family and Blake's family are in business together. Not sure about the rumors of Hayden being the owner's son. Hayden wouldn't say and you saw his name tag, right? His last name isn't Alloy, it's Pierce. But some say that Alloy Insurance is just a name and not the last name of the people who own this place."

Her emerald eyes twinkled, brimming with knowledge of a secret she couldn't wait to share. "If it's true and Hayden changed his last name to go under the radar, I don't know why they gave Blake a managerial position, but are making Hayden work with us regular people." She placed her hand on my shoulder as some sort of reassurance. "But don't sweat it about your job. I'll stick by you if anything goes down. Blake was just throwing a tantrum because he met the only two girls in this town who won't drop their panties and bend over just because his parents' come from money."

"Your hate for him sounds...personal. I thought you didn't really know Blake?" I paused, wishing I could take back my question.

She placed her hand on my desk and flipped her dark hair over the shoulder with the other. "His family is just...weird. There's word going around that the Grants have ties to some pretty shady people." She glanced over at Hayden's empty chair. "That one's different so far. Blake's kissing his ass like I'd never seen before. I wonder what his deal is. From what I could pull from him, he said he was once a quarterback for some big name school. He was supposed to go on to law school, but flubbed it thinking he would get picked up by the draft his senior year. Didn't happen. His stats in his last year sucked. He wouldn't say what happened to him, but he wound up riding the bench for half the season. Screwed himself hard on that one."

"Is that why he's here?"

"He's been here for a few months, so maybe." She shrugged. "I didn't dig into all of it. He's one of those people who's hard to get a read on. My theory? I think he got sent here for screwing up." She examined me. "I saw the way you looked at him. If that torch is lit, don't worry. I was only talking to him because I've seen him hanging around the guy I'm crushing on. If you want me to hook you two up—"

"I...don't really know him, and I'm not interested in him." The veracity of my statement could've been called into question. The dark magnetized the light and consumed it. My murkiness was a hole consuming every other black hole in its vicinity.

Hayden appeared to be too pure, too nice, and too mild in his behavior for

---

courtney lane

me to be attracted to him—and I deemed that a good thing. Still, something about him drew my interest.

"Denial is not just a river in Egypt."

"I have a boyfriend," I blurted out the lie, needing to grasp some aspect of my isolation to avoid being pulled into social behavior when I couldn't afford to engage.

"Oh?"

"It's a long distance thing, but it's very serious."

"Well, you can't keep that money if I don't go. I'll go with you."

My sudden panic nearly choked me. "Don't worry about it. I'm going to return the money."

"It wouldn't be right. You have three jobs, don't you? I know you need the money, Whitney." She placed her hand over mine. "I don't think he'd accept it if you returned it to him any how. Well, I don't want him to have something to hold over you, believe me he will." She sighed. "I'll go and hook you up with Hayden."

26

# THREE

ALTHOUGH I HADN'T BEEN in Bebletown for long, I looked forward to the non-threatening low-grade storms. The rain came in sideways with a hard pounding. The air remained slightly warm, and the cold wind chilled the moisture on my skin. The trees bowed and bent with the winds. The streets and the ground flooded with several inches.

I stood on the farmer's porch to my home in my white sundress. My entire body was soaked by nature's shower.

My thermally straightened long hair whipped around in the harsh winds, slowly reverting it back to it's natural texture—curls that wound perfectly around my thumb. The wind kicked up, whipping my rain-drenched dress around my legs.

I closed my eyes and held on to the banister, the wind threatened to move me. My eyelids slowly retracted to the gray-toned scene in front of me. My mouth fell agape when I caught sight of a familiar man running against the wind, soaked from head to toe: M. Reid.

He paused not far from the walkway to porch to catch his breath. He bowed, his back erratically moving with heavy breaths and placed his hands on his thighs. His shirt was made transparent by the moisture. A full view of his back exposed the striations of muscle and bulk. He turned sideways, regarding the distance. His hair drew down in waves across his forehead, threatening to fall into his eyes. When he stood tall and faced the sky, his enviable bone structure never looked more surreal.

The second he turned in my direction, I slipped behind the closest pillar, hoping it hid me well. The whistle of the wind and pounding violence of the rain rushed inside my ears.

I peeked around the bend to find him standing at the end of the walkway leading to the porch stairs.

"You shouldn't be out here like this," he said, his deep voice battling with the sounds of the angry weather. His white T-shirt clung to every peak and valley of his chest and abs. He might as well have been shirtless.

"Neither should you."

"The wind gives me a good fight and the rain keeps me cool. I can't sit on my ass and aim to keep up the body you can't stop eye fucking."

The pressure of the wind beat at the skirt portion of my sundress so brutally I was afraid it would fly up. I gathered the hem in my hands to keep it securely down.

As his gaze skated down my body, his mouth twitched up at the corner.

An uncontrollable stream of suggestive thoughts clouded my mind.

"But I think I bit off more than I could chew." He took a few steps at a time to stand in front of me. "Goddamn, Whitney, I can see everything underneath that dress. If there were any other men around here, I might have to do something about that." His moves were predatory, his posture strong and intimidating. The brandy in his eyes darkened to a well-aged whiskey and flickered at a crack of thunder that startled me into jolting backward.

He was right; white lingerie and a white dress were a horrible combination. The darkness of my pubic hair and my brown nipples were easily seen though my soaked clothes.

My back banged into the front screen door with enough power to make me wince at the pain. I covered my breasts with my arms.

"That's not working." He circled a finger in the air toward my crotch. "I like that you don't shave."

The band that kept me bound to the woman I dressed in every day had snapped until it broke apart, sending a surge of dread through me. Left open and unable to determine what I would've done had we continued our interaction, I fought against unearthing the deadly thoughts, knowing they would put an end to the fake version of myself.

"Do you live too far from here?" I blurted out my question and pushed myself further against the screen door of the house.

"I can tell you I live too far away to run back in this weather." He only took his eyes off me for a second to contemplate the scene in front of my house. "Are you going to invite me in, or are you going to make me swim back to my house and probably drown? After all, you can trust a small-town police officer, right?" He seemed too enamored with me to be affected by anything around us. I hadn't been noticed by anyone. I was a wall they spoke to but never really took the time to acknowledge directly. M. Reid regarded me as though he was looking through my exterior and discovered the muddled core.

Every word he said and every sweep of his stare loosened a grip on what I had kept stowed away.

"You can...come in until it stops," I offered, the words falling as uneasily from my lips as equally as I meant the offer. The screen door flew out of my hands the instant I tried to open it. Opening the main door, I stepped inside. He followed and worked quickly to secure the screen, locking it in place prior to closing and locking the front door. He turned to me while wiggling out of his trainers and scanning around the house.

"Mason."

"What?"

"My name is Mason, does that help? Because the whole shaking like Bambi thing, while on the one hand, turning me on, on the other it's making this very fucking awkward. I'm not sure you're shaking for the reasons I'd like you to."

"Whitney."

"I already knew that." A charming smile revealed sparkling straight teeth.

"The bathroom's down the hall if you want to dry off." Standing between the kitchen and the living room, I pointed to the hall leading to the bedrooms.

"Sure you don't want to go first?" His gaze drank in my body, and he licked his enticing lips as though he liked the flavor coating them. He gripped the hem of his shirt and slowly lifted.

The sight of bumpy ridges and lines outlining his eight-pack stomach pulled me to turn away from him. A shocking electric jolt of lechery left my skin tingling with a renewed awareness. "Jesus Christ," I muttered.

"Careful who you say that around in this town. It's considered blasphemy"—he stepped beside me, his scent a mix of the rain and a woodsy spice—"punishable by multiple public spankings."

I shuddered, involuntarily and embarrassingly. "I have things to change into in my bedroom." I gestured toward the hall with wide eyes. I was afraid if I closed them, the fantasies that had almost abandoned me when I came to Bebletown but recently returned to trickle into my thoughts, would reconstruct grand scenes and play repeatedly though my head.

His silence drew me. A battering storm behind his very light brown eyes entranced me. Taming his grin, he brushed past me, heading toward the bathroom.

My breathing no longer ragged, I inhaled freely, sucking in oxygen and expelling it as though I had surfaced from drowning. I clung to my soaked dress and headed to my bedroom and closed the door. Intending to dry off, I seized the terrycloth robe hanging on the hook above the door to my closet. With my skin no longer soaked, I rummaged through my small closet and decided to change into a pair of jeans and a T-shirt. I tucked my long curly hair up into an effortless bun and checked myself out in the mirror prior to exiting the bedroom.

With the lack of a defined bone structure, bee-stung lips, and large dark brown eyes, my mother would often call me her dark-skinned porcelain doll. My features aligned with one, making me appear much younger than the twenty-seven years indicated on my driver's license.

I began to primp and prim as I stared at my reflection. I shook my head, chiding myself for caring in silence. I couldn't afford to care.

Shuffling down the hall, I was a bit alerted when I didn't find Mason in the living room.

I entered the kitchen and grabbed two mugs along with matcha powder to fix us both a cup of tea. I ignited the gas under the kettle to bring the water to a boil and waited until the kettle whistled.

As I poured cups for the both of us, I held on to the belief that the purpose of my gesture was to extend my hospitality, instead of a tactic to make Mason stay longer. I almost believed it.

A flutter of movement drew my eye. With a cup of tea prepared for him in hand, I swiveled to greet him.

Mason stood in the doorway wearing nothing but a smile and a black towel. The low position of the black terry cloth material revealed his V-shaped muscle and presented me with an unexpected view.

The mug slipped out of my hands and shattered on the ground. The burn on my foot took a minute to register, and when I did, I couldn't hide the signals of pain from setting on my face.

Mason acted swiftly and walked toward me. He wrapped his hands around my waist and plucked me up out of harm's way to set me up on the counter. "You're kind of a klutz." Annoyance nor amusement could be detected.

"I'm not usually. Gorgeous men, whom I don't really know, standing half-naked inside my house tend to turn me into one." My words were lost to the thickening air between us.

His smile was drenched in sex and deviance. "This happens often?"

"No."

It was so soft and mumbled I couldn't have been certain, but I could've sworn he'd said, "It better not."

Feeling guilty over him cleaning up my mess, I offered to lend a hand. "I can do that. You don't have to—"

A cutting glance dictated silence and compliance toward permitting him to clean. He gathered the shattered pieces of the mug in one hand and dumped the pieces in the trash. My consideration landed on places on his body it shouldn't have as he moved around.

When he was done, my floor was left more spotless than it was prior.

He placed the kettle back on the grate and turned on the gas. Turning his focus back on me, he glanced down at my foot. "Now, to take care of you." The breathy promise could've easily been considered a sexual innuendo.

It pulled a contemptible and involuntary trigger inside my body. What was once hot turned cold, and what was once cold became scorching. Thick dense clouds shrouded my ability to make sense of the changes occurring inside me mentally and physically.

He turned to the freezer, grabbed a few ice cubes from the tray, and placed them in a towel. A chair was scraped across the floor and set in front of me. Making himself at home in the chair, he plucked up my foot in his brawny and well-veined tanned hands. He slid an ice cube on my burn and left my foot to rest on his lap.

"I'm sorry about the tea," I offered up a sincere apology. My gaze focused on the separation in the black towel, wondering if it would open to reveal more.

"I'm a coffee drinker anyway." Upon noticing where my eyes were glued, the crook of his mouth turned upward. "I don't think you have clothes for me here, and I didn't want to get your furniture…wet."

"It wouldn't have bothered me," I said, my regard momentarily darting out the window of the backdoor, and for the first time, wishing the rain would stop soon.

"Did you notice anywhere in there where I said something about it bothering you? Because I didn't." He finished his statement with a wink. His thumb began to mindlessly rub at the arch of my foot, sending a tingle of shock up my thighs. He slipped a piece of ice from the towel and placed it directly on the pulsating burn.

I jerked in a failed effort to wrangle my foot from his hold.

He rocked the ice back and forth. A stronger pull coursed up my legs and hit me with an unrelenting intensity between my thighs. I pressed my ample lips together to stifle a moan.

"Feel better?" He continued to manipulate the ice in small circles against my skin while daring me with his eyes as they turned into insistent slants.

Nodding, I wrapped my hands around the overhang of the counter until a numbing sensation worked through my fingertips. "Did you get any new leads on the guy who died?"

"If I could tell you...the answer is no. Might be because my main lead decided to give me the wrong number." Something dark crossed in his eyes as he blotted my moist foot from the completely melted ice cube. He tossed the towel full of half-melted ice on the counter beside me, lolled back in the chair, and put his arms behind his back. The muscles in his arms swelled fully behind his head. "Off the record and between us, don't worry about it. We haven't gotten the toxicology back yet, and in a town like this, it will probably take forever. Personally, I think he was a drugged-out kinky vagabond who should've had someone with him to spot him when he jerked off while he hanged himself. Really a fucked-up way to die, isn't it?"

Moments of silence passed where I had no idea what to say, and he silently urged me to engage him in conversation.

The kettle whistled, alerting us that the water was on boil.

It was a natural reaction to get up to retrieve it after having lived alone. Mason was the first to get up and when he did, I caught a glimpse of what hung between his thighs between a temporary widened split in the towel. And he knew that I had. The smile on his face couldn't have been any deeper.

"I'll get the tea." Devilry doused his eyes and his smile.

As he poured a single mug of tea, he kept a stray eye on me. "I'm kinda pissed about you letting me inside your house so easily when you live alone."

I sat down on the seat he vacated and stared at the sky in the distance through the windowed door. I wished nature would hear my wishes and make it stop raining. The temperature in my home had become stifling hot.

"The town is usually really safe. And...you're a cop. You said so yourself. I'm safest with you, right?"

"Doesn't matter what you think of this town. You should *never* let your guard down."

"You didn't say anything about…you. That I'm not safe with you."

Leisure in the way it spread across his lips, a dark smirk contorted his delectable mouth. "Define safe."

The chaotic sounds of the storm had dissipated, but the rain hadn't. The seconds behind my shuttered eyelids exposed uncharted surprises.

*He rips off his towel and stalks toward me. His eyes are hungry for blood and his hands reach out ready to bruise me. He picks me up and throws me down on the table, stomach down. One hand holds the back of my neck pinning me in place. The other hand spanks me through my panties with the flat of his palm until the pain sensors in my flesh render my behind numb.*

*"Stupid fucking bitch. You think you can open a door for a complete stranger and not have this happen to you? I told you, you weren't safe." He rips off my underwear, and I feel his closed fists pump his cock against my behind. Without lubricating me, he thrusts his cock deep into my untouched ass and makes me scream.*

Snapping of fingers and brisk air at my face coaxed my eyes open. Mason's sculpted chest muscles tensed as he extended a cup of tea toward me. "You mutter to yourself when you daydream." He sucked in a breath and grinned. "Underneath the shy girl routine, you have a very dirty and fucked-up mind, and I have to say, I really fucking like it."

His expression dared me to pull at that part of myself again, and he almost succeeded. Whether my eyes were open or closed, the scene with him as the featured co-star replayed in a cycle. Before Nick, in my waking hours, I clamored for the ability to control the mortality of others. A dream of giving up my control to someone else shocked me.

My colorless desires had been rearranged without my knowledge and wanted to be fulfilled by a very attractive man.

I wrung my hands with such viciousness it changed the pigment in my fingertips. To protect him and myself, I dashed off and closed myself up in my bedroom, locking the door.

As I paced my bedroom, I grabbed a belt from its position over my doorknob and wrapped it tightly around my hands. If I thought I could will myself to fantasize about the familiar—his neck surrounded by my belt and at my mercy—I was wrong.

Persistent knocking on the door made me inwardly groan. "Whitney, don't be embarrassed. Talk to me."

"I'm sorry. I felt a little sick all of the sudden." I pulled at the belt until my pain sensors screamed louder than any other sensation. I demanded my thoughts turned to more familiar territories, instead of the uncharted course I couldn't make sense of. The course that left me panting with a greedy hollow. "You should really go."

The ill-fitting door shifted as though he might've leaned on it. "Was it me teasing you about your dirty mind?"

*Yes.* "No. Not at all."

"Hey, I know what happened has to affect you. If you really want me to go, I will. But I need you to tell me you're okay to be alone and make me believe it."

"I'm okay to be alone. Leave your number with me if it makes you feel better."

"I'll do that, and I expect you to use it. I have to use your phone since mine shit the bed, then I'm going to get dressed and head out. Call me tonight, Whitney. That's an order."

"Okay." I stated the simple word because I couldn't find something more suitable to say. There was no safe way to broach the topic of him influencing a bad part of me and churning out new complications.

Fifteen minutes after rocking on my bed and staring at the moving shadows from underneath the crease in the door, the honking of a horn emanated from the front of the house.

"That's my ride," Mason called out from the other side.

Lost in a billow of appropriate things to say and unable to pluck one out from the massive cloud, I remained silent.

The front door closed, echoing into my room and shuddering the door. I slipped off the bed and raced toward the front door to lock it. I scattered to the bay window at the front of the house and pulled the curtain open for a peek.

Standing beside a black sports car, far too expensive for a call center employee at Alloy Insurance, stood Hayden. He exchanged a few passionate words with Mason. Riveted with the knowledge that the two men knew each other, I continued to spy on them.

Mason held up a finger, and the incoherent soft voices stopped. They both turned to look toward the window to my house. I stepped back allowing the curtain to fall back into place and waited until I heard the loud rev of the powerful engine. I double-checked and made sure they had left.

During the time I left Mason alone in my house, he had tidied the kitchen area. The mugs were cleaned and neatly stowed away in their proper place.

The box of matcha powder wasn't exactly sealed the way I'd like them to be, with the inner baggie folded down. The paper lid was open. Mason's phone number and name was scribbled across the white space. I ran my fingers along the edge the box lid, toying with the idea of throwing the box away, or drinking the tea tainted by Mason's touch. I closed the box and secured it back in the cabinet.

Reeling from our interaction and wishing he hadn't been so enticing, I locked all the doors and windows and prepared for my nap before my night shift at the hotel.

# FOUR

THE DEATH OF THE homeless man was a dart veering in my direction, threatening to kill my chance at a new life. I tried to take on another client shortly after Nick's death in an effort to reassume a life that wasn't my own, but the one my mother constructed for me.

The next day my client was found dead in his apartment. It was said the cause of death was erotic asphyxiation and not suicide. I left my mother the same day the report was disclosed.

The circumstances surrounding the death of my date and the homeless man were coincidences. I refused to correlate the death of the man in the hotel to that of my client's.

Regardless of my desire to hold on to the idea of the events having no correlation, it made me leery of the town's allure as a safe place when it might've been a clue to the sickness of sexual suppression, instead of oppression; the former was a deadly state for anyone to be in.

Small tinges of fear drove me to want to connect with someone—anyone; my family crossed into my thoughts as the people who I could run to. I told myself I would never call, but there were times when I missed my family—my sister and my mother—so badly my finger hovered over their numbers. The compulsion to hear their voices and know they were all right suffused my thoughts. While my family was far from perfect, we loved each other the best way we knew how. At times we weren't able to get along easily, but we were a family.

I watched the time on my phone, counting the hours until I would have to work again. There was too much time. Instead of outing myself and allowing my family to find me, I called Penny and gave her my address—going against everything I had promised myself I wouldn't do.

PENNY WAS AT THE curb with Marion, Penny's friend and a waitress at Wingettes, ready to take me to Hayden's residence. We exchanged inconsequential chit chat along the way. No matter how minor it was, it deepened my need to find a friend by reminding me of my loneliness.

The destination was one of the four large sized homes located in Bebletown. It was a sprawling ranch with horse stables an acre behind the house and an in-ground swimming pool.

As the music loudly resounded, shaking the immediate ground surrounding the house, my sense of trepidation returned and made it difficult to continue the path inside with Penny and Marion.

"Whitney? Why are you dragging your feet? Come on." Penny beckoned for me with her hand.

"I'll catch up with you guys in minute." I gave her a tepid smile and waved them forward.

Her expression was one of pleasant encouragement. It did very little to persuade me to believe what was false. I didn't belong there.

I promised her a lie: I would later join her. With a shrug, she linked arms with Marion and ambled toward the house. They subsequently disappeared behind the closed front door.

Rain drizzled from the sky, misting everything in sight. The clouds threatened to rob the full moon of its light, darkening the poorly lit areas bordering the house. My steps followed where my eye was trained: the stables. Finding them empty, the sinking pit of disappointment added to my down state.

On the brink of exiting through the back of the stables, Hayden and Mason's unexpected presence piqued my curiosity.

The clouds receded, permitting the full moon to outline their general features. As they walked deeper into the barn and closer to me, the moving silhouettes became more clear.

I couldn't make out much of what was said. The moment I grasped a word in a foreign tongue, the conversation transformed into quiet whispers.

I stepped closer while keeping to the shadow side of the stable, hoping I'd be able to uncover the language they utilized. The drizzle outside turned into a downpour, hindering my ability to eavesdrop.

With his back facing me, Hayden paused all movement, standing frozen in place. In an instant, too quickly to allow me to react, he peered over his shoulder in my direction, and Mason followed his line of sight.

Worried that they might've seen me, I scattered into an open stable.

"We can hear you," Hayden called to the other end of the barn, startling me. "You can stop playing hide and seek and step out of the shadows."

The thumping in my chest pained me. My feet were firmly planted on the dirt floor of the stables.

Mason and Hayden exchanged a look with one another and nodded at the unspoken.

Mason's steps were hard and heavy thuds as he swiftly moved toward me.

My senses finally returned to me and directed my steps toward the opening of the stables. I bumped into the doorway and tipped over a rake. It fell with a loud crash, sending a shuddering echo throughout the barn before I could catch it.

I stepped out into the hard pounding rain, intending to run. Moisture pelted me and threatened my view. Unsure of where to run, I pressed my back against the galvanized iron walls.

Mason halted at the barn door, shielded from the rain. With a menacing tilt of the corner of his mouth, he regarded the sky. "Think mother nature is giving us a do over?" His eyes settled on me. "This time you won't be able to run in your room and lock the door." Hastily, Mason ripped off his shirt and thrust it down to the ground. With one large step forward he held his body under the hard-hitting shower.

Mason paused a good distance in front of me to remove another piece of clothing and threw it toward me. His pants landed a few feet shy from where I stood.

Blinking through the onslaught of moisture soaking my lashes and my skin, I cast a pleading look toward Hayden who stood a fair distance away. He stuffed his hands in the pocket of his jeans and leaned against the far wall of the barn. I could've sworn he was smirking.

Control became something I no longer had. My attention was pulled to Mason like my life depended upon it. Rivulets of water streamed down his body, traveling down the caverns of his form, and slowly drizzling down the protruding muscles in his shoulders, arms, chest, and abdomen.

Straightening his spine, he palmed his dark blond hair back, appearing brown by the water and the lack light, as it began to drape across his forehead from its once straight and sculpted barber-tapered hairstyle. Beads of water kissed his light tan skin tone. The artery in his neck rolled and tensed. The ball of his Adam apple rolled and receded with his dramatic swallow.

The urgent clearing of his throat drew my eye back to his face. Eyes reflecting the color of espresso in the dark narrowed at me. "I know how much you like it when I'm...wet."

Keeping my eyes low, I allowed myself to only view Mason's feet.

Grabbing either side of my face, he jerked my head up and bent to touch his forehead to mine, forcing me to look at him. I gasped in reaction, shocked and unsure of what to do. I held my hands out aiming to push him away. No longer able to see Hayden for Mason clouding my vision, I stopped hoping he'd step in.

"Why do you do that so much?" The quiet in his voice was mixed with a heady promise. The rhythm of the rain pinging against the ground served as background noise. "Do you think no one can see you, or do you think you can steer clear of seeing anyone? Is that why you ran from me? Is that why you didn't use my phone number when you were told to?"

"I have a boyfriend," I blurted out. "I only came with—for Penny."

His smile spread slowly and the sight of it entranced me, ensuring I remained immovable. "Do you believe your lies, baby? Because I don't."

"It's not a lie," I protested weakly, shivering and soaked.

"What do you want me to believe you came here for? Free beer?"

"I hate beer."

"Are you going to tell me what we both know you came here for and stop pretending?" He chewed on his lip for a moment as the corner of his mouth began to tilt.

"It's a horse stable. I thought—"

"Ten feet away and I think you could hear how silent it was in here. You could've left, but you stuck around, and we both know why."

I looked down only to be met with him firming his hold on my head to the point of hurting me.

"Look...at...me." The grit and hoarseness in his voice shattered my composure. A face that belonged in pictorials or not, his voice and his demeanor commanded; the trepidation he elicited forced compliance.

I obliged, despite wishing I had the strength and will to do the opposite. "I wasn't trying to spy on you." I stared at the droplets darkening and thickening his dense dark blond lashes as the rain began to taper off.

Swallowing hard, I allowed my gaze to trail lower, to nearly hairless and defined abdominal muscles. His heather-gray boxers were rain soaked and revealed the imprint of his cock. It throbbed and hardened.

He caught my notice and bit into the corner of his curled lip. Pretty brown eyes smiled at me. "No, I know you didn't come here to spy. Every time you see me, you tell the truth without saying a word. You stayed for one reason." An open mouthed grin made me shudder. "A fuck."

"I'm sorry if I gave off signals at the house, but I'm not interested in you."

"You know what I think?" His chin touched his chest, the shadows added to his daunting presence. "I think you're very fucking interested in me. Keep fighting it. Keep misdirecting. I'll chase you and fuck you sore for the game you're playing." His teeth sank into the plumpness of his lips, lips I couldn't steal my gaze away from. "The way you can't stop drooling over my cock, you can't tell me you don't daydream about me plugging it down your throat."

"You flatter yourself way too much." I stared perplexingly at his soaked boxer shorts. His cock throbbed again, revealing it's long and thick shape.

He ducked down into my view, disrupting me from my bold and unabashed act, forcing me to look into his eyes. "My face isn't down there, baby."

"I'm sorry I didn't call. I'm sorry if you think I'm giving you mixed signals. I'm not. Let me go." I clutched his hands, trying to remove them from my face. He began to walk, forcing me backward. In my steps and spaces of my view, I noticed we were now alone.

My back slapped the horse enclosure with a resounding hard thud.

"You're a cop. You said you were safe. Why are you doing this? A power trip?"

"Do you really remember the chat we had? Because I know I said our definitions for safe weren't the same." He laughed low and softly. "I get it. You think because I put my job first and didn't grab you by the hair into one of the hotel rooms when we met, or break your bedroom door down and fuck the cock-teasing ways out of you like I imagined doing, it makes me a nice guy? A *safe* bet?"

A tingle inched down my spine and awakened the area between my thighs. Embarrassed and ashamed by my own body, I quaked in anger—at him and myself. "Stop it." I flailed my arms, intending to push him away; a stark contradiction to what I wanted—for him to continue.

He lurched forward, completely erasing the space between his body and mine and wrapped his hands around the galvanized rod.

"You shouldn't have worn a skirt, Whitney." He touched his lips to my nose, subduing my struggle to make him stop. "I can smell how wet your pussy is from here."

My craggy breaths and erratic movements gave myself away even if I wanted to object. I wanted to picture him under my mercy with a leather strap binding his neck. Instead, it was me on my knees, willingly giving up a power I held sacred.

He reached down and touched the inside of my thigh. I smacked his hand away. A mistake I regretted. My wrists were gathered in one of his brawny and heavily veined hands and directed to rest on top of my head.

"You came here for a fuck, and you don't know how badly I want to give you that. To slam your face against the fence and plant that ass on my cock and fuck you so hard; you would swear the impossible happened and an earthquake came to Bebletown. I'm going to fuck you sore, Whitney, and you're going to take it." He winked, giving me a wide mouth and skewed smile. "Turn around and grab the fence."

"You're unbelievable," I said through a gasp. "You can't talk to people this way."

"I'm talking to you, not other people, and I've already planted my flag on your body. You are my territory to do whatever the fuck I please."

"I'm not your territory, and there's nothing I want from you, especially not now."

"Here you are…standing here and letting me say whatever the fuck I want to you." He let his thick, rose-hued bottom lip disappear between his teeth. "Let's not pretend, baby. You like it just as rough as I want to give it to you."

I couldn't hide the shudder nor the reminder of the visions that infiltrated my thoughts when I was with Mason inside my home. If I ever gave in to what I denied, he was destined to fulfill my fantasy. He offered it to me in an offensive way, and I was close to swallowing down a pill laced with razors like an addict unable to get clean. A poisoned pill never looked more decadent.

I lurched forward, my breasts mashing against his chest in an effort to push him away. Acutely aware of my wet, sensitive, and hardened nipples brushing up against his damp form, I moved back. He increased the contact of our bodies, pushing his bare chest against my breasts, pressing them to his body as his chest muscles twitched and hardened.

"Let me go, or I'll scream." My weak pleas were whispers in the dark of night.

"I'm not going to let you go until I make you scream." Fire ignited his words, burning me to cinders.

"Y-you don't know me. You don't know the things I've done and what I could do to you. I could hurt you."

He remained impenetrable. "You think you're a match for me?" He paused for a stitch. "I'll take you on and make you into someone you never thought you were. I will fuck up your world and make you like the wreckage I leave behind. Understand this…I know everything going on inside that twisted and dirty little mind. And you know why? You told me."

He was a symbol for good in a once safe, albeit hypocritical, town. He wasn't supposed to be the temptation or the windowless space for my bad to flourish. "I've met a lot of men like you." I writhed my wrists in his hold. The wet skin against skin contact created a pleasurable friction. "You're just a bully."

Brandy colored eyes dipped into darker hues. Spearmint-scented breath splayed across my face. "Apologize." His anger was barely bridled, having revealed the struggle he maintained to keep it at bay within his gaze.

The rapid pace of my heart resounded inside my ears. The swirling pit in my stomach began to migrate. The snappy comebacks I could've stated slipped away, falling out of my reach.

He removed his hand from my wrists only to join with his other to move across my throat, obstructing my ability to swallow. "Fucking apologize to me."

I didn't gasp or struggle. I fit my neck fully into his hand, daring him to leave marks.

My gesture softened his features. "You like that?" His soft lips swayed down my nose. "I'm going to have so much fun with this body. Not tonight. Tonight you're not ready."

The thickening heat intensified, leaving me without the ability to breathe freely. My wet clothes weighed more than they should have. A disturbing itch manifested all over my skin. Everything in me screamed yes, pining for weightlessness and an itch scratched until I begged for more.

Scared of what awaited me at the end of the descent, I fought to divert and deny. "Let...me...go." My shallow breaths weren't enough; I began to feel faint. Desperation toward filling the unfilled impulses left me weakened.

"I'll let you go after I give you the full view of what you couldn't take your eyes off of yesterday."

"You're wearing underwear."

He moved one hand down and pulled down his boxers, pulling something out of them.

I searched his eyes, willing myself to keep my curiosity at bay. My lips parted, and my skin was set ablaze with a scorching fever every word, every glance, and every touch elicited.

Unable to manage the formulation of words, I shook my head.

"You're going to do what I told you to do and look at cock. Because if you ignore me again, I'm going to force it down your throat and make you gag on it." His deep baritone voice assaulted my ears with its quiet and deep hum.

The blood rush, resounding loudly through my ears, left me without the immediate use of my sense of hearing for a few seconds.

I quickly glanced down at his cock, standing erect and thick in his hands before rolling my eyes up. My fists clenched into little balls torn between punching the cockiness out of him or baiting him for further beautiful punishment. "Can you let me go now?"

His steps receded as he pulled up his boxers. "I'll play your game, Whitney." He nodded to the stable door. "Get the fuck out of here before I arrest you and take you to the station for trying to steal the home owner's jewelry. You know this town. Who do you think they'll believe? Don't fuck with my patience, because I really like the idea of you being stuck in the small town jail, alone...with me." A sinister flash sparked in his eyes. "Someday."

I shook with anger and embarrassment over being turned on by his degradation. "You're an asshole."

"And you don't know when to stop adding to my list. I have a very long memory." Storm clouds possessed his eyes with each passing second. It stole every stitch of sense I had. In that moment, I'd never wanted something so wrong and so badly.

With a satisfied smirk, he gave me space to leave.


"What's wrong, hun?" Having run straight into Penny, her arm around a distraught Marion, and unable to hide the evidence that Mason had affected me, her concern was warranted. "Oh my god, you got caught in the rain? And you're covered in hives. Are you okay, hun?" She released her friend and reached out, wanting to touch me.

I quickly withdrew and tucked my hands underneath my armpits in a defensive stance.

The anger toward myself for my reaction, and toward Mason for implanting thoughts inside the shadiest parts of my mind that should never have existed, coursed through my veins. Closing my eyes, I counted my breaths until I calmed down. "I just want to go home." I glanced from Marion to the house. "What happened in there? Is she okay?"

Penny exchanged looks of disgust with her friend. "The-so-called party wasn't what we thought it would be. No one from town was there, not even Blake. Have not a clue where they came from. It's not for us. We…didn't feel safe."

"G-garen," Marion forced through sobs. "I was flirting with him, but it was innocent. I told him I liked someone else, but he wouldn't take no for an answer. He—he tried to get me alone and take me down to the basement and, and…" Marion burst into tears and covered her face.

Penny wrapped her arms around Marion as she shook with dramatic sobs. "That's all I can get out of her. She won't tell me what she saw down there. I think Garen scared her into not telling. I'll get it out of her soon, so we know if we should go to the Sheriff's office."

"I won't talk about it," Marion professed, struggling out of her friend's grasp. "I will never talk about it." She held herself and plodded away, moving swiftly toward Penny's car.

"W-what happened back there?" I asked Penny.

With a sullen shake of her head, Penny shut down the conversation. "Let's just say we're never coming back here again."

# FIVE

THE UNASSUMING SINGLE BLACKED out door, leading to a modest brick building swooshed closed behind my entrance. At the counter, a haze of long red hair disappeared behind the glass display case with a hissed curse. Whomever it had been, it certainly wasn't Robert, the man who usually worked at this time of the day. I approached the counter and lifted up on the soles of my feet to gain height. A woman huddled behind the glass display case of expensive hand-blown glass sex toys with her arms over her head.

"Penny? Is that you?" Shocked that she was behind the desk, indicating she was a new employee, my mouth gaped and my steps remained still.

Uncovering her hands from her head. Her emerald eyes widened and her fair skin reddened. "Hey, Whitney!" Her greeting matched the theatrics of her smile.

It was surprising to see her there, being that Kylie boasted about Penny's vow to God to remain a virgin until marriage. "A job is a job. It doesn't get to say who you are. I won't tell anyone…as long as you don't tell anyone I come here, occasionally." I gave her a sheepish grin that seemed to relax her.

"Whew." She relaxed. "My mother is a total controlling succubus, if she knew I worked here, she'd have a fit."

I slid off my plaid fedora, smoothing the ponytail of my straightened blue-black hair that hit the middle of my back. I looked at her with question, feeling skeptical about adding to my collection being that she was someone I knew would scrutinize my purchase and either shame me or judge me for enjoying indecent behavior. She couldn't have looked more uncomfortable in her new job.

"Is…Robert working?" He usually supplied me with what I needed under the table.

"Nope. He left. I think he went back to his home country or something. Avon isn't selling much in our town, and you know how bad unemployment is. You were really blessed to get three jobs." She glanced down from the television playing a porn movie. An expression falling between a grimace and a smile contorted her mouth. "The lingerie and costume section is on the right."

I'd frequented the store at least weekly and could navigate the departments and its shelves while blinded. Robert had told me the only other store to find the films he sold me in secret were within a good distance. While the acts were realistically faked, they were generally frowned upon in adult stores and not easily found. Despite my searches, I never uncovered a shred of truth to the myth of snuff films—despite Nick telling me that they were real and a guarded secret of very powerful men.

Robert's departure and the likelihood of him taking his stash of snuff-inspired films with him, would force me to drive five counties over to satisfy my depraved fix. As I debated my next steps, my gaze settled on a poster featuring Nick Kent.

Scanning the poster that caught my attention, she nodded. "A few girls who came in said the poster was morbid. I don't know who he is. It's not that I watch porn a lot, but I've…never seen him in one." She clasped her hand to her head and sighed. "Don't tell my mom that, either. She'll send me to a convent. I'm not kidding. She's such a hypocrite, I can't stand it."

The television located in the upper left hand quadrant of the store displayed a very explicit threesome scene.

She knew where my attention trailed but refused to look at it. She frenetically waved her hand in the direction of the screen. "The girls told me about what happened to Nick. I asked the manager about taking it down, but he won't let me. He claims that because they never found his body, he's not dead. I guess that gives him a good enough reason to keep it up."

It didn't matter if they had found his body; Nick Kent was dead because I was the one who'd killed him. If there was anything left to be found, it would be his decayed body. Even in death, the man's ghost haunted my mind. Guilt over what I had done maintained a strangled hold on my thoughts.

Leaning over the counter, she gestured for me to come closer.

Taking my time, I took short strides toward her.

"People don't want to remember, but Nick was raised in Bebletown—well, sort of. He was raised in the house where the party was last night. I went to grade school with him."

"I never knew that." The veracity of my statement added to my awe. The coincidence was nearly shocking. "Do you know about his parents? The people who own that house?"

"Just some old rich Russian woman, I think. No one's seen her in town. They say the place was a vacation home, and she had some nanny raise Nick while she traveled. I think some drama happened and Nick was taken away. Whatever happened, he came back to her for good." She wrapped her well-manicured hands on the counter. "I'd never been inside the house until last night. Never will again."

"Speaking of, is Marion okay?"

"She's got the eye of the guy she wanted so everything is all good now. Whatever it was, it couldn't have been that bad if she forgot about it." She lifted her eyebrows in question. "Was there something I could help you find?"

"Robert…usually has a private selection of films for me." I expected her to be perplexed, but instead there was a tinge of surprise in her features.

She cupped her hands around her mouth and spoke in hushed tones to me. "Robert left a few things. Movies." She regarded the counter for a few seconds before drifting her eyes up to me. "Is that what you were looking for?"

"Can you explain them to me?"

"Erotic torture porn films. One of the other girls who works here told me about them. She said Nick's in a few of the movies Robert left. Have you heard of those kinds of films? They are like fake snuff films because you can't do the real thing. My coworker said in one of them he kidnaps"—she paused to use air quotes around the word kidnaps—"a woman and pretends to rape and beat her to death."

"Never seen one," I replied innocently. "The things Robert gave me...were different." My guilt over the lie likely gave me away. It appeared it would be a lie easily slid past her.

"The owner doesn't want them destroyed even though it bothers us girls who work here," she whispered. "I don't really know why he keeps them in the back."

"Hate to say I'm curious."

"Are you sure?" She smiled broadly. "I would've never guessed you were a closeted freak, Whit. Since when have you been into those kinds of movies?"

"Since I was thirteen and found one of my mother's old porn tapes."

Not a single thing on her person moved with the exception of her mascara laden eyelashes batting rapidly. After a few awkward seconds, her apricot-stained lips slightly parted.

"I didn't mean that the way it sounds," I said quickly, my cheeks hot with embarrassment. "It wasn't a scene with her. At least not the first one. It was a scene with a man dominating another man and..." I pressed my lips together to stop talking. I'd already said more than I should've said.

She finally moved her head, swaying it from right to left. "Your mother was a porn star?"

I hoped in remaining silent she would forget what she had heard and change the topic.

Taking a moment to make me uncomfortable with her stare again, she turned on a dime and motioned for me to follow her towards the back.

The curtains to the viewing rooms swayed, providing glimpses of the men held up in the small booths. I kept my eyes forward, following her to the end of the hall. Three short steps led to an access door. Painted in blaring red was the warning: "Mangers Only."

Using her key ring, she unlocked the door to the narrow room, outlined with boxes of unopened and opened shipments of DVDs. She shuffled through them to a particular place hidden behind a framed poster of a porn star. With a few turns left and right of the lock, she cracked it open and pulled out a small gift box. She handed me the box. "Just don't tell anyone I gave it to you for free. I really need this job and don't want to get in trouble."

I slid the top off the cover. In black marker was the label: "Dirty Cop." Behaving less than giddy about something I was embarrassingly excited over, I took the DVD and slid it into my messenger bag.

She closed up the safe, placing everything in order, and led me back toward the merchandising area.

My head was turned to the exit, intending to quickly bid her goodbye and head home.

"So what's new?" She grabbed my hand from across the counter and leaned over it. Eyeing my chipped manicure between her red gel nails, she made a face and dropped my hand.

"Oh, nothing," I said, keeping things casual. "Still working three jobs."

"You're going to work yourself to death, Whit. You need to take care of you." Her gaze shot up to mine and was riddled with traces of a plan. "You need something to do…like a boyfriend. Not saying you need to have sex, just someone to spend time with. I swear I'll talk to Hayden the next time I see him about taking you out. Maybe we could double date?"

I toyed with the strap of my messenger bag as I rummaged through my thoughts in an effort to find the best answer. "I don't plan on staying in this town forever. I'm saving up to go somewhere else when the time is right."

"How close are you to your goal?"

"Close."

She released a suppressed laugh. "I think I remember my mother saying that you told her that a week ago."

Shame and embarrassment pricked my skin like tiny pokers laced with acid. I said it once in passing in the rare occasion Kylie actively engaged in a conversation with me. I had no idea she actually internalized the small tidbit of information. "You and Kylie…chat about me?"

"They should call Bebletown the gossip center because that's all we have to do. Talk about people. It's never anything bad about you. We're both worried."

"I'm not really that interesting." I shrugged sheepishly. "Why did you want to work here?" I hoped to move her to another topic.

"I have to help my mom out with her bills. I want to save up what I earn here and get us out of this town. I'm tired of the women with nothing better to do judging my mom and spreading mean lies about her." She pointed to me and beamed. "I bet you can relate to that with your mother being who she was, huh?"

I fingered a speck of dust from the metal support bar on the glass counter, having no intention of broaching the subject of my mother. "Do you make a lot here?"

"I wouldn't have accepted the job offer if I didn't." She sat upright, resting her hands at her sides. "Are you looking for a fourth job?"

"It's not like I have anything else to do."

Her bottom lip protruded as she shook her head in sadness. "That's so sad, Whit. You know you can always hang out with me if you're lonely and don't want male company." Puffing out her cheeks, she sent forth a steady stream of air. "I only started this job a week ago, but it's okay as long as I don't run into someone I know."

"Sorry."

"No. No." She rejected my apology. "You're the most interesting thing to happen today."

I was debating taking another job after I received a call in the morning with last minute changes to my usual workday schedule. My hours were reduced from full time to part-time on the night shift. It couldn't have been a coincidence; it was retaliation from Blake. "The call center recently cut my hours. The manager claimed I wasn't meeting the monthly goals."

"That's too bad, Whit. You'll be okay. Keep saving and you'll get out of this place for good."

# SIX

"ORDER UP," I PROJECTED my voice through the small window toward the prep area of Wingettes and moved on to my next ticket.

From the other side, Cinda gathered the baskets of chicken and placed them on her tray. Fixing up the fries, she used a squeeze bottle and applied chemically manufactured spicy cheese.

At Wingettes, things were mildly different. I was able to stick to my mantra of interacting with little to no one and stuck to the kitchen duties. Thankfully, I hadn't been given the job of being a member of the wait staff. The requirements imposed on them drew attention from customers. They were front and center and the co-stars to the central feature: the food. The makeup required to be worn by the all female wait staff was inspired by the fashionable and daring women in the '50s: thick winged liner, heavy lashes, and red lipstick. The uniforms were high-waist red seersucker mini-skorts or high-waist shorts with white button-ups that had the Wingettes logo on the right breast pocket. Hair had to be up in ponytails or high buns with a red bandana knotted forward. The few men who waited tables simply wore white short-sleeved button-ups and slacks.

The town adhered to biblical law inconsistently. A restaurant toting secular and immoral values could remain because it meant resources for the town. The town ostracized who they considered to be the less savory of the population, who then loitered at the hotel considered a dirty secret—the hotel where I was employed. It made very little sense to me. Drug addicts were considered to be the devil's pawns, but a restaurant promoting scantily clad women was deemed acceptable.

"Whitney," the manager, Baxter, barked as he stood on the other side of the prep station and beckoned for me. Sweat beads decorated his forehead. His face and large bald spot glistened with oil like a beacon. Ill-fitting white button-up and slacks loosely hung on his stout form.

Fending off a rush of nerves, I removed my plastic gloves and walked around the counter. "Yes, sir?"

He busied himself with his phone as he pointed toward the corridor leading to his office and the employee locker area. "Got a call in. Uniform for you in my office. You're up front today."

My nerves had taken to choking me, leaving me unable to speak right away. "But, sir—"

"You want this job, go get dressed and wait tables. You can shadow Cinda if you need to."

"Are you kidding?" Cinda, a longstanding young waitress at Wingettes, entered the food prep area. She flicked her long blonde ponytail to one side and set her bright blue eyes on me. "The way this girl whizzes through orders and watches me, she doesn't need any training. Put her on the floor and see what she can do."

*Shit.*


"Oh, my god!" Cinda squealed and tried to grab my arm. I dodged her to save myself from dropping my order, but instead, I lost half the order anyhow. I groaned inwardly as I stared at the scattering of fries on the ground. The day just continuously became incrementally worse. "I have a table of obnoxious brats. If I piss them off, Baxter will have my job. Please take my section. You'll do fine. Keep being quiet like you always are. I'll trade you a Saturday, plus half my tips from three tables."

Much to my chagrin, it seemed my promotion was permanent. "I want to help, but I need my weekends." I multitasked, keeping the tray still as I pushed the fries out of my path with my foot.

She clutched my arm a little tighter, expressing her eagerness. "I'll cut you in five tables at my section."

"Who are they?" I began to walk out of the kitchen galley toward the dining area.

"Thanks for taking the abuse," she said without answering my question.

I finished serving my waiting customers and checked on a few more before I grabbed a few waters and approached the table Cinda claimed she couldn't take. My steps stumbled when I discovered who was at the table: Mason and Blake.

Blake was a regular at Wingettes. While the place was known as the hangout for the local law enforcement, I hardly ever saw Mason there until a week after I was hired, and then he became a regular. They were both notoriously known for being very difficult customers.

From what Cinda said about watching her retaliatory behavior from them, they both had to have exerted power over the town that allowed their behavior to remain unchecked.

I found solace in the fact that I'd never have to be a waitress serving their table—until today. Hayden appeared with them. Having never taken the time to sit down and commune with his friends, he walked past their table in the opposite direction while clutching his phone, and headed out of the entrance doors.

I stopped by the side of the table and placed the waters down on the dark wood surface and caught Mason's eye instantly. Dressed down in a pair of jeans and T-shirt, his hair free of any gel and falling toward his forehead, I fought back the more vapid emotion. As he watched me, the shift in his eyes was palpable. My day hadn't stopped its descent into hell.

I repeated the scripted spiel with my shoulders held back and my head held high: "Welcome to Wingettes, home of a hundred and one flavors. I'm Whitney. I'll be your server this afternoon. Our specials today are twenty buffalo wings for ten bucks and draft beer for a dollar. Are you ready to order or would you like a few moments?"

I wasn't used to the leering. When it occurred for a little too long, I made a silent promise to find some way of making the waitressing position temporary.

I nodded and pointed my pencil to the pad in an effort to get them to get on with their order.

"Why couldn't you be braless?" Blake continued to drool over the cleavage revealed between the open part of my shirt. "You could move from a four to a six if you were."

Mason, no longer carrying an easy expression, leaned across the table and glowered at Blake.

"I was just kidding, man." Blake appeared suddenly nervous.

Willing myself against untangling the web set before me to uncover what had unfolded between them, I held up my smile. "I'll come back when you're ready to order."

Mason gripped my wrist in the middle of my stride. I yanked my arm back and repeated my sentiment.

"Oops." Mason slipped his eating utensils off the table, sending them to the ground nearest the adjacent table. "Can you get that for me, baby?"

I squatted down to pick up the silverware and placed them inside the pocket of my apron. "I'll get you a new set, sir."

The instant I turned to do that, Mason swept his arm across the wood surface. His friend's utensils propelled into the air and clipped my hip before they dropped to the ground. "I like the way you call me sir." He pointed to the silverware on the ground. "Might want to get that bending over directly in front of me...or who knows how many other forks might go flying off the table."

Subduing the anger bubbling inside my chest, I bent over to pick up the items. Feeling a hand on my back of my legs, I jerked upright. Mason stood before me, holding one of the glasses of ice water I had brought to the table. He poured the contents of the glass down the front of my shirt. Shocking ice water doused my breasts and manipulated the protrusion of my nipples.

Lifting the cup high above my head, he dropped it on the ground. "When you're done cleaning that up, I want you to give me a smile, a real one, and ask how you can help me. Don't forget the sir."

A sharp and cutting "fuck you" was on the tip of my lips, but it wouldn't come forth. Mason tripped a wire, creating an explosive sensation inside me that made it hard to breathe much less maintain the stance of a woman who wouldn't have allowed him to treat me this way.

A few patrons and staff pretending not to stare, had noticed. My humiliation was put on display. My skin teemed with a scorching heat. My entire being bellowed for more. I'd never experienced a sensation that left me feeling so…fallible.

"Why are you being such an asshole?" In my denial of what Mason evoked, I questioned him like what I assumed a normal woman would've. "Is it because I called you a bully; you feel like you have to play up the part?"

A hint of surprise followed by a flare of bedlam filled his eyes. "Why am I doing this? You really want to pretend I'm the one corrupting *your* mind? You asked me for this, and I'm doing it because I know how it makes those thick thighs moist with the juices from your pussy." He touched my chin with the pad of his thumb. Quiet little threats were served through his light brown eyes and sent a flushing heat to drape my face.

The man had turned me inside out, and I no longer knew my exterior from my interior. He latched on to a small seed inside of me I didn't know existed and watered its roots.

Squatting down, I gathered the utensils in my unsteady hands and stuck them inside the cup. Standing tall, I gave him a plastic smile. "Is there anything I can get for you, *Sir?*"

"It makes me hard when you obey, baby. Very." His voice was quiet enough to ensure privacy between us. His eyes skated down my body, staring at the private parts of me as though they were bore to him. "Give me a real smile and not the fake one you give to people who don't matter." The grin he carried spoke words he didn't: *"I am the man who owns you. You've been mine from the second I laid eyes on you. Tell these people who you belong to."*

In a state of self-loathing over my unwelcome craving, I managed to fight through it and give him a genuine smile, confirming that he had begun to etch the first letter of his name on the gateway to my void.

Satisfied with himself, he slid back into the booth. "Give us the special three times over and keep it coming." Glancing at his empty cup I clutched in my unsteady hands, he added, "And another ice water."

"Of course, sir," I said through a smile. "Is there anything else I can get for you?"

Rubbing his lips, his eyes drifted up my body, pausing at every place as though I was his freshly bought and prided piece of machinery. "That's all I need right now. Thanks, baby."

On the heels of my departure, I heard Blake ask Mason. "Are you two dating?"

"My name is branded on her ass, and that's all the fuck you need to know," said Mason.

Shivering against the icicles of anger fueled by needs split between retribution and having Mason fulfill fantasies only he seemed to elicit, I fought against shutting my eyes and watching the scenes of his abasement replay behind my dark eyelids. He didn't deserve it, he deserved the other side of me.

"Take a break." Baxter caught me at the prep station while I was in the midst of handing off my order on the trolley. My hand shook severely; it became a painstaking process.

Bewildered and concerned my job was in immediate danger, I swept away the anger, imploring Baxter to give me a chance. "But I—"

"Take a break, Whitney." Baxter pointedly nodded to the Mason's table.

"I can do this. They won't get to me again. Don't take me off their table. I need the tips." I more or less referred to Cinda's promise and not to a kind duty to serve the assholes at the table. Blake and Mason were known for leaving menial tips for waitresses who didn't indulge their—more or less, Blake's—antics.

I understood why he took a very particular stance on the situation. Five years ago, Baxter was slapped with a lawsuit by an ex-employee, claiming Wingettes was a hostile work environment. She lost her case and immediately afterward, the townspeople turned on her and bullied her into leaving town. Inhabitants of Bebletown didn't like the thought of the town's money-maker receiving negative publicity or threats of closure due to court and lawyer fees.

Complying with Baxter's wishes, I took off my black bar apron, balling it in my hands as I exited the prep area. Navigating down the corridor, leading to the manager's office and employee lockers, I rushed out through the delivery door.

Pinching the material of my shirt, I fanned it to trap more of the cool June breeze against my skin and dry the water stain on my shirt.

A few feet away, Hayden paced the sidewalk with his phone glued to his ear. He immediately ended the call and seemed perplexed by the interaction. He cast a passing glance my way, but for some reason or another, allowed his eyes to settle on me for a burdening amount of time. As I returned his stare, his expression dissolved away from anger. "What?"

"I'm waiting for an apology."

He contracted both brows, appearing boggled. "For?"

"Your friend Mason cornered me and said some pretty rude things to me at the stable for your party the other night. You could've stepped in, but you didn't."

His eyes whirled in his sockets and he pinched his nose as he exhaled a stream of wavering air. "First of all"—he dropped his arm and swayed his head at me in contempt—"I don't remember seeing you at all yesterday, which makes sense because I never left the house last night."

"I know what I saw."

"Psychotic episodes and paranoia. You really, really should see someone, Whitney." The concern in his words threw me completely from straddling the line of determining his personality type. "I'm not going to apologize for something that didn't happen.

His believable reference to his absence brought my sanity into question. It wasn't the first time I might've saw things that weren't there. Since Nick died, at times I thought I saw him in the faces of strangers.

Hayden rolled his shoulders and contemplated the azure sky, filled with cumulus clouds intermittently hiding the sun. "I'm sure you have somewhere else you'd rather be."

"I'd honestly rather be here."

My words widely missed plucking the vein to agitate and provoke him for some unforeseen reason. Reclining against the wall near the back door, he ran his hand wildly through his dark hair, leaving it in less of a structured messy state.

Gearing up to dig at an issue that perplexed me, I inhaled a breath of courage. "You don't remember anything at all about what happened in—or outside the barn?"

He turned squarely to face me. "What do you want, Whitney? An apology for not being your shining knight when I don't remember being in a place I know I wasn't?"

"I'm not a damsel, but that doesn't excuse you from being a gentleman." My sarcasm was cutting and plucked the vein I missed previously.

His body tensed. His lids lowered, casting a haunting shadow over his hazel eyes. "Again, I don't remember what happened that night, but I do know you're being a bitch and it's completely uncalled for."

"Me?" I pointed inward, my simple question marred with incredulity. "Why can't you remember walking away and letting your friend have at me? He's… not right. I can't imagine the things he could've done to me."

"But…he didn't do any of the things you imagined he would, did he? Things you probably wanted him to do deep down." Unable to hide his grin, he showed his straight white teeth and just how deep his dimples dug into his cheeks. "I'm sorry for not doing things for you that I don't remember and know didn't happen, Whitney. Does that solve your issues with me?"

"I'm not the kind of person to hold a grudge." I rolled my shoulders up, keeping my hands casually in my pockets. I dropped the issue because I was no longer certain if I imagined it or if Hayden was screwing with me. "You're newer to this town than I am, but you seem to have fit in pretty quickly."

"Because I'm the pillar of fucking everything."

"And here's the world's smallest cricket playing the world's smallest violin." I yanked my hands out of my pockets and pantomimed playing the instrument.

Covering his mouth, he chortled. "You should be this girl more often." His demeanor sank, his face held a more grim expression. "You're new here, so the town gossips say, but I can tell you want to continue to fly under the radar. You're not exactly doing a good job of it." He stepped forward, and I stepped backward.

"I'm blending in as well as I can."

"You don't blend, Whitney. A few of us here don't."

"You seem to."

"I don't. Mason, as much as he hides in the protect and serve position, he doesn't blend, either. We are very mixed up and can't meld with anyone outside of people who are like us. Our colors are too dark and messy to fit inside the lines this town creates."

"People like us?"

"From the second I met you at work, I could see it. You're wading in a pool of dark, Whitney. You're in denial about it."

My unreliable determination of the real world became clearer, sending blaring red warnings inside my head. Last night did happen, and for some reason I couldn't discern, Hayden needlessly denied the events.

Misgauging the curb during my stride toward the back door, I lost my balance. I flung my arms around in an awkward attempt to regain my equilibrium.

Hayden grabbed my arms, yanking me forward. I pulled my arms back abruptly and shifted my feet backward, providing myself with much-needed personal space.

"What's wrong with you?" Hayden's eyes were wild with wonder. "Do you have a phobia of people touching you?"

"I don't like it when certain men touch me, especially without asking permission first."

"You're one of *those* women?"

The word "those" and "women" were said with a disdain, and it left a sour taste on my tongue. "What exactly is that supposed to mean?"

"It means you're self-righteous and a huge hypocrite. You've also taken up to stalking me and formulating daydreams about our interactions."

"I work here, and I did not make it up. It happened, and you know it did." Recalling the shifts in Mason's behavior from when I first met him to today, there had to be a reason for the slight change. He was always domineering in our interactions, but never so overtly staking his dibs on me that he felt the need to publicly shame me. "Did the two of you set that thing up outside the barn to test me?"

More blinking and stunned looks. "This isn't an attempt at a joke; you're starting to concern me."

Unable to endure much more of the way Hayden purposely pushed my buttons, I turned away from him having the full motivation to leave. My blouse clung to me, reminding me I didn't have a change of shirt fit for waiting tables.

I abruptly spun around to be met with Hayden standing inches in front of me, assaulting me with his inquisitive stare.

"I came out here for a break." The words burst forcefully from my mouth. "Not to bother you...or for you to bother me."

Amusement ignited a glow in his cheeks. He was enjoying this far too much. "Technically, you provoked the conversation."

"You would've said something even if I didn't, because for some reason, you are getting a kick out of making me think I'm psychotic."

"Maybe you're a little too crazy for me, Whitney." The muttered words, no matter how low and quiet, stung me beneath the surface. He dropped his chin for a moment and shook his head. Shielded by his dark lashes, his eyes leveled up to me with his chin flushed to his chest. The mirth was siphoned from his expression at a pace faster than I thought possible. Hayden's eyes sliced and diced me into near oblivion. "How good are you on your promises?"

"Excuse me?"

"I asked..." The intensity in his gaze strengthened, darkening his expression. "…how good you were on your promises?"

"My word is my bond, usually."

"Then make me a promise, if you see me again, don't speak to me. Like you wish you didn't, pretend I don't exist."

It was impossible to pilot the sharp summits and rifts of his mood. They changed in an instant and never came with a warning.

"You can't be this way and expect me to sit there and take it," I snapped at him as I tried to work through dismantling the man underneath the mercurial behavior. "I didn't do anything to you, so whatever residual anger you have over college not being what you hoped it would be…or whatever it was that made you come back to this town, it's not my fault."

He stepped backward, his eyes searching the ground in many moments of silence before they turned up to glare at me. "How are your hours at Alloy?"

Feeling the crushing weight of an incorrect conclusion, I stilled. I assumed Blake had something to do with my lack of hours at Alloy; Hayden was seemingly a call center employee. How could it have been that he had the power to cut my hours?

I restrained my shock and gave him a smile, intending it to be dour. "I feel very lucky that you took such a special interest in me."

Without ceremony, Hayden turned his back on me and disappeared into the parking lot.

Upon my return to the dining area, Cinda caught up with me. She was liken to a container of effusive energy when she stuffed several twenty dollar bills into my hands.

"The sun is shining on us today. I ought to give you my tables more often. Mason never tips like this when I wait on his table, then again, he's usually not as bad as he was with you. Usually Blake is the difficult one. Ah! Who cares, look at the tip he left." With a wink she was gone.

I opened my hand to find two hundred dollars.

A small town cop's salary didn't pay well enough for him to be free with his money—Mason must've had a hand in other things. Immoral or not, I needed the money and quickly pocketed it before I changed my mind and returned it to Mason.

# SEVEN

It was an uneventful weekend night of warming up a microwave dinner and watching television. After finishing two cups of my favorite tea, I cleaned up my home and decided to indulge in a habit I hadn't allowed myself to since I came to Bebletown. I collected the DVDs from Robert and kept them stowed away in my chest at the foot of the bed. I never watched them as I had many times prior to leaving my old life. It was dangerous behavior to hoard a collection of the things that reminded me of my illness and sent my self-reproach into overdrive. I convinced myself it would build my strength for resistance.

In the still of night inside my dark bedroom, Mason flooded my head with delicious, demeaning acts. I craved an increase in the severity and toyed with the idea of his claim on me.

*"My name is branded on her ass,"* he had said. I touched the side of my hip with a smile. Maybe someday it would be.

To thrust it all aside, I rummaged through the chest and found the movie Penny had given me and loaded it inside the player.

Stripping off my clothes, I sat on the floor between my bed and the vintage television—so old it needed a convertor—and watched the scene on my screen unfold.

The man's screams as he was impaled with a knife filled the quiet in my room. His body rocked with the violence of Nick's poundings. Nick removed the knife from the man's back and lifted it in the air. The harsh slushing sounds blanketed the muffled wails of his victim. The sex was real, the violence, as usual, was not. The special effects mattered little, the sensation deep inside my core demanded more violence and was easily fooled. My hand rested between my thighs and began to dally with my wet slit.

Nick's face was shielded by the aviator sunglasses he wore. The policeman cap was pulled low over his forehead. Sweat draped his skin, making the intricate and frightening tattoos decorating his body come to life.

Nick brought his hand down abruptly on his victim's back. The sharp metal blade disappeared into the man. Gurgling sounds were heard. The camera panned to the man's face in the midst of a death wail. Watering dark brown eyes became glassed over, his mouth fell agape as though experiencing pleasure.

My eyelids grew heavy, feeling the weight of exhaustion steeling my consciousness. I worked my hand faster. Another slid up to cup my breasts and pinch my hardened nipples. As the eyes of Nick's victim began to change, I came so hard, the world went black.


*Red light fills the room. I catch a glimpse of Nick's figure in a cop uniform before he lurches toward me. He grabs me up, his large fists folding around my neck, and thrusts me back on the bed. Our surroundings become increasingly tinted in a darker shade of red. He plucks up my hand and shoves it upward, directing it around my neck. He pushes in, pressing his palm against mine to restrict my breathing. His sunglasses serve as shields across his eyes and are exactly like the ones he wears in his movies. His tattoos, peeking underneath the short sleeves of the dark blue uniform top haunt me and mock me.*

*Fear rifles through me, settling inside my gut.*

*I'm sure he means to kill me—I can't fight the building sensation, desiring nothing more than to feel the ultimate orgasm.*

*The badge and name tag with no discernible markings of who he is shimmer in the red light, sending a glow across my bed.*

*He pins me down, his hand over mine, restraining me and stealing my oxygen. A hand slides down his body and unbuckles his belt, unzipping his pants with a delayed pace. His hard cock pulses in his hand. He increases the pressure on my throat, forcing my neck to angle and my gaze to rest on him. With a deviant smile drenched in sex, he shoves himself inside me hard and fast.*

*A groan, stuck between pain and desire, unfurls from my throat.*

*The bed rattles underneath me with violence.*

*He thrusts inside me deeper as though he intends to make me bleed. I want him to. It's a need outside my mental capacity to comprehend.*

*In my reality, I don't naturally like the pain or crave someone else to take control of me. I can't ever easily give up my control. But he demands it by taking it and threatening me in silence not to challenge him. He commands my desires by the sheer will of him being inside me, manipulating my body.*

*The harder he thrusts, sending an echo of our skin slapping, colliding into each other to resound between us, the firmer he holds down my hand, forcing me to choke myself.*

*"You're a filthy little whore," he grumbles, straining through panting breaths as he pushes into me harder, slapping his balls against the swell of my ass.*

*His voice is shrouded and deconstructed like it is in his movies.*

*"A filthy whore who likes dirty little things, aren't you? Your cunt is soaking my cock. Do you think you deserve to fucking come, you bitch?"*

*I know the nature of his question, and he isn't referring to a traditional climax. He means his definition of the unmatched orgasm—my death. "Yes," I croak, the admission merely a whistling whisper through straining breaths.*

*"Then, die."*

*It's not his command that wills it. It's the friction of his thrusts, claiming me and ruining me for any man to come before or after him. My thighs shudder around him as the electric pulses consume me in one full sweep. His hips recede, withdrawing his erection. Directing me forward, he positions me until my ass rests on the tops of his thighs. A devilish grin imposes on his lips.*

*He pushes his hips forward, intending to pierce something not easily open to him. I feel him inside my ass. I try to scream but he presses his hand down on my throat until I can't. I push at his hard chest weakly with one hand.*

*"You like this, you know you do. Stop trying to scream. Don't fucking fight me. Take it like a good whore." Showing no mercy, he fucks me with a brutally that marks how much he hates me.*

*It defies logic or anything I can make sense of. The pain has transformed into an exquisite burn. As I come physically and mentally, he pulls out of me and shoves me back on the bed with one harsh, fluid movement until my behind no longer rests on his thighs. He leans forward, using my throat to guide his weight through the pressure of his hand on mine. He begins to pump his erection, soaked in my blood and arousal, on my stomach. He kisses me hard, biting my lips, making me taste the metallic flavor of the blood he evokes from my lips. He kisses me until my mouth is sore and battered then goes for my tongue, clenching it between his teeth until rings of pain vibrate through my senses.*

*As he pumps hot streams of white, sticky fluid on my stomach, he presses my hand down on my throat.*

*I can't breathe. I can't swallow. I can't think. I know better than to struggle. I stare at him as he seems to look down on me, relishing in putting me out of my misery. I succumb to the lure of the endless chasm and close my eyes, intending to rest for eternity.*

GASPING—STRUGGLING FOR AIR, I jolted upright. My vision foggy, I blinked repeatedly until I could better register my surroundings. I was on the floor, not far from my bed. My legs were spread and a pink silicone dildo was not far from the apex of my thighs. Dried arousal and specks of my blood decorate the soft cylinder.

The pain hit me all at once: between my thighs, inside my throat, and my ass. The most sensitive and vulnerable part of me throbbed with a searing ache. I struggled to stand upright, but my body screamed at me to stay down. I sealed my lips against a protest and worked through the agony, staggering into my bathroom across the hall from my bedroom.

After flipping on the light, I touched between my thighs and drew back flakes of dried blood. In the vanity mirror, I caught my reflection. My full lips were swollen and red. Finger prints marred my skin with purplish black bruises. I lifted my hand, fitting my fingers to the marks. They matched perfectly.

The darkness I ran away from had returned to haunt me in an uncharted way. My mind had increased the brutality and extended outside the confines of my prison to punish me. I did this to myself as I dreamt about Nick in a fantasy that became twisted around and deemed me as the one who needed dominating.

Opening the medicine cabinet, I braced myself against the counter through the painful pulses threatening to rob my body of its strength. I retrieved a bottle of pain medication and popped it open, taking more than the recommended dose and chased it down with a handful of water from the tap. I slid my foot across the cold tile floor to the bathtub to run hot water for my bath to soothe my soreness.

The hot water embraced me in its comforting warmth. I remained in the porcelain tub, filling it until the water turned cold, and the stitches of pain transformed into a dull throb.

Lifting myself out of the water, I plucked up the terrycloth robe hanging on the hook implanted in the door, and wrapped it around myself. Moving with care, I entered my bedroom and gently planted myself on the edge of the bed.

My burner phone was hidden securely underneath the mattress. I reached down between the separation of the mattress and the box spring. Clutching it in my trembling hand, I dialed *her* number.

It took only seconds before she picked up. My number registered as unknown.

"Whitney?" Dreya's voice bled through the other line. "Speak to me and tell me where you are. We can fix this, Whit. Talk to me."

The doorbell rang and threw me back into my new world, bringing a clear vision of the repercussions of my decision. If I told her what happened to me, she'd make me work for her again by reminding me that it was my panacea. My hands couldn't be responsible for taking another life. Whatever happened with Nick, it brought me back to a place full of shame and deluged me with the desire to be normal. Previously, I never cared. Performing the acts required of me for a decent amount of cash, numbed me until it no longer solved the issues I had but made them worsen. Wrong or right, morality used to have no place or a purpose with me. But with Nick, the dirtiness stained my hands to such an extent, my regret manifested into waking nightmares, seducing me with the demeaning and attracting me with its indulgences.

"Whitney?" she called again, her voice wavering. "Come home."

I immediately hung up on my mother.

Since the house I rented was situated in a private and mostly secluded area, the sound of a car arriving could be heard from miles—it gave me enough time to escape, if needed. This time, I had been distracted, and whomever was at the door decided they were tired of waiting and knocked with persistence.

Holding my phone to my chest, I ventured into the living room that opened to the front door.

"Whitney? Are you here?" Penny's voice rang out from the other side of the door.

I slid my phone into the pocket of my robe and opened the door for her to come inside. "Penny? I didn't know you were coming by." Because she never would. I assumed she had no knowledge of where I resided.

She slipped past me and searched around the house. "With all that's going on, I was worried about you being here alone."

"What do you mean?"

"I thought you heard, they are closing the hotel and won't say when they'll reopen it." The confession cinched her delicate features.

"What? Why?"

"How didn't you hear about it? It only happened a few hours ago. Another person died at the hotel late last night—a homeless addict, I think. Some say his throat was slit, others say he was hanged. It's all over town. No one wants to use the word serial killer, but I think it has to be. There is no way two men did this to themselves in the same exact way.

"The Sheriff is having a town meeting tomorrow night and it might be about a proposal for a curfew." She glanced around the living room, searching for a television. She wouldn't find one, the only one I had was kept inside my bedroom.

"You live like I thought you would…minimalist." She pointed at the sparse furniture before sticking her nose up in the air, smelling the scent of my cinnamon and vanilla bath oil, fresh on my skin. "What are you cooking? Will it go with this?"

She grabbed the paper bag she left on the coffee table and slid a bakery box from it. "I bought chocolate strudels from the bakery in town. I really wish we could have a drink. We both need one. Jesus turned water into wine and the town wants to make it a sin? It should be an invitation to drink all we want, if you ask me. I hate that the county is dry."

"I haven't started anything for dinner." I returned to the kitchen, keeping my movements fluid and unrestricted to avoid giving her clues about the condition of my body.

I rummaged through the freezer to find something to prepare. As I checked the time on my phone, I was shocked to learn I'd slept through the next morning and the day.

Penny's company was welcomed when it shouldn't have been. After what occurred last night after watching Nick's tape and knowing another death had stained the reputation of the town, I didn't want to be alone.

"Were you hungry? I don't think I have enough of anything for the two of us. I can make you something different from what I make myself, if you want." I clutched my stomach as it grumbled. "There's chicken and fish—salmon."

She placed her hand over mine and directed me to step away from the freezer. "Are you okay, hun? You don't seem like yourself right now."

"The news about the man who died." I looked at her hand holding mine, oddly comforted by it. "It scares me."

"Then we'll have a slumber party until you feel right again." She flipped my hair over my shoulders. "Go get dressed. I'll figure out what we're going to eat and whip something up."

I headed down a short and narrow hall back to my bedroom.

"Maybe we should order out?" she shouted down to me in my bedroom as I searched through my closet for something to wear. "I invited a friend over. She should be here…soon."

I dropped a pair of jeans and a T-shirt on the bed. "Like who?" I carefully wiggled into the tightly fitted jeans. I regretted my decision to wear them after they seemed to exacerbate the pain not yet numbed.

"Marion."

I immediately flopped down on the bed, wincing as the apex between my thighs hummed with pain. Moving at a sedated pace, I walked across the hall into the bathroom to retrieve another dose of meds.

Her voice resounded closer, as though she was standing in the hall. "We have to stick together, especially with all these weird deaths popping up." She tapped on the doorframe, announcing her presence. "I hate to bring this up again, but maybe a plutonic male friend wouldn't hurt, either?"

"No, thank you."

"What about Andrew? Marion has her eye on Hayden, so he's out. But Andrew is a cop who works with Mason, and he's single and nice."

"Andrew?"

She gave me a smile and fanned her face. "It's only because Mason… he's…" She paused to swoon. "He's the guy I've been crushing on. He won't give me the time of day, but I'll be damned if I give up. He's like…ice cream in a town that has triple digit weather all the time. A double date might do it. Did you mind or anything? I've had a huge crush on him since he got here a little over a few months ago."

As I sipped tap water to move my pill further down my throat, I choked on it. "I thought he'd been here longer?" My voice held a rasp due to my irritated throat.

"Nope. He transferred in from another police department somewhere—Chicago, I think."

"Well…I'm not interested in either of them…because…"

"Right. You have a boyfriend." She gave me a wink and shook her head.

"Penny, are you here? The fun has arrived," Blake announced his arrival from the living room.

"Come out, come out wherever you are." Mason's voice magnetized the pace of my heart, sending it soaring into a rapid rhythm.

Penny gaped at me "I swear to you I only invited Marion," she whispered, grabbing my hand, leading me out toward the living room where the entry door opened.

Blake's arm draped around Marion. He held her close and kissed her while staring straight at Penny as though she was supposed to be moved. Penny glowered at her friend, but it was clear it wasn't due to jealousy over her coupledom with Blake, it was confusion.

"I have something for you, but considering I had to drive three counties away to get it, you have to pay for it." Mason approached me, a mischievous grin deepening the outlines of his bone structure. Simply dressed in a white T-shirt and dark blue jeans, his hair a little less tame than it usually was. I couldn't deny the man's attractiveness, nor my unwanted attraction to him for reasons I couldn't fathom. He dangled a brown shopping bag in the shape of a bottle in front of my face.

I followed his brandy-colored eyes as they glided over my body. "I can give you your money back for the tip you left if that's what you want."

Penny slipped her hand from mine on the brink of her grip cutting into my skin.

"No," he drawled, his gaze boring into me, "that's not what I want." Tilting his head down, he chewed the inside of his cheek while staring at my hips. "I like the way those jeans struggle across your ass, Whit."

"You're disgusting," I snarled.

He cowered forward, a serious warning settling in his eyes. "Very soon, baby, I'm going to teach you how to think before you speak to me." He clutched the back of my head and pulled me forward for a kiss.

The burn elicited from his soft lips on my mouth shot straight to my core. His mouth insisted and claimed. He used his tongue to tickle my lips and chipped away at my waning will. A hand slipped down my ass. Fingers probed dangerously close to the separation of my behind and my sore opening. Pressed against me, the warmth of his body singed my skin. His scent overwhelmed my senses. Deeper still, he fucked my mouth without mercy, leaving me burning in the brightest, highest temperature flame. A chaotic chorus filled my head, unearthing everything I buried and forced me to make sense of it.

I wiggled out of his hold, only able to get free because he released me. My confusing onset of emotions sent a dense fog over my vision, and I didn't see through the murkiness until it was too late.

Penny was crestfallen over what Mason had done. While his display of affection was meant to affect me, it hurt her.

She plucked up the brown bag from Mason's grip and slipped the bottle out of the bag. "Cabernet sauvignon? Nice. It's like you answered my prayers." Plastering a smile across her lips, she headed into the kitchen.

I quickly joined her. I checked back in the living room, only finding Blake canoodling with Marion on the couch. "I'm sorry. I don't know why he did that." Unsure of how to steer on the bumpy road, I turned apologetic. "Penny, I really like having you here, but the others have to go."

She rummaged around my cabinets with persistence. "Why don't you have any wine glasses? It's like sacrilege or something to drink wine this good out of plastic cups." She clutched one of my favorite mugs and shook her head. "Or these."

"Penny?"

"Huh?" She turned around, clutching the mug as though she had awoken from a dream. "Did you say something, Whitney?"

Shaking my head, I glanced back at Blake. He grabbed Marion into his lap by her hair like some sort of neanderthal and directed her to straddle him. All the while, he checked for signs that Penny had noticed.

76

The back door leading to the yard was left ajar, when I knew I had left it closed and locked.

"I'm going to order a pizza. Are you particular about what you want on it?" Penny picked up her phone and began to fiddle with it. She hadn't once held my eye contact since Mason kissed me.

"Order whatever you want. I need to get some air." I walked back toward the kitchen and exited through the door, leading to the back yard. The glimmer of light called my eye. Sitting in one of the lawn chairs I thought were lost in sea of overgrown grass sat Mason.

Tension took over my muscles, leaving me in a rigid state.

"Relax, baby. Just because we're alone, it doesn't mean I'm going to punish you like I've been promising. We'll get to that at the right time." He grinned at me, his smile holding a bit of depth beneath what I was sure he meant to be shallow.

"You should leave, and please make your friends leave as well."

"I'm not their fucking keepers, and they sure as hell aren't my friends." Mason rolled his shoulders and ejected from the chair to stand on the edge of the concrete patio with his back to me.

Sitting down on the porch swing, I watched Mason retrieve a small pack of cigarettes from his back pocket and hold it up over his shoulder. "Smoke?"

While swinging slowly in the rocking bench, the sway oddly soothing, I stared at his back, watching the bumps and ridges in his back flex and stretch underneath his white V-neck shirt.

With a raised brow, he turned to look over his shoulder at me. "Answer my question, instead of staring at my ass in silence."

I stuffed my hands underneath me and let my gaze fall elsewhere. "No thank you."

Deciding against keeping up the distance between us, Mason sat next to me, adding weight to the swing and halting its slow and soothing sway. The notes of his pleasant cologne wafted around my nose.

Words and gestures paled in the shadow of his existence; the man had a tangible presence that touched me every time he neared me. Denied sensations were suffocated by his silent and spoken promises of debauched pleasure.

While wincing, I slid to the other end of the bench, keeping a fair distance between us, and tucked my feet underneath me. The jungle of the back yard I never cared for nor had the time to find someone to keep it well-manicured served as a backdrop. It was a graveyard for all things broken, left over from the previous tenants. I was certain a few animals were probably hiding in the three-feet-tall grass, as well.

"Someone needs to take care of that." Mason eyed the yard, dressed in dark green from the dim lights of the night.

"The stuff was here when I got here."

"And you still rented this shit hole?" His eyes shot to mine, matching the same mild indifference in his tone.

"It was the only property available, and I meant to get rid of the stuff eventually."

"I wasn't talking about the start of a junkyard, I was talking about the grass." He flicked his ash to the ground and pressed the cigarette pinched between two fingers to his lips.

"When I first moved here, I did really well at keeping the yard up, but the lawnmower broke down. I accidentally blew the motor."

A shift in the wind ruffled his thick, dark blond hair, barely moving it from its gel-laden style. The reflection of the waning quarter moon shimmered across his warm light brown eyes. "I could do it for you, and I'd even gift you with doing it without my shirt."

I exhaled, pretending his offer didn't entice me. "Don't you have other things to do with your time?"

He rolled his shoulders, swelling the muscles in his chest and arms before resting a hand on the back of the bench, leaving it dangerously close to touching me. "Used to do it all the time when I was a teenager for the people in the neighborhood. The pay was shit, but I didn't do it because I needed the money."

"Why were you forced to do menial labor when you come from money? Wouldn't you have better opportunities?"

He abruptly turned away from me, dropping his arm to the side of his body as he stared at the twinkling midnight sky. "What makes you say that, baby?"

"The house…you live in that house with Hayden, right?"

He exhaled a ring of smoke into the air. "Why are you fighting me so hard, Whitney?"

"Where did that come from?" I asked, unable to hide my stun and dismay at his abrupt change of topics.

"Answer the fucking question." While not marred with irritation, the roughness in his voice exerted authority.

"I don't fit into a neat little box, Mason. And I'm not sure what I did or said that makes you think I want the things you so eloquently offer me." I abruptly grabbed the cigarette from his hands and brought it to my lips, inhaling and immediately exhaling. A coughing fit attacked me right away, calling Mason to guffaw.

"Try it again," he directed, barely containing his laughter. "This time hold the smoke a little before you exhale. Do it…slowly."

I brought it to my lips, taking in a deep breath, and held the smoke in my cheeks. I unfurled a breath, permitting a smoke cloud to form around my face. "I don't get the point of these things."

He slipped it from my fingers and smoked it deftly. "What's the point of anything?"

*Good question.* A flutter on my arm brought my attention. I sat still enamored as the mosquito began to prick my skin. I smacked it with my hand before it could fly away and wiped the remnants on the bench. "Who are you, Mason? I can't figure you out. You're too mercurial to figure out."

"Ask me one question, and I'll answer it," he effortlessly flowed into the question

"Why did you transfer here?"

He inhaled his cigarette smoke and exhaled Penny's name with a bitter amount of blame. "I was a cop in Chicago on my way to being the youngest officer who took the detective exam and passed. Hayden fucked it up for me and the rest is for the fucking birds."

"Did he convince you to come here?"

"Are you hard of hearing, baby? I said one question." He paused for a beat to take a drag. "A word of friendly advice about this place, some of us can control the rumor mill and feed it false shit." He tilted his head back. His prominent Adam's apple ebbed and flowed with his dramatic swallow.

Hearing an odd sound emanating from the house, I trained my eye to the back door. "I think I picked up on you speaking Russian to Hayden. Were you born there?"

"Maybe I was. Maybe I wasn't." He flicked the ash from the cigarette. "That's two questions I answered." I could feel him shutting down and observed him tensing. Clearly any deep conversation with him was deemed off limits.

"Do you want something from me?" I inquired if he had any possible questions for me.

"Fuck, Whitney. There are a lot of things I want from you, and you're going to give them to me…eventually."

Resting my elbow on top of my thigh, I placed my chin on my fist and stared at him until he acknowledged me. "You really want me to believe I'll change my mind about you? All the signs are telling me to stay away." The lilt in my voice was quiet and more acceptance-seeking than I intended. I cared and couldn't be sure why. "And it's not just for my protection."

"I've met a lot of fucked-up, deranged people in my life, Whitney. You don't scare me at all. I know what you want and that you're shy about outright asking for it. But no, you have to fuck with me and mumble about what I'm doing to you in your daydreams."

A flush of heat filled my cheeks with their temperature, expressing my embarrassment.

"You know a fuck isn't going to be just a fuck with me." His upper half leaned forward, closing the space between us. "I know what the rumors are about you being a shy virgin, sometimes a bitch, but I know so many things no else does."

"You were right about the rumor mill. The thing about the rumors in this town, most"—I cleared the sudden grit in my voice—"of them are untrue. If you behave a certain way, you'll be labeled a certain way. It's a perfect way to reinvent yourself if you know how to work the small-town grapevine system."

He flicked the smoking cigarette ash with his fingertips.

"The truth is I have a very happy and monogamous relationship with my boyfriend."

"Boyfriend?" The odd contortion of his mouth mocked me.

"You don't believe me?" I lifted up from the bench, fending off the tinges of pain from showing on my face.

"As far as anyone else is concerned: You have a boyfriend and his name is Mason Reid."

I laughed, and somehow it awakened the pain in my core, forcing me to temper it. "You're crazy, you know that?"

He stood only inches from me. "I'm not crazy. I'm fucking psychotic, and so are you."

Chilly air surrounded my body and made me quake. He inched toward me, decreasing the frigid air. A sound made us both freeze. I turned my ear toward the sound of moaning coming from the front of my house—from my living room.

Investigating the sound, I rounded the house, halting when I reached the partially retracted curtains that offered a view into the living room. Through the separation in my white chiffon curtains, I happened upon a sight that shocked me for a less than obvious reason. Hayden, who I didn't know had arrived, and Blake were in the midst of a rough sex session with Marion. Penny was nowhere to be found.

Marion was bent on top of my coffee table with Hayden behind her and Blake in front of her. Her naked skin was decorated in red marks here and there. Her eyes watered as Hayden plunged into her from behind. I couldn't have been completely certain from the angle, but I was sure he was fucking her anally, and the condom had a reddened hue.

Hayden was arguably more rough with her than Blake. Eventually deciding it wasn't for him, Blake removed his erection from Marion's mouth and pulled up his pants, leaving my line of sight. Hayden barely noticed Blake's departure. He folded the only thing remaining on Marion's body, her T-shirt, over her face and secured it at her throat with his hand. The veins in his hands popped to the surface, displaying the strength at which he suppressed her breathing.

I couldn't make sense of why he felt free to do something like that in my house, not knowing who I was and if I followed the strict law of the Bible in the town. I could've been anyone, and they trusted me enough to do something that I'm sure they didn't want the town to know about inside my home.

Hayden tugged Marion's blonde hair hard with the jerk of his wrist. A muffled screech resounded from underneath the T-shirt. Her body jarred with the violence of Hayden's thrusts, shuddering the table and nearly pushing her off balance.

I was riveted and unable to take my eyes away. A tingle worked its way up my thighs, leaving me gasping for air.

"Close your eyes." Mason stood uncomfortably close behind me. He shifted my hair to one side of my shoulder. The exhalations of his breath moved the fine hairs down my neck.

"No." My muscles tensed, uneasy over the threat of my exposed secret.

His hand went over my face, doing it for me. Behind the dark I saw the scene only seconds ago. Except I was Marion and Mason was Hayden.

"What do you see?"

"Nothing," I stated with quiet and false indifference.

"You see me fucking you the way Hayden's fucking that bitch right now. You see yourself enjoying it. You see yourself coming the hardest you ever had. That's what you see." He slipped his hands down my eyes to rest across my sore neck.

I attempted to save face. "That's not what I see. I don't know why he would do something like this when he doesn't know me and doesn't know if I'd spread rumors."

A free hand gripped my waist. "You think that's why this is happening?

Because he has no other place to go?"

I gasped at the action, but didn't fight, even as he held me closer, bringing my back to his chest. He leaned down on my shoulder, blowing a stream of tepid air through his open mouth around my ear.

*Shiver.* "Is it supposed to entice me?"

"You might want to make me think it doesn't, but I know it does. And you might want to fool me into thinking I'm not in your twisted little fantasies when you rub your pussy at night, but I know I am. You won't tell a soul about what you're seeing, will you?"

It wasn't a threat, in fact, I couldn't be sure of what it was. "How do you know I'll stay silent?"

With few actions, he twirled me around and backed me up against the siding of the house. He imprisoned me between his body and the front of the house, resting his closed fists outside my arms. "Your mother was a very jerk off worthy porn star during the '80s, and when she retired she became a high class whore. I would've thought it was all bullshit until I found some information about you during my background check." He flipped my hair back behind my shoulder and leaned into my ear. Open-mouth kisses injected with his tongue worked their way down my neck and paused at the bruise. Delaying for agonizing seconds, he shoved a hand in my hair, jerking my head back and placed a dizzying kiss full of preludes to explosive sex across my bruise.

In reaction, my hands slid up and slid down beneath the gap in his jeans. The back of my fingers grazed against trim pubic hair.

He parted his mouth from my neck to stare down at me. His eyes danced, a skewed smile spread across his lips. "I know you won't tell because you came here to hide. The last thing you would ever want is to bring any attention to yourself."

Panic hummed in my throat, keeping me from immediately responding.

"Did you think if you hid in a town full of a bunch of Bible thumpers you'd be safe? That they would be safe? Can I tell you how fucking false your assumptions were? You see it. You know it. You've settled into a town full of people who pray for piety but secretly fuck with the dirty little sins of the secular world."

"Why did *you* come here, Mason? You didn't finish the story. I heard about why Hayden came here from other people. He was forced to be here. Were you?" The back of my fingertips brushed against the base of his throbbing cock, eliciting an even darker grin to appear across his lips.

He picked up the cigarette, miraculously still laced in between his fingers and plucked up my hand from underneath his jeans. Thumbing the space between my thumb and my index, he began to grin.

The contact reached beyond the surface and worked as another deadly temptation, attaching an additional tether to my body.

"Don't move or I'll stop talking." With delay, he placed the burning cigarette at the place where his thumb touched me, going slow to prevent snuffing it out for too long. The sound of my sizzling flesh and the bite of the burn hit me at once. My reserved strength fueled by my hunger for more ensured I remained immobile.

"Hayden and I grew up in the same place. When we were eight, we were separated because no one wanted to adopt us together. I had a new life, and I never looked back. A good fucking life. Twenty-one years later he shows up at my doorstep with a sob story. I followed him here because he needed my help. Don't ask what he needed help for. It's not your business. Does that answer your nosy fucking question to your satisfaction?"

Through watering eyes, I blinked rapidly at him and gave him a slighted nod.

He pressed the butt down hard, snuffing the cigarette out on my hand. I withdrew the hand remaining in his pants in protest.

"Ah," I cried out as the moisture stung my eyes.

"Shh." He lifted my hand and kissed the burn. With the other, he ran his fingers through my hair. "Feel better?"

I nodded at him, and I couldn't have been sure if it was a lie.

A finger brushed alongside my jaw. Moisture trickled from my watering eyes and trailed down my cheek. "Get this through your thick head, don't believe everything you hear about me from the shit-heads in this town. It's all a fucking a lie you will never find proof to prove or debunk unless I decide to tell you. And I'm not going to reveal who I am to the woman who is running away from the truth and living a lie." His eyes darted to mine. "Don't worry your beautiful head over what I know. I won't use it to turn the town against you. Like you, I have a few secrets I'm very motivated to keep."

"And what was this for?" My gaze darted to the cigarette burn on my hand.

He seemed surprised by my foray into indignation. "To get you ready and to test you."

"Test me for what?" My voice shook with contradictory emotions. Vexed over allowing him to burn me and the tingles of lascivious thoughts that warmed my core, I soared into a state of a persistent emotional war.

He smiled at something on the ground. He shook his head, mumbling underneath his breath, "I'll see you soon, Whitney."

When he was out of sight, I clutched my chest, sensing the pace of my racing heart.

I couldn't have been sure of what had occurred. I could barely swallow it down. It was too bitter and too jagged to digest. Staring at my shaking hand with a dark textured mark, marred by cigarette ash, a small smile stretched my lips.

I turned back to the window. Marion was on the ground, trembling in pain. She crawled toward Hayden, kissing her way up his body as though she was begging for more. He rejected her advances easily, stepping over her body as though she were roadkill.

He stood clear in front of the window, his pants undone but his erection secured. He brushed his hands over his dark brown hair while he watched me with a crooked smile on his face. "You're next," he mouthed and puckered his lips to kiss the air.

I stepped away from the window, and took a walk, vowing not to return until they left my home.

# EIGHT

THE SUMMER RAIN MADE pinging sounds on the roof of my one-level home. Since my schedule had changed at Alloy, I had more time during the weekday to spend alone. I hoped with the doors locked and the lights off, I wouldn't receive an impromptu visit from anyone.

The feelings I kept contained from everyone had begun to hemorrhage for Mason. He treated me to indignities and moments of tenderness in the optimal mix. He was becoming the perfect picture of the man I never thought existed outside of my fantasies.

I had worn out my welcome in Bebletown.

I checked my phone for places with a small population, but none of them appealed to me. My mind was anchored into the town.

A few moments after the sun set, I used the light on my phone as a guide. Searching around the footlocker at the head of my bed, I rummaged around the locker to find the movie Penny had given me.

The aspiration to adopt a different life—the life of a person who hid her cold-blooded monsters in a secure place—disintegrated in front of my eyes. The malignant spirits hidden inside me were no longer hungry to play god. They wanted exquisite devastation.

Sitting on the floor with my legs spread and the remote in my hands, I played the movie.

The camera panned to a man bound and gagged, his dark brown eyes watered. Sweat drenched his face. The camera zoomed to showcase Nick, dressed in a cop's uniform. He removed his clothes, but it didn't matter. Most of his face was obscured by the shadow of his hat and the strategic dim lighting in the room. Only his tattoos—the ones I memorized—made his identity clear. The one on his chest couldn't be mistaken, the terrifying skeleton head.

As the bound man began to dissent, Nick drew back his hand, landing a bone-crushing punch to the side of his prisoner's face. The bound man's face snapped in the direction of the punch, and his naked body was thrown on the threadbare mattress to lay on his stomach.

The anticipation awakened my core. I hit mute on the volume and clenched my thighs together.

Nick spit on his hand and spread it on his erect shaft. Gripping the man's hips in his hands, he forced them to tilt upward and speared him. From the blood increasingly coating Nick's cock, it was clear the man had never been taken that way. Behind the darkness of my closed eyes, visions of Mason taking me like Hayden took the waitress, or recreating the scene in front of me controlled my thoughts.

A pressure formed inside my chest as my hand lightly moved between my legs. Worried that what happened once before would occur again if I went there, leaving me waking up to more bruises, scarred skin at my own hand, and lost time, I forced myself to sit on my hands.

I closed my eyes and leapt from the floor, extending my arms out to the television. Peeking one eye open I touched the on/off button, shutting off the vintage television.

The chime on my phone resounded loudly. I picked it up with a less than nice cadence. "What?"

"Easy, baby," Mason purred through the phone.

A tinge of schoolgirl glee strangled my need to frown and pulled my lips into a smile. Extending my legs, I crossed them at the ankles and rested my elbow on my thigh. Another hand worked on its own accord and rested on a place that increasingly throbbed with need. "Mason? How did you get my number? Never mind. Please don't call me again." My hand moved to press end call, but I couldn't. Expectancy kept me on the line.

"You're moaning into the phone. Are you rubbing your pussy while I'm talking to you?"

I removed my hand from beneath my panties, forcing it to rest across my other thigh. "What did I do to tip your radar and make you become so interested in me?"

"You existed."

I fought hard to overpower the laughter from spilling forth and failed miserably. "You're going to get tired of chasing after me. I'm never going to stop running."

"I have more stamina than you give me credit for." An exhaustive sigh hummed through the speaker. "What are you so afraid of, Whitney? There's nothing sick or depraved about what you want." He returned to the familiar and protective guy I first met.

"You would be the only one who thinks that, Mason."

"It's really all that matters, isn't it?"

"It's not so easy. If I allow it to happen, I'm scared about what will happen to me afterward."

"You're right. You won't be okay after I do what I plan to do to you. You'll never be the same again."

"Mason." I gasped. "Stop."

My phone lit up with an alert for a text message. I took the phone away from my ear and pressed the message icon on my screen. It was a picture of Mason. He was naked with a piece of paper strategically placed over a certain part that read:

**Stop fucking with me and you'll have what already belongs to you.**

"You're so cute." My sarcasm was diminished by my breathy voice.

"I can make it hurt very, very fucking good, Whitney."

The snapping sensation of a rubber band all over my skin threatened to pull me under his spell. "Why me?" I whispered.

"Some things don't have a pretty little explanation. I think you know that."

I glanced at the picture again and sank my teeth into my lip. *Damn.* "But you're not. I mean, you can't or won't. You shouldn't want to. That's the whole point."

"I can tell by how you're getting all flustered you're looking at the picture again."

I craned my neck looking around my room, wondering if tonight would be the night I indulged the devils filling my head. "Mason?"

"Whitney?"

"Come...over."

"I'm on duty in thirty, but...give me an hour."

My cell phone lit up. *Call Ended* blared across the screen. Panic rifled through me at the predictive visions of him showing up to my door in his cop uniform.

I immediately regretted my invitation.

The abruptness of unfolding my legs to stand left my body scrambling to adjust to the sudden new position, and I stumbled to my knees. A gambit of emotions seeped into my actions as I flittered around my room.

Taking the movie from the player, I secured it inside the chest I kept at the foot of my bed. I threw on a white T-shirt, a pair of off-white jeans, and my red Converse sneakers. I caught myself in the mirror, appearing haggard and tired. I returned to my bedroom and did a few adjustments to my face and my hair, pulling it into a neater bun.

Without a destination, I took the keys to my beater from the hook and nearly burned rubber as I pulled out of my driveway.

Rain drizzled from the sooty sky in a fine mist, making everything appear doused with a gradient of moody lights. The musky and earthy scents permeated my nose. I pulled off the side of the road to catch some air. In the background stood the same house where Blake had a gathering for Hayden.

Hayden was outside attending to something underneath the hood of his car.

My tread moved up the driveway, ignoring the suppressive words filling my head, telling me to leave him alone.

"Hey."

Startled by my voice, his head popped up and nearly hit the hood. He grabbed a rag, wiping the grease from his hands. "Whitney. Surprised to see you here."

"I'm hiding from a stupid decision I made with Mason," I admitted.

"You escaped to come see me?" An inquisitive tilt of his head was juxtaposed with a smug look possessing his face.

I rubbed my clammy hands up and down my light-colored denim jeans, leaving cream tracks in the thread at their trail. "About what you said the night you were with Marion inside my house, I don't know what made you suddenly interested in what you called a four, but I have a boyfriend—"

"I know, and his name is Mason. As for what happened that night, I remember very little. I was drunk and woke up with a wicked hangover. If I said something to you, ignore it."

"He's so fucking crazy. He's not my boyfriend." I fingered the wet cloud of condensation from the window of the car, the cold glass a welcome reprieve to my sweaty hands. "You didn't look drunk. Why did you do what you did at my house unless you were trying to seduce me?"

"Seduction? That's your idea of seduction? I'd call it opening your mind."

"Or...leading me on. I thought you didn't remember what you did?"

"I don't remember what I *said* to you, if I said anything. I wasn't aware I had enough of your attention to lead you on. You quibble...a lot."

"I have an issue with Mason, and it hasn't stopped him from claiming we're something we're not."

He rubbed the back of his neck and fought back a grin, his dimples betrayed him and appeared as deep indents in his cheeks. "This stays between us, but I think in his twisted way, he's really taken with you."

"I don't know why. I can't wait until he finds someone else to focus on." I rested my back against the car and stared out into the massive acreage surrounding the property.

A touch of incredulity fell across his face, one that couldn't be blamed.

I was running away from what I wanted out of fear of where it would lead me. "Does Mason speak about me, about the things he claims to know?"

"I know nothing." Hayden dismissed me, but he seemed less than convicted about the lie he tried to sell. "Leave it at that." The corner of his mouth curled up as he seemed pleased with an unshared thought. "I know what I saw when you watched me with the waitress from Wingettes." He glanced at me periodically, eventually doing it for an elongated time.

"Something wrong?" I questioned his weighty stare.

"You've never had an orgasm with someone else before, have you?"

I didn't want to broach the subject at all. I couldn't compare my orgasm to any other woman, because I wasn't sure of what theirs felt like. I only knew of others from what I saw while indulging in my private poison and what I witnessed from the waitress a few nights ago. Nick forced orgasms on the men he was with—or at least it seemed that way. I couldn't have been sure since many of the men were authentic in playing their roles as victims. The circumstances surrounding what Nick did with other women were unknown to me. I knew the recordings existed, but I chose not to watch them.

"I have orgasms just fine."

"Fine? Fine?" He chuckled and chastised me with a shake of his head. "The word fine and orgasms should never be in the same sentence."

"Can we"—I shifted my feet, suddenly burning with the sensation of hot coals—"talk about something else?"

"No. I want to talk about this, and I'm going to keep broaching the subject until you converse with me about it."

"Why do you care, Hayden?"

"Never said I cared. I'm curious."

"A woman's body is complicated. I'm sure not all of us have screaming, convulsing orgasms like the women who fake it in porn."

"And you would know that because of your mother, wouldn't you?"

Alerted by his answer to my previous question, I dissected him with my caustic stare. "Don't be that way. I never have and never will talk about those things with Dreya."

A look of astonishment creased his features over my use of my mother's given name. "Here's the thing, if you're screaming coherent sentences you aren't having a good orgasm. During the act, you shouldn't be able to say much of anything, but after...yes, scream your head off. I don't think your body is that complicated. I think you're too frightened to give in to what you know would get you there. Stop being a bystander and be a participant."

I shifted again.

"The shame on your face could weigh down a Mack truck. Can I tell you something? Your dirty little private fantasies aren't exclusive. A lot of people have them. Find someone who gets you and will fill them."

"I'm perfectly fine with what I'm doing. Thank you."

He gesticulated for me to follow him with his hand and circled around the car, heading toward the stables. Slowing his pace and shooting a pointed glance at me from over his shoulder, he said, "That was an invitation, in case you didn't know."

Comforted by the knowledge that he wouldn't take me inside, I followed his path.

He led me back to the stables and paused at the large entry door. No longer empty, something stirred in one of the stalls and released a resounding snort. Excitement elicited my speedy tread forward. The third stall to the right was occupied by a large black horse so sleek her coat had a reflective shine. I always had an unrequited love for animals. My mother never allowed my sister nor I to keep a pet, claiming they were too this or too that. I admired horses from afar, deeming them beautiful, mystical creatures I never had the ability to interact with.

Being with her and just short of touching felt therapeutic; it made me forget about what pestered me daily. It reminded of my humanity by washing me in a hodgepodge of emotions: awe, serenity, and delight.

"Come here." Hayden stood closer to her than I could, inviting me over with warmth in his eyes. "She won't bite."

"I like horses, but I'm..." I stepped back, clutching my trembling hands, revealing my debilitating nervousness threading me into its uncomfortable web. I wanted to touch her so badly, I inwardly cursed my actions.

Hayden opened her stable. From the hook he retrieved a bridle and pulled it over her head. He led her out by the lead.

I stepped forward, taking my time.

"Touch her here," he said, referring to the side of her flank.

I held out my hand but couldn't connect.

"Touching you and not asking permission." A hand wrapped around my wrist, imprisoning me in his grip. I was pulled forward with a tug when Hayden forced me to make contact.

At first, I went rigid, but as he moved my hand into continuous stroking motions, I started to connect with the horse and do it on my own. I smiled as she nuzzled my head.

"I think that's the first time I've ever seen you do that since I met you."

"W-what?" I asked, snapping out of my daze. I didn't like the way Hayden was looking at me...it was different.

"What's the issue with anyone touching you? Why do you react this way?"

"People talk about the healing power of touch, but every time certain men touch me, I feel like they're pouring acid on my skin."

"You ever think it's the way they touch you?"

"What do you mean?"

"Nothing." He shrugged. "I would ask if you wanted to ride, but with the rain, the owner of the house would pitch a bitch. It's her horse."

"I've never ridden a horse before. Too scared I'll break my neck." I withdrew, shoving my hands in the narrow pockets of my jeans. "I've heard rumors about the woman who lives here. Did you know her or any of the other people who lived here?" I hoped my cryptic question, to clue me into whether or not he knew Nick, would've yielded a return.

"I could give you a really simple answer for a really convoluted situation. But I think that would bother you more than me not answering the question."

"I don't think I've ever seen the owner in town. Are you housesitting for her?"

His jaw clenched as a precursor to his proverbial shut down. "Why did you pick this town, Whitney?" he asked with his scrutiny directed past me. "You could've gone anywhere if you were looking to hide."

"It's silly." I slouched my shoulders and gave him a subdued grin. "I was on my way to nowhere, and I saw a postcard for Wingettes laying on the ground at the gas station. I came here to visit, and after getting a job easily, I decided to stay." I stepped back from the horse, looking toward the exit. "All right. You don't have to keep being nice to me. What good word do you want me to put to Penny or Marion? But I'm not sure why you'd need one for Marion, she seemed pretty taken with you that night, and Penny has a crush on Mason."

He lifted both of his brows with a wry smile. "You think that's what I brought you here for? A charade to get you to become my wingman?"

"Getting to the woman you want through me? It's an old trick, but I get it."

He nodded, seemingly contemplating my words.

"What's going on with you and Mason?" I questioned.

"There are a lot of things wrong with him," he said softly, answering only half of my question. "It would take a lifetime for me to tell you all the things that made him that way and all the things I've done to help him."

"That's interesting, because he claimed you showed up at his doorstep and asked him for help."

He shook his head as sadness swept across his eyes. "We've been through a lot together, and endured much more apart. We are all we really have in this world. We used to be close. Things felt different. Right. Calm. If he wants to think he's helping me, let him…" His words trailed off into silence.

It was hard to take my eyes off him. There was so much humanity and vulnerability in the moment I couldn't hide my awe. I never thought we'd have a thing in a common, but he gave me a glimpse into a past and a present that told me we did. His relationship with Mason reminded me a little of my situation with my sister, Sloane, when we were together.

Hayden's general statements added layers to Mason when I once thought the man was full of shallow water.

"Don't tell Mason this…" I delayed my confession, unsure if I should've admitted it to Hayden. "But he's getting to me. It's not a good thing. It doesn't matter if I think he's perfect for me. I will hurt him. If you care about him like you say you do, tell him to stay away."

"If I wanted to, he wouldn't. I'm not going to tell him either way. It's up to you to deny what you want, but I'm not going to help you live in your delusions." He cleared his throat and swiped away the bits of humanness with a mask of stoicism. "Come on. I'll walk you to your car."

I CLOSED THE DOOR to my car and moved to head inside my home. A sense of hyperawareness drew me to the view across the street. Mason was curbside, in his uniform, leaning against the passenger door of his cop car. A ghostly chill worked through me, pushing me to be urgent in my need to get inside the house and lock the door.

As he watched me, the baleful grin on his face became crooked.

My steps were hurried toward my door, hoping to lock myself in and away from him. He stopped me the second I turned my key in the lock. His strong hand gripped the handle and slammed it closed. I turned and was pinned against his body. The natural scent of the outdoors were taken over by the strong undertones of Mason's cologne: peppered, woodsy, and pleasant.

"It's very fucking rude to invite someone over and then take off. Where the hell did you run off to?"

I rocked on my heels, discomforted by his attention as I tried to cross my arms around my breasts. He pushed forward, his heat and the pressure of his form impeded on my ability to breathe. "I'm sorry. I had somewhere else to be."

The worst ideas swirled inside my mind. He'd been privy to my secret. The unknown trick hidden up his sleeve threatened to unhinge me at a cyclic rate. No matter what I tried to run from, my feet were firmly planted in curiosity and the alluring unknown and ill-advised path.

His lids shuttered his eyes, revealing a deflated view into his warm-toned light brown eyes. "Don't go out with Hayden again." His accurate summation shook me to my bones. "You won't get far with him, and you'll only piss me off more than you already have."

Huffing a seething breath of annoyance, I shoved him to no avail. "I don't even know you. And would you stop claiming we are together?"

"Test me and see how much my word is the fucking law. If you ever keep me waiting again, you won't get a damn choice in what I'll do to you, and you won't decide when it happens."

A part of me begged in silence, wanting nothing more than for him to make good on his promise. "Hayden and I are becoming friends." I had no idea why I admitted anything to him or confessed where I had been. I felt cornered and the need to explain. "I had to leave…"

"Why?" An angry curved brow arched over his eyes darkening with every passing second.

"Because it was a mistake to invite you over."

A curt smile contorted his soft pout. "Were you hot and bothered thinking about me when you were finger-fucking yourself that you had to leave? Were you scared of what I was going to do to you?" He thumbed the corner of my mouth, his eyes danced with curiosity and a warranted confidence in my answer before it was spoken. His questions weren't really questions but cocksure statements to what he knew to be true. He was toying me, forcing me to face my behavior.

"I have a boyfriend."

His jaw tensed, the muscle rolled and spasmed underneath his tanned skin. Silence interrupted us and surrounded my body in a brisk cold. "The long-distance boyfriend? I don't fucking buy it. You have me, and that's all anyone in this town will ever know." He grabbed my shoulders holding me still, his face hanging only inches from mine. He grabbed my right hand bringing my fingertips to his nose and slipped them down his lips to be teased by his tongue.

Inside I was breaking apart. My need was a painful burn on my skin. I wanted him so badly my body began to quake. I was near to asking him inside. I punished every thought, disgusted with myself. "Please go."

"You're lucky I have to work." The second he released me, I scurried into my house and locked the door, engaging the deadbolt. I immediately did a sweep of the house ensuring all the windows and doors were locked. I cuddled up in bed, staring at the door as though I expected Mason to come for me.

There was no denying what I felt between my thighs. Mason, for no logical reason, had begun to exhume parts of myself that I'd tried to entomb.

# NINE

"I'M SORRY, MA'AM, YOUR account is overdrawn," the bank rep on the other line told me.

In the morning, recent events coaxed me into formulating an exit strategy and trumpeted above all other thoughts. The last thing I needed was an entanglement with a member of the town's police force. No matter how the picture was painted, I was a criminal who was allowed to live freely because no one knew of my crime. My subconscious had taken to punishing me in my dreams. There was no limit to what my mind would do if I allowed it to flourish outside the bindings of morality.

I did a quick sweep of the back hall inside Wingettes before turning back to my phone. "That's not possible. I'm the only one who has access to this account."

"I'm showing a record of a Dreya Langston who's also on this joint account. She closed it yesterday afternoon."

I made the mistake of making a phone call, and my resourceful mother called my bluff by hitting me where it would affect me the most. Always careful with my withdrawals and deposits, I made certain to use banks in different counties for every transaction.

"I have a limit on how much can be debited."

"Yes, ma'am," the banker stated, maintaining her professional disposition. "That all but covers electronic transfers where the routing and account number are specifically used."

"What about savings?"

She fell silent for a moment. "I'm showing a zero balance, ma'am."

A sinking sensation inside my gut weakened my posture. "No. That can't be right. There was at least ten-thousand in there."

"I'm showing a zero balance and your checking account is overdrawn by two hundred dollars. Ma'am, I have a notice here about an envelope left for you in a safe deposit box by Dreya Langston. Your yearly rental expires in a few days. Is there a time you'd like to schedule to come in?"

The trip to New York was unnecessary. The envelope presumably contained a note from Dreya; a trap to cajole me into returning home.

When I heard whispers on the other line and the banker stressed that the bank manager wanted to speak to me, I immediately ended the call.

My situation left me stuck between two decisions: Remaining in Bebletown while somehow finding a way to open an account, or returning home and allowing my mother to feed me lies.

"I don't pay you to stand around. Your hair isn't regulation." Baxter scolded me the moment I returned to the prep area. "You still have thirty minutes until close. Tend to your tables."

"Yes, sir," I conceded, unwrapping the rubber band from around my wrist and using it to gather my hair, left in its natural curly state, into a ponytail.

Cinda approached me with a tray full of dirty dishes in hand. "I heard your chat." She set the tray down on the window for the kitchen staff to take it and transport it to the dishwashers. "If you need more money, I could use a cheap babysitter."

"I'm okay," I assured her with a smile, hiding the high degree of my irritation.

"We have work that needs doing," Baxter barked at me. "Bus down the bar. Marion's leaving."

I collected myself and moved to the bar to relieve Marion. There were two older gentleman sitting at the bar who didn't seem inclined to leave.

I politely reminded them in a roundabout way it was closing time, but they didn't catch the hint.

"Gentleman, it's fifteen minutes past closing," I finally said.

"Welp, time to go see the old ball and chain." The older bald gentleman slammed his money down on the mahogany bar, clearing his tab for the night.

"It's a damn shame, I tell you," the graying man said as he stared at the sports channel reviewing the scoreboard for the game. "That woman was a little harlot anyhow. She probably ran off with one of the hundreds of men she invites into her bed. You know she tried to hit on me once?"

"It happens," the bald man stated as he stood. "Some people aren't good enough for this town and Kylie was one of them. Shame she'd leave her daughter like that with no word. Poor girl thinks someone took her." He reached in his pocket and unfolded a piece of paper, placing it down on the counter.

I peered over the other side of the counter to have a look at the paper. The graying man took it before I could determine the information contained on the small poster. "Can't believe that girl shares the same genetics with that tawdry woman. It's not right for the child to not share the same name as the mother because she had that child out of wedlock."

His statement hit close to home. I wasn't able to share my mother's last name because my father was married to someone else. My sister, Sloane, was in a similar situation, but her father left his wife for my mother, and once he did, my mother decided she no longer wanted him. Sloane's father was very active in her life, while mine couldn't be, for extenuating circumstances. Both our fathers were in the porn industry. Sloane's father was a former star and mine was a producer turned born-again Christian who had a large church in New Mexico—if I believed what I was told by my mother. I had never remembered meeting him.

Cinda breezed over, I thought to help me, but stressed more interest in the two men. "Who're you two talking about?"

"Didn't you hear?" The balding man continued. "Kylie's been missing for two days, and her daughter has been posting 'have you seen her' posters all around town."

I stepped away from the bar and picked up my phone from the pocket of my apron. Calling a number I was given a while ago and never used, I hoped to get a hold of Penny. The call went straight to her voicemail.

"Penny, it's me...Whitney. I heard about what's going on and...if there is anything I can do, please call me."

After closing, Baxter insisted we walk together and repeatedly asked me if I had some sort of weapon to protect myself before allowing to me to get inside my car.

I PHONED PENNY ONE more time as I unlocked the front door to my house. Unable to juggle so many tasks at once, I dropped my keys. In the middle of squatting down to retrieve my keyring, a box at eye level on the other end of the porch captured my attention.

It was a small black box, neatly taped up without any markings referencing a return address. In typewriter font was the printing of my name.

I took the box inside, locking the front door behind my entry.

Transporting the package into the kitchen, I set it down on the counter and went in search of a knife to cut the tape.

A plethora of styrofoam peanuts filled the box. I dug around the odd shaped foam and drew back a plastic DVD case without a cover insert. The DVD was labeled in black marker with the words: Dirty Maid.

My hands shook as I held the disc, torn between viewing its contents or destroying it before what was on the tape damaged me.

During my delay and silent pondering, I drank two full cups of my favorite tea before I garnered the courage to investigate the movie.

The tea swirled around inside my stomach with a powerful current. Dizzy and out of sorts, I could barely keep my eyes open. My steps were lazy and soft as I moved toward my bedroom in the dark. The scenery around me was draped in brighter hues, appearing surreal enough to be the backdrop to a dream.

I started up the player and had trouble loading the disc into the tray; violent tremors unsteadied my hands.

I sat back on the edge of my bed as the screen illuminated my dark bedroom. I grasped the remote and pressed play.

Tears soaked her face. Mascara created paint streaks on her cheeks. A filthy white rag was stuffed inside her mouth. Her green eyes pleaded into the camera. Evidence of fear was more real than any of the actors in the torture scenes I had watched.

The burning and churning inside my abdomen couldn't be ignored. This wasn't staged, this was real.

The camera panned out, and the woman was revealed: Kylie.

Shadows darted around the dark room. The subtle trembles of the screen indicated the camera wasn't on a tripod. A man emerged from the shadows. The tattoos on his hands and arms were slowly revealed.

*It couldn't be. It can't be.*

Nick's broad jaw came into focus. The sunglasses and cap barred a view of most of his face, but I knew his identity. No one had the unique tattoos that adorned his body. The uniform he often wore in his movies was fresh pressed —brand new.

Nick approached Kylie's naked body. All four limbs were spread and secured to the iron wrought bed with twine. The mattress was covered in a rubber fitted sheet. I continuously fought to silence my thoughts, fooling myself into believing no matter how real it appeared, it wasn't. It couldn't have been. Nick was dead.

Unable to tear my eyes away, I observed the scene unfold on the screen.

Nick approached her body, a night stick was held in one hand. He settled himself between her legs and fucked her anally with the device. Her screams were genuine. The blood he evoked from her was real.

My head swayed at a delayed pace in disbelief. The room began to spin around me in an impossibly swift pace. Acid burned and bubbled inside my throat. My spine curved as I fought the urge to release my sickness onto the floor. "No…I killed you. I *killed* you. This isn't real."

Nick withdrew the nightstick, coated in dark liquid, and began to beat her with it. The cracking of her bones, her heartbreaking cries pulled my heart into my stomach. Her screams curdled my blood and shocked me to the core, sending gooseflesh up my spine.

Every blow made me shudder as though I was the recipient of Nick's brutality. Her screams muddled beneath the cloth as he continued to beat her. Blood spurted forth, soaking the cloth affixed to her mouth. He pulled a knife from his back pocket and directed it toward her sex.

A tingle pervaded from between my thighs. I lied to myself and said it was anticipatory pain.

I turned my back on the gruesome scene of a woman's labia being skinned and stabbed in her most sensitive place by brutality so filled with hateful savagery; tears stung my eyes. Her death wails flooded my ears and threatened to haunt me for the rest of my days.

When all fell silent, I swiveled around to face the television. Steady on the black screen, written in white was the question: "Did I make you wet, Whitney?"

Harried and bloated with fear, I turned off the television and disconnected the converter connecting the vintage screen to the DVD player. Using the hem of my shirt, I wiped down the DVD and placed it back in the case, wiping my prints off it as well.

I LEFT THE HOUSE in a hurry to travel to the very small police station on Main Street.

Acting swiftly, I dropped the DVD off at the unmanned counter. The barebones staff of two people seemed occupied with other matters and barely noticed me. I returned to my car and tried to catch my breath.

TEN

Lacking the confidence to take a daring adventure out of the confines of my home, I called in sick to all three jobs the next morning. I was unceremoniously fired from my position at Alloy over the phone when I called the human resources representative.

The call to the hotel was unnecessary, the shutdown was still active with no plans to reopen it.

For three days, I was glued to my bed while the television remained on a local network. I hoped to stumble upon a new development about the DVD I dropped off in secret at the police station. Nothing ever came of it.

Stuck between wanting to leave and lacking the resources, it took a call from Baxter at Wingettes before the blanket covering my reality was removed. If I wanted to leave and avoid involving my mother, I had to work.

Halfway to my car to start my shift at the restaurant, I received a text message from an unknown number:

**I give you a present, and this is how you treat it? The police will**

**never find the evidence, and another will die because you're an ungrateful bitch.**

A picture of the DVD with the scrawling of "Dirty Maid" was sent a second afterward, placed on the hood of a car. The rusted paint job and the shape of the hood were both very familiar, because it was *my* car.

Retreating back inside the house, I closed and locked the door.

I paced my room as though the movement would help me find a way out of my increasingly tangled situation. My phone buzzed with a text. I approached the bed as though it was teeming with a disease. The sight of Penny's name put me at ease:

**Five minutes to your house.**

As I waited for Penny to visit me, I placed a kettle of water on the stove, and stood watch at the front door.

She pulled up to the front of my house, arriving punctually in exactly five minutes.

"Did you hear the rumor about Hayden?" Penny greeted me as she came inside my home. She looked tired and haggard, unlike her usual gorgeous self. She wrestled with a pizza box I dutifully took off her hands.

"Not sure," I said quickly, looking around in a skittish manner. "Penny, about your mother—"

She held up her hand and shook her head to stop me. "I want to escape right now. With two deaths in a month and my mother missing, I'm not thinking I'll find her alive." The catch in her throat made it difficult for her to continue. She cuddled up on my couch, looking around for the television. Remembering herself, she stood up and headed toward my bedroom.

I reluctantly followed after her.

"Do you have any good movies?" She looked around my bedroom, specifically eyeing the garish floral wallpaper devoid of any pictures or

106

photographs. "Do you mind if we move this into the other room?" She gestured toward the television. "We can set it up on that server table you keep in the kitchen."

Nodding in agreement, I began to remove the wires from the television. We worked together, setting it up inside the living room.

While she settled on the couch, I moved to the kitchen to grab a couple of plates, fix us both a cup of tea, then brought them to the living room.

"We don't need plates," she said with a humorless smile and popped the pizza box in her lap while patting the space next to her.

I slid a slice of pizza from the box and placed it on the palm of my hand to guide it into my mouth. It remained a breath away from my face. My stomach was too raw to eat anything. "What happened with Hayden?"

"I can barely believe this one. At church today, one of the members said a recording of him and another man from college made the rounds at his school, and have been going around in Bebletown. It was said he was in bed with another guy on the team when he was at school. That's why he abruptly changed and messed up so bad he had to come back here. Couldn't pass, couldn't go to class. He couldn't handle the harassment. He withdrew from school—he wasn't kicked out."

Keeping up an act of disinterest, I busied myself with shoving a bite of the pizza in my mouth to quiet my grumbling stomach.

It couldn't have been true and didn't compute into what I knew of Hayden. Mason warned me most of the rumors were untrue, and I believed I could count this as one of them. I was beginning to see what others said about this town.

"It's hard to believe."

"I know." She snapped her gaze toward the television and remained silent the rest of the night.

I STRUGGLED TO FALL asleep on the hard couch with the inability to stretch my long legs. It was more important that Penny was comfortable, so I gave her my bed. The sounds of the house settling and the wind banging the loose screen door bothered me enough to do something about it.

*My eyes peeled open.*

*The room clouds in crimson hue, announcing Nick's reappearance in my conscious nightmare.*

*He looms in the hallway near the doorway leading to my bedroom where Penny sleeps. I stand up, debating running to her defense—but this isn't real. She's not in real danger.*

*He looks in the bedroom as though he sees her, making my nightmare more real than it has ever been. My environment hasn't existed to him the time before, but on this night, it does.*

*Nick...is dead. I know it with every part of me. I held the belt around his neck until his heart stopped and his chest ceased its rise and fall.*

*I can't discern what to do: Trust my own mind and believe this is a dream, or trust my intuition and believe this was somehow real.*

*He puts a finger to his lips and makes a soft shushing sound.*

*Shaking my head in disbelief and wonder, I step backward. His steps quicken and catch up with me. He secures me against the wall, wrapping his hand around my throat. "Did you think I wouldn't come for you, you ungrateful cunt?" The nightstick skips down my body and wedges its way between my thighs.*

*"Why don't you kill me and get it over with?" I plea.*

*"I'm having too much fun with you." His voice sounds altered. But the face... the face belongs to Nick. It's his face, his body, and his tattoos. The end of the stick slides underneath my panties and rocks up and down the lips of my sex.*

*In one jerk, he shoves the stick inside me, pumping it in and out. He shushes my whimpers with a hiss, warning me to be silent. "You want this. You like it when I destroy you."*

*"Yes," I admit as the words fall in unsteady waves from my lips.*

*"Why fight what you want? Why do you want to die when I can do this to you for the rest of your life? Treat you like the dirty, deceitful bitch you are." He pumps the thick black stick faster.*

*My legs shake so severely they feel numb and Jell-O-like. The hold he has on my neck restricts my movement and my breathing. He withdraws and runs the stick draped in my moisture along my thigh, leaving a trail of my arousal there. An insidious curl of his lip warns me of a punishment to come. He pulls his arm back and with a brute force, flogs my sex.*

*The hollow sound of my sensitive flesh being attacked hits my ears faster than the sensation. Pure unrequited agony throbs from my sex and rifles through my nervous system. The pain elicits a scream I'm sure will wake Penny. Having a full view of her in my bed, she simply rolls over to find a comfortable position.*

*Maybe he's not really here. Maybe I'm dreaming and Penny is a part of that dream.*

*A hand covers my mouth as he pulls me to look at him. "I just got started. Stay awake. I'm not done with you."*

*This isn't real. This isn't real...*

THE LOUD GRUNTS OF a man rang inside my ears. The fog over my vision began to clear. I tried to move, but the soreness shooting through my body slowed my movements. In front of me played a video.

The man on the screen couldn't be mistaken, it was Blake, naked and bound in a way that kept him bent over. A naked and battered Marion kneeled before him, lazily taking him into her mouth. Her gaze shot to the right—to someone off camera. Supplication held in her blue eyes—a desperate request for approval from an unseen person.

The man off camera swept in as though he were an aberration and appeared behind Blake. Dressed in a T-shirt, jeans, and a cap pulled low over his face it nearly shrouded his identity. The peek of his hands and jaw unveiled the man—Hayden.

As Hayden unzipped and placed a condom on his erection, he angled Blake's hips, preparing him. With one jerking motion of his hips, he impaled

Blake. The blood on the condom and Blake's struggle made me question if any of what I witnessed on the screen was consensual.

One thing was apparent; I had sought refuge in a town with secrets as dirty as my own.

A flash of movement in the corner of my vision, called my attention.

Penny stood not far from the couch with her jaw unhinged. She stared at the television, illuminating the room with various lights. "What's this? Is that Marion and Hayden? What the… Why do you have this?"

"I don't know how it got here. I—" I tried to turn the television off, only to fumble, slowed and made clumsy by the throb between my thighs, and turned up the volume by mistake.

"You? You were the one who spread this tape around?" Her green eyes shot to mine in accusation. Splotches of red suffused the fair skin on her cheeks and neck. "Do you know what you did to Marion's reputation? To Hayden's?"

I wrangled with the dials and finally turned the television off. "I wouldn't do something like that."

She angled her head to the side and slanted her eyes at me. "But it's in your DVD player, and you were watching it, right? Am I crazy? Is this some crazy dream where we'll both wake up and my mom will be okay and you won't be a back-stabbing harpy? You can't, can you? Why would you do this? Is it for Mason? Did you think you'd get more of his attention? I mean, why not, right? You already stole him from me, even when I told you I was crushing on him. This is a really messed up thing to do to me right now."

She picked up her shoes from beside the door and slammed them down, wiggling her feet into them. "Don't ever call me again." She signaled with her arms, halting me from stepping forward. "Don't speak to me again. Ever."

My mouth opened to plead my case, but Penny was already halfway out the door by the time I could.

None of it made any sense. Between a once crime-vacant town experiencing three deaths in such a short period, the video of Kylie's death I couldn't have been sure really existed, and the video I had just witnessed featuring Bebletown's golden boy, the town was no longer as innocent as it once felt to me.

I needed the cash now more than ever, and I only knew of one person who might've had it. He, more than likely, needed an exit plan as badly as I did.

# ELEVEN

PRIOR TO MY ARRIVAL, I sent a text to Hayden, but it was still required I show my I.D. to the security guard when I reached the gates. Extra security was hired, and the gates—usually left open—were closed.

Slurs and derogatory terms were all over Hayden's car. Contractors busied themselves cleaning up the graffiti decorating the house. The faults residing in the small extremist town ran deep.

A man with hulking muscles and a shaved head greeted me at the front door. His blue eyes were unwelcoming. He gave me a once-over and shot an intimidating glare in my direction.

"I'm Whitney, Hayden's friend," I introduced myself.

"Garen." The harsh emphasis on the vowels alerted me to his Russian accent.

The same Garen who had spooked Marion?

"You'll have to excuse Garen," said a woman with less of a heavy accent. Dressed in a head to toe leather skirt suit, her long dark hair tied up in a sleek ponytail, her lips painted the same shade of red as her stilettos—she was a formidable and stylish woman. Unnatural stretched skin around her eyes, lips, and jawline indicated she might've had work done. "Aksyna Babikov. This is my son, Garen." Her introductions were offered quickly. "You're Whitney? The boys talk about you all the time. Quite a nice sandwich there, eh?" She elbowed me with a broad smile.

"Yes, well…" I followed her blue eyes as she scanned over my hair and clothes. "I've never seen you in town. Are you here often?"

"I have many homes," she stated, her genialness falling away, "and occasionally come here when I want quiet. The boys needed me."

"Hayden and Mason? Are they your sons?"

She and Garen stared at each other and laughed boisterously in reply to my question. "Come. Hayden is in the back." She grabbed my elbow and pointed toward the right hallway.

Wiping away the perplexing look I was sure had crossed my face, I started to walk there. Halfway down the corridor, I glanced back at Aksyna, but she had disappeared. Garen, standing stone still, glowered at me, chilling me with the frigid temperature of his presence.

"It was nice meeting you."

Garen remained motionless and continued to strip my comfort with his eyes steadily on me.

Returning to my purpose, I ambled down the massive hall toward Hayden's bedroom.

The area of room was equivalent to three times the size of my room. In fact, it was bigger than my entire house. A living room, theatre area, and sitting area amongst the massive bed were included in the room.

Hayden was perched on the couch, watching a science fiction movie on the curved television mounted on the wall.

I wondered even more now what the Babikovs did for a living and what sort of life Nick had growing up with Aksyna. Garen couldn't have been Nick's father—he was at the most in his thirties. A connection had to be traced to the fact Mason and Hayden spoke the language and resided in the house. I found it difficult to find one beyond my original assumption both of them did something illegal—something pertaining to what the Babikovs had done to gain their fortune.

I plopped down on the other side of Hayden on the couch. "I don't believe I've met the Babikovs before, but they were...very strange acting. Is everything okay with them?"

Hayden took a moment before he looked at me. "Strange how?"

"Secretive." I purposely refrained from using the highly appropriate word—frightening—when referring to Garen. If he and many others like him were the sort of people Penny and Marion encountered during the party, I couldn't have blamed her for her abrupt departure.

"Maybe you're reading into things." Irritation seeped its way into Hayden's remark.

"Or...maybe not."

"Not everyone has your type of paranoia, Whitney. Blake lives here on occasion, and he took an impromptu vacation at the spur of the moment. They're worried. That's all you're seeing."

"I don't blame him for leaving for a while. I'm sure Aksyna came back because she heard about all the things going on here. The disappearance of Penny's mother? The deaths? At this rate, I don't believe the motel will ever reopen again so I can work. Some really strange things are going on. I don't feel safe here...anymore."

"Don't work at the hotel again," he said evenly. "I would go so far as to make sure you walk in pairs when you leave Wingettes. I have a feeling things will get worse."

"You think there was something more to the deaths? That the men were murdered?"

He adjusted in his seat, winced, and carefully leaned back.

I couldn't find any wounds to determine why he suddenly seemed in pain. "Are you...okay?"

"Fine," he offered curtly. "Pulled a muscle when I worked out this morning."

The television became my focal point as the action star was thrust into the middle of an epic space battle. "I wish I had a choice about the hotel, but I can't afford to not work. When it reopens, I'll go back."

"If it gets you to stop working there, I'm good for the money. I could find something for you to do if you'd like honest work. You could take care of Aksyna's horse."

"I can't take your money." His concern for my safety was surprising.

He continued to contribute to the quiet and stale air as he stared back at the television screen in melancholy.

"I don't know how to segue into the thing you're probably uncomfortable talking about. It's the commercial break after that live television show where someone says something unscripted and controversial. Story of my life. I know why you didn't come to me about it. It's not my business. You should know I don't care about your sexual orientation."

Snapping his head in my direction, he considered me, pushing me to continue talking in order to remove the sudden thickness forming between us.

"If you were...gay, bisexual, or unidentified...I wouldn't care."

"Wouldn't you?"

"No. Why would you think I would?"

"Everybody cares. This is Bible-town, right?" He moved into a new position, the strain in his face signaled his discomfort. Crouching forward with his hands in prayer position over his open lap, he closed his eyes tightly, creating tension lines at the corner of his eyes. "I can't stop questioning why you came here. Why this place of all places? The town centered around religion to such an extreme and hypocritical way. The town is centered around a book that labels homosexuality a sin. It's a town of group-thinkers. But you, Whitney?" His newly opened hazel eyes landed on me. "I think I know your flaw. You are one of the biggest sinners here. Were you hoping this town would save you?"

Thrown from a steady path, I regarded my hands.

He jolted up from the couch and approached the billiard table at the far end of the room and flicked a few balls around. Better at hiding his pain than he was before, he wore a disguise of impassivity.

"I could understand why you'd hide it, but you have to admit—"

His eyes darted to mine. "What makes you think I am? Am I wearing a sign?"

I rolled my shoulders, sliding my hands into the pockets of my white apron dress. I looked down at my feet, noticing I needed to throw my Converse shoes into the wash soon. "I have maybe a thousand in cash right now. We could both blow this town with whatever money you have and go west."

He leaned across the table, clasping his hands across the green and rested his chin on his hands. "You barely know me and you want to run away with me? Not very smart. What do you think will happen with me and you? Do you think Mason would ever let you go off with me alone? We leave and do what?"

"I'm sure you want a new start just like I do. This place is temporary for the both of us, right? We don't have to land in the same place. I really, really have to get out of this town." Mason and the deaths were my two driving forces. It was hard not to stereotype Mason. A minor sliver of me recalled the darkness he had yet to reveal to me. I pegged him as deranged enough to be the town's killer—if Hayden's coded assumptions were correct in asserting that something happened to the homeless men.

He couldn't have known Kylie's fate—even I wasn't sure. I refused to believe Nick was alive. Succumbing to that thought would've questioned my sanity. Nick was dead and someone else had to have mutilated, violated, and killed Kylie. I knew of Nick's crimes; he admitted them all to me. He was unwell and thrived off his sickness to extremes; he only saw one way to end his ailment. He couldn't have been the one who possibly killed her, no matter what I saw. My mind could no longer be trusted.

My biggest fear was that if Kylie was murdered, her killer had plans to find me. The DVD made it clear the murder was about me. I was certain with my life Nick had died. I left quickly as he instructed me to and trusted he made arrangements.

Nothing assured me my red dreams were anything more than lucid nightmares. I wasn't losing control of my mental faculties. There was a killer out there who looked a lot like Nick, and for some reason or another, had taken to tormenting me.

"Why would I want to go away with you? Why would you want to go away with me? Why would I want to be anywhere with you for more than an hour? I can barely stand you for five minutes."

"Tired of your moods and the way you screw with me." Standing quickly, I moved to leave.

His steps swiftly and loudly hit against the hardwood floor. He caught up to me, spinning me around and encaged me against the wall. "I'm not gay."

"I told you, it doesn't matter to me if you are or aren't. You don't have to convince me."

"No. I mean it." He slightly relaxed, leaning in the doorframe. "Mason has this very bad habit of fucking up anything positive I have in my life. Whether it's intentional or not, it's what he does. The sex tape that went around town is his responsibility. I know it is. What I did in the film was for one purpose, and it had nothing to do with getting off, or getting the guy off. I have never and will never want to be with a man that way."

Perplexed over his denial, being that I had seen video proof, I had no idea how to navigate our conversation—or if we were referring to the same movie. Was I the only recipient of the movie with him, Blake, and Marion?

How it could've been that both brothers blamed the other for their lot in lives was something I could identify with; my sister often vilified me.

"Maybe you're bisexual? Did you enjoy it? Being with him?"

"I...am...not...gay."

"Hayden, I saw the video. A recent one, and not the one of you at school. I wasn't bothered by some of it, but the other? Marion looks in bad shape and Blake...did he consent to it?"

He pushed against the door, backing away from me. I only saw a second of the pain in his face before he turned his back on me. "It was consensual. Everything beyond that was a complication."

"You can talk to me. I can understand quite a bit, Hayden."

"I'm not saying it's complicated because I think you're incapable of understanding."

"Then why?"

"We never have a two-way exchange, Whitney."

"I don't understand you, Hayden. Why do you care? I'm a four—a psychotic four who's too crazy to befriend, right?"

"I still think you're psychotic, but I never thought you were a four." Turning to me, he slowly smirked. "But you knew that, didn't you?"

What I thought of myself mattered little. I wanted to be just a fixture no one really noticed. "Are you now saying you rated me that way to bother me? Why are you so hell bent on being an asshole with me? I don't like that part of you."

"But you like Mason's type of asshole?"

I hesitated and stuffed my hands in the back pockets of my dress. "Mason...has these protective moments with me that are unlike anyone I've ever been with. I've never been one for sweetness and romance. The fact he isn't that way doesn't bother me. His type of asshole is different, because in reality he's calling me out on what I'm..." I shook my head and shut down the untamed spilling of my secrets from a mouth that couldn't hide its smile. "Doesn't matter what I like. Every time I'm with him, he sends off these deafening alarm bells."

"I get it." He exhaled and his face sank slightly. "He's the bad boy you'd fuck and not tell anyone about, and I'm the dependable guy with a pinch of asshole who you'd consider a friend?"

"What about what I said?" I shifted my feet back and forth no longer comfortable in my once comfort providing shoes.

"You haven't answered why you want me to go with you."

"Do I need reasons? I was going to go alone, but with what's going on with you, I thought you'd come with me."

"I assume you need more money to go. Is that the only reason you're inviting me?"

My head swayed left to right with a profuse motion. "It's not the only one. I've been waiting for the right time. Right amount of money. I think I was waiting for the right person to go with. You don't even have to go the whole way with me. Maybe take me halfway?"

His eyes drifted to the floor for many silent moments. "Meet me at your house in two hours."

Feeling relieved and warmed from within, I couldn't help but grin. Finally, this was my chance to get away. I was hopelessly optimistic this time I'd be able to outrun my past. "Really?"

"Really."

"Okay…I have to work tonight, but can we meet up right after? I should get home at about midnight." I clutched my bag to my chest and headed for the door.

"Hey, Whitney."

"Yeah?" I swiveled around to face him.

"I'm not gay, and for some reason, every time I'm around you, I can't fight the urge to rip off your panties and stick my hard cock deep inside that tight, wet pussy and make you viciously sore. I saw you with him outside the barn. Watching you with him made me imagine all the ways we could split the duty of claiming your pussy as ours and no one else's. When I fucked Marion, it was just a preview. Every time I fuck Marion, I imagine she's you. She could never match up. Your body is built to handle more than I have ever given her."

I choked.

He smiled, receding into his bedroom and closed the door in my face.

AFTER AN INTENSE SHIFT at Wingettes, I dragged my feet home, barely sure if I had enough energy to pack for my great escape with Hayden. The instant I opened the front door to my home, a pungent odor burned my nose and forced me to wretch. The stench I couldn't place overwhelmed my senses at the closed door to my bedroom. I froze at the entryway, surveying my surroundings making sure nothing was in disarray. With a few seconds of delay, I opened the door.

An arctic freeze encased me in its hold. The prickly tingles of abject terror stunned me in place. He hung lifelessly from a belt wrapped around his neck, tied to my ceiling fan. His face was grayish in tone, his eyes swollen and verged on falling out of his sockets. A black tongue hung out of the side of his mouth. A dried, gray, indiscernible mess coated his lips. Between his parted legs, staining my bed, was a white flakey mess. Jeans were pooled around his knees exposing his sex. I stumbled into a tripod affixed to a camera and fought to steady it. Torn between the sight of the camera and the grotesque death scene, I walked backward out of the room.

The noise in my head screamed at intoning volume to get my things and move on, no matter what little money I had. The sound of police sirens increased the dramatic thumping inside my chest. My lungs were squeezed with a heavy, painful weight. The task of taking in steady breaths became laborious.

"Show me your hands and get down on the ground." The command in Mason's voice startled me. It wasn't laced with sex or innuendo. With his weapon unholstered and his hand guided to it, I took his threat seriously.

I slipped down to my knees with my hands above my head. He rounded my position and took one hand down, locking it in the cold handcuffs and took the other, encaging it in the rigid metal as he read me my rights.

In a daze, I watched as his partner, the same one who belittled me at the hotel, made a few choice remarks about what would happen to me while staring in disgust at the scene inside my bedroom.

Mason patted my body down, checking for a weapon. He paused at my hip and leaned in my ear. "Shh," he said of my tears. "I'll get you out of this, baby. I promise." A hand jammed down beneath the waistband of my shorts to find my sex. His fingers on my clit through the thin lace fabric of my panties awakened me out of my state.

I sucked in a wheezing breath as though surfacing from the threat of drowning.

"Trust me. I'll take care of you. You won't go down for this." His hand moved faster as he pushed me away from the doorway, ensuring his partner couldn't see us. "You trust I'll make everything better for you and you'll stop running from me?"

"Yes," I groaned, thrown into a pit of confusing pleasure adorned with sharp tinges of dread.

"Good answer. I thought you'd fucked up and forgotten whom you belonged to." He kissed my ear gently and removed his hand. Guiding me by my hands behind my back, he shoved me forward just as his partner exited the room. "She's all yours."

# TWELVE

Tired and confused, I remained silent as the sheriff questioned me in a small room that looked as though it doubled as a break room. I was sure the most action the police station saw was the occasional bar brawl, domestic dispute, or drunken and disorderly persons who were thrown in the drunk tank. There was only one large cell in the back hall and not much else. The front lobby had one chair and a small desk in front of a work area with four smaller desks. It wasn't a place equipped for serious crimes. I feared if evidence proving my innocence wasn't found before my bail hearing, the state police would get involved and make a horrible situation indescribably worse.

Mason stood watch by the door, shaking his head at me anytime I threatened to crack and plead my case. From Sheriff Taren's questions, I plucked threads of truth about what had occurred: They received an anonymous tip that a possible murder was under way at my address. There was no sign of a struggle of any kind to prove he didn't know his "attacker." Blake had been dead for more than a few hours.

No one paid attention to the glaring evidence, proving Blake had killed himself. If there was no struggle, he was another coincidental death. A man who felt so ashamed over his fetish and the reveal of his sex tape, he ended his life. Perhaps Blake's shame was a rouse. I knew the mess I saw on my bed, and I couldn't help but ponder why he'd do such a thing inside my home, or how he managed to enter a locked house.

I could've argued that Blake did it to himself, but Sheriff Taren didn't want to paint the golden boy with such a dirty brush. From the way he spoke highly of Blake, he wanted someone to take the fall and it was apparently supposed to be me.

Sheriff Taren pounded on the desk, startling me as he insisted I provide an answer to his questions.

"Sheriff, can I speak to you in private for a minute?" Mason's request was bloated with irritation. Sheriff Taren simply nodded and followed Mason out of the room.

Several minutes later, Mason returned, and slid a cell phone across the table toward me.

"Do you have someone you can call?"

"I didn't do this." My dry and parched throat strangled my confession.

"I know," he said, shocking me with his gentleness. "The assholes want someone to blame because Blake had a little clout in this town. No one wants to believe he had a fucked-up fantasy." He leaned forward, brushing the back of his hand down my cheek. "I'm glad the sick fuck is dead. If I had caught him in your room, it would be me who they would've had to arrest."

He thumbed my chin for a moment and flashed me a smile. "You won't go down for this. The police force here is full of a bunch of yokels who don't know their cock from their ass. But to be on the safe side, make your phone call. I think you know because I'm a cop who arrested you, I can't directly help you. But no one said I couldn't indirectly get you out of this mess." With a wink, he left me alone with a cell phone. There was only one number in the phone with the title "Lawyer." I ignored it and called the woman I'd been avoiding for months.

"Dreya."

It was once a coincidence I refused to correlate to the death of a man I had dated for a short while that sparked my need to leave my mother's side. I could no longer convince myself of the lie. The occurrences were no longer a happenstance.

"It's happening again, and I'm stuck," I confessed to her. "I don't know what to do. I'm in jail for something I didn't do."

"Give me the address of the police station and I'll call the nearest and best lawyer I can find." Her tone was dead calm, true to her nature as an unflappable woman. "I'll be there as soon as I can be. I want you home, Whit, and out of whatever mess you got yourself into. Where are you?"

THE DIN EMANATING DOWN the hall leading to my cell began to slowly wane. Alone in the cell with no other occupants, my thoughts ran wild. No matter how much I rationalized recent events, one resounding truth filled my head; I was losing my mind.

The slow clomp of dress shoes echoed down the hall. I huddled in the corner of the metal bench with my knees tucked to my chest. The ping of the gates being hit with a metal bar vibrated inside my head.

Mason appeared outside my cell in his full uniform. Pieces of Nick possessing Mason's face infiltrated my vision. Upon sight of the brown fast food bag in his hand, my perception found its clarity and revealed the truth.

Double-checking the path toward the front of the station, he used his key to unlock my cell. "The last officer on duty just left. It's you and me." He locked the cell door behind his exit and sauntered over to me. Placing the bag down between us, he sat down on the iron bench. "Eat."

"I don't think I can." My voice was hoarse and dry.

The storm cloud turned its gaze on me, demanding compliance. I picked up a soda cup and began to slowly sip.

"I know what you're thinking." He lolled back hooking his thumbs in his belt. "Why does all this weird shit keep happening in this town? Why did it

124

happen to me?" He reached out for me and tucked a stray curl behind my ear. "Don't worry about this. The camera in your bedroom was missing a memory card, but they'll find it eventually. You have an alibi for his time of death. Someone is playing you. They moved his body to your house to fuck with you. Hate to say it, baby, but I warned you about the company you keep. I'm the only one you can trust in this town."

I slammed down the cup and receded to the other end of the bench. "If someone is playing me, it's you. Maybe you haven't killed anyone...maybe you have. But I know you're the one who called in the tip."

His eyes darkened a tad more, the muscles in his broad jaw began to twitch as he said through gritted teeth, "Do you think I'd fuck with you that way?"

"Hayden once told me the three of us would never blend in here because we were cut from the same cloth. If that's true—"

"You've been speaking to Hayden"—he sat ramrod straight and turned to me—"about me?"

I ejected from the bench and walked to the other side of the cell.

He jolted up and lunged toward me. A hand knotted in the back of my hair and yanked my head back to stare up into his eyes.

The tightness of the tension in my scalp induced a wince.

"You're very hard of hearing." He plucked up my hand from where it rested on my side and guided it to his zipper, slowly moving my hand down to unzip it. "Let me speak in a language you understand."

"Why can't you leave me alone?"

He bowed forward and the second my hand slipped inside his undone pants to stroke him, he paused. A sensuous and devious smirk contorted his lips. "You don't want me to leave you alone."

"Doesn't matter what I know about you—what I assume about you—I want it *too* much."

He placed a thumb to my lips and pressed in forcing me to open my mouth. "You don't know anything about me other than what I want from you. Show me how much you want it, baby. Wrap those pretty little lips around my cock and prove you want it."

His dare tingled up my spine and shot straight up my thighs. Common sense and the threat of my life began to drift away. It was the danger I wanted to avoid. I couldn't afford to become lost in anyone. No matter how bad they were for me and how badly I wanted it.

"No." I managed to get free of his hold. I stood in the corner of the cell, daring him with a drift of my eyes to come for me.

A loud clicking sound flicked off the lights, leaving only the dim safety lights that barely lit my cell.

"Hello? Is anyone here in this Podunk town." A shrill man's voice created needed division between Mason and me. "I can't see a damn thing in here. These better not be the usual conditions, or my client and I will sue."

"This will fucking continue," Mason warned me as he zipped up.

He locked my prison before heading toward the front of the station. When the man loudly protested he was my lawyer sent by Dreya Langston, ready to put up my bail, the relief spread over me.

# THIRTEEN

THE SECOND I WAS able to return home four nights ago, I took a long, hot bath while the lawyer conducted business in my living room and wouldn't leave until my mother arrived the following morning.

Dreya offered nothing in the way of comfort and barely spoke to me other than to say when I wrapped up my business in Bebletown, I was to return to Manhattan with her.

The next morning, gossip spread pertaining to the discovery of the recording of Blake's death. I never heard the details of what was contained on the recording. The evidence was substantial enough to clear my name. The Sheriff came by personally last night to apologize for my wrongful arrest.

I was so thankful to be out of the running for Blake's death, my bedroom became my safe place, from which I hardly ever left.

THE LOUD HUM OF a motor and the smell of coffee disrupted my sleep. I sat up in bed, drunk with exhaustion and listened in until I could better decipher the sounds outside my window—a lawn mower. I slipped on a thin white jersey dress and removed the protective silk scarf from my head.

As I traveled into the kitchen, my hair fell down from my wrap haphazardly—I'd straightened it last night and wanted it to remain that way for at least a few days.

My mother stood at the counter drinking her coffee while gazing out of the window.

"Where's Henry?" I asked of the newest man she had taken an interest in. Henry made a lucrative salary as an international trade manager and often took my mother with him on his excursions. Behind closed doors, he was her dutiful submissive.

The packing boxes were the first things I noticed; she'd been very busy this morning.

"He had business in New York," she answered. "I'll be joining him this weekend." She passed a cup of coffee my way, instead of the matcha tea I drank exclusively, while she continuously gazed out the kitchen window. "Quite the view you have over here."

I joined her side and took the cup of coffee from her as I followed where her attention rested. Mason busied himself doing yard work and had transformed the space into something worthy of being labeled a back yard. My shock was undeniable. My head felt like it had been spun on its axis and no longer knew which end pointed up.

Dreya wrapped her long, sculpted fingertips against her mug as it remained on the counter. "It's great of him to do that. I researched the terms of your lease and wanted to make sure you would get your deposit back. When I spoke to Henry on the phone, he was willing to pay a gardener. I was in the middle of calling someone when he showed up. He fixed the lawnmower, mowed the lawn, and trimmed the hedges." She turned to me and gave me a tame smile. "He deserves a little reward for all he's done for you, don't you think?"

A small glint of knowledge was in her eyes. She laid on her request a tad too sugary—a tone unnatural to my mother. "What do you know about him?"

"Enough."

I placed my hands on my hips and rolled my shoulders waiting for her divulge more information. "Does it have something to do with the Babikovs?"

She pointedly looked around the house, and I drew my conclusions.

I rented from a person who served as broker for the home. The company name on my lease was Alloy Properties. If Hayden somehow had the power to cut my hours at Alloy Insurance, I may have found the connection. The Babikovs owned the Alloy name and the companies that used the name. I questioned if the reasons behind my ability to rent the only house available in Bebletown weren't altogether innocent.

"Dreya...what do you know?"

"I know enough, and that's all *you* need to know. Why don't you bring him a glass of lemonade?" Viewing me from the corner of her eye, she discharged a long stream of air with dissatisfaction. "After you shower and make yourself up," she added with puckered lips. "He'll be out there for a while. Wear that pretty purple sundress that makes your skin look like it's glowing. I know you brought it with you."

I poured my mug of coffee down the sink, having no inclination to do as she had asked.

"Whitney." She used a tone she didn't usually use on me with one narrowed eye. "I told you to do something."

"Why? Because you know something I don't about him?"

"Do you know why I'm not telling you, Whitney? Because your priorities are mixed up. You came to this town for God knows what reason to live like... this?" She gestured around my house. "You're better than this, and you know it. You also know we can't outrun who we are, even if it's unacceptable in the normal world." She grabbed a lock of my hair and flipped it over my shoulders. "Normal is synonymous with monotony. Go. Do what I told you to do because it's obvious that man has your scent on his nose. Go make me proud. Maybe he'll give you pocket money to shop with when you get to New York. If you play it right, he'll continue to give you pocket money."

I stared at her, wondering what she knew that I didn't about a small town cop who tipped her interest with a bank account balance not befitting an officer of the law—Dreya wouldn't have asked me to give him the time of the day if he didn't earn a certain amount.

It was silly, but there I was, waiting outside in my pretty dress for Mason while holding an ice cold glass of lemonade. Almost done by the time I got there, he finished up the last of what he had to do with the yard.

His fleece pants were low on his long waist, revealing the V-muscle. The white T-shirt, soaked in moisture, clung to his tight body. A baseball cap hung low on his head, making his broad jaw more square in appearance.

I found it difficult to tear my eyes away from every part of him. At every chance, behind my closed eyelids, my dark fantasy featuring him came to life.

*He rips off his shirt and charges toward me. "Show me you're thankful." He grabs me by the hair and forces me closer to him.*

*I nod demurely and kiss my way down his body. His salty taste is an aphrodisiac. Rivulets of sweat tread down the bumps and ridges of his body. I trace the lines in his stomach with my tongue and pull down the waistband of his pants while wrangling his erection from underneath the fleece material. Opening my mouth, I tease him by swirling the tip of my tongue along the bead of arousal drizzling down the head of his sex. Winding my hair around his fist, he holds me still and begins to brutally pump inside my mouth.*

*"This is how you thank me, you fucking whore."*

A snap in my face pulled me out of my daydream.

"You do that a fuck of a lot around me. It makes it worse for me to control myself when I can hear what you're thinking." He dabbed his face with the hem of his sweat-soaked T-shirt and sported a broad smile. "Your fantasy is standing right in front of you, baby. You don't have to close your eyes to see it."

I shoved the glass of lemonade in his direction. Glancing back at the window, I noticed my mother was no longer standing there. Instead she stood in the doorway, snarling at Mason. "You're going to take care of my daughter, correct? As in, you better not leave her side and you'll keep her safe while I'm gone."

"That's the plan, ma'am," Mason told my mother with a smile that charmed me more severely than it persuaded her.

"I'm holding you to that." She gave me a nod and pointed behind her to announce her departure.

I stared after her path, stuck in a little awe. She would never have left my side unless... "Did you have a conversation with Dreya while I was sleeping?"

"I did," he replied, his grin tongue and cheek. "I brought her breakfast and had a very, very long, nice talk about you."

"Why are you doing this?" I asked. "Hayden said..."

The genialness fell from his face. "And I told you to stay the fuck away from him. Anything and everything you need, I'm the one who provides it. Not him. Not anybody else."

In front of Hayden, my snappy words were usually easy to say. With Mason, he'd collared me with an invisible strap of leather and tugged whenever I thought about revealing my unfiltered thoughts with him.

"Should really take a shower." I glanced over the massive amount of sweat that bled through his white T-shirt and clung to every ripple and wave of his body. My incisors began to attack my bottom lip.

"You were missing a we at the start of that sentence." He sucked his ample bottom lip. His brandy-hued eyes reflected the color of clover honey by the sun peaking from underneath the lid of his baseball cap.

"I'm not joining you."

"What you're looking at tells me something different, baby."

I tore my eyes away from ogling his crotch. "Your pants are low. As in, I can see things I shouldn't low."

"You've seen it before, and you will see more soon." As he sipped the drink I gave him, he leered at my legs.

I plopped down on the patio swing and spread my legs wide so my floaty dress arose, revealing my lacy white panties. "You've seen what you wanted to see, now can you please go?"

He rubbed his bottom lip, leisurely gulping down the remainder of the drink while keeping his eyes on me. His neck drew my eye and not because I wanted to wrap a belt around it and leave his life hanging in the balance. I wanted to bite it, suck on his Adam's apple, and feel him…

In few motions he was in front of me, pinning me into the swing with his fist on either side of my body and his face only inches from mine. "You don't get to tease me, Whitney. Show me everything."

I looked around the back yard for any wandering eyes.

My chin was pinched between his fingers and forced to obey his motion. "Take…them…off." A flash of his eyes hit between my legs.

I maneuvered awkwardly and slipped them down my legs. He gave me room to breathe and picked up my leg, leaving my panties dangling around my ankle. Using his teeth, he slipped them off my feet.

"Keep those pretty eyes where they belong—on me." He sucked his fingers and dipped them inside his glass, retrieving an ice cube. Stuck in his trance, I only caught a glimpse of his fingers sliding inside me. The cold tinge of the ice made it near impossible to keep quiet. I shuddered and pressed my lips together, unable to tear my gaze away from the thunderous clouds held in his eyes.

He pumped two fingers in and out, circling his thumb over my clit. I reached out and held the swing to steady myself and sank my teeth deep into my bottom lip. His fingers began to thrash inside me, stealing the strength in my spine. Painful shocks worked up my spine, verging on exploding from my core. Close to the edge, I bucked against his hand.

He went down on his knee, slowing the place of his fingers. Unable to speak and tell him to keep going, I squirmed, hoping to encourage him to do more. He withdrew his hand completely and folded my skirt up to my waist while trailing every small movement of my eyes with his. He grabbed my thighs, yanking me down until my bottom hung half was off the swing. Staring at me, he waited until my erratic breathing normalized and the fire once rising inside me began to subside.

Swooping down between my legs, his lips and tongue worked in a whirlwind on my sex. He licked me from my opening to my sensitive nub and back around again. His arm snaked around my hip. A thumb reached down to strum at my swelling nerve center as his tongue darted in and out of me.

Cool surges of intense pleasure built up at my core, threatening to explode and make me break my silent pact to stay quiet. With his eyes on me, he worked his tongue upward, flicking it back and forth across the bundle of nerves, leaving me squirming. Surrounding the sensitive flesh in his mouth, he began to suck on the swelling nub…and I shattered.

I clasped my hand over my mouth to keep quiet. The shrill shock hit me so hard my eyes watered. He sucked harder while running his tongue in circles repeatedly over my bundle of nerves. I wanted to push him away. I felt like I was soaring on an even higher peak with every little suck of soft lashing.

My back arched and my toes curled as I climaxed. My body shuddered and convulsed violently. Remaining quiet was no longer an issue, I couldn't speak much less breathe.

He kissed my wet slit with a loud smack and withdrew. My muscles were tense; I was left unable to move.

He slowly put me back together with a cocky grin staining his face. He moved the brim of his cap down lower to cast a daunting shadow over his eyes. "You owe me every goddamn piece that makes up everything you are. I own you. End of fucking story." His hands laid on either side of my body, palming the seat and halting the swing from its slow rocking motion. He stared at me as the sweat from his body dripped on my dress. He neared my face, leaving only inches of space between us. I could feel his heavy breaths against my face, trailed with the scent of my arousal. The bulge in his pants drew my gaze and my want.

"I need to hear you admit the obvious, Whitney."

I placed my clammy hand on his lips. He slightly parted his lips, allowing my fingertips to slip inside his mouth. His tongue cradled my fingers while his top teeth gently sank into my knuckles. As I withdrew my hand, he smiled, subdued from his previous mood.

I looked at his sweat-soaked hair, peeking underneath his cap. I twined my fingers in the silky strands. In the sun it shone a brassy dark gold, darkened by his sweat and clinging together. I clasped my hand to his jaw, making him close his eyes. Extending my spine to reach his height, I brushed my mouth against the soft texture of his lips. With his mouth open, I exhaled a cool stream of air, whispering my confession, "You own every part of me, and every part of you belongs to me."

He sank against me, tipping his hat up and resting his damp forehead against mine.

"But you're worse for me than I am for you." *Because somehow I know we're both killers.* I quickly withdrew from his space. "Thank you for taking care of the yard."

He bent at the hips and kissed my closed fist as it rested across my lap, misfiring he rubbed his open mouth against my abdomen. The thin material of my dress made sure his heated open-mouthed exhale was immediately felt.

My thirst for him and my discomfort burned me to the quick and elicited a sharp gasp. I jolted upright to stand in front of him and pushed my body against his. "I don't have a way to repay you."

"You do have a way, and you will repay me until I say you're paid in full."

"Go home, Mason." My lids became heavy, and my shaky request was lost in a gust of hot wind.

A hand was shoved in my hair, evoking a sharp inhalation in surprise and satisfaction. He snapped my head back with one hard yank. "Did you think you could decide? You don't."

"Why are you doing this to me?" I nearly whispered.

He ran his fingers through my hair and inclined down to me. "I'm selfish and obsessive over the things I own—to the point of being driven fucking crazy. I want you, and I don't have enough of what I want because you keep fucking with me. Don't toy with me and what I want anymore. That's a threat, Whitney. Take it very fucking seriously this time."

His words wrapped me up in a dark, thick blanket and sent an adrenaline shot straight to my veins. My head and heart throbbed together with one purpose, whispering, *"Don't stop. Possess me. Own me. Remind me why I'm yours."*

"I can't understand the way you make me feel, Mason." I questioned the grasp he held on pieces of me when I couldn't recall when I'd given them to him. "I don't know if I like it or hate it."

"I haven't started yet, Whitney." He slid my panties into his pocket with one hand and rubbed his nose against mine. "You will end and begin with me, and you will love every fucking thing I make you feel."

# FOURTEEN

"Whitney, you can't sleep all afternoon. Come help me pack up your things." My mother was dressed in a costume to clean with pedal pushers and a tightly fitted T-shirt. She considered it beneath her to lift a finger to do any actual cleaning—it was her submissive's responsibility.

I dragged my body out of bed and moved to the bathroom, forcing myself to look presentable before I greeted my mother.

She wasn't alone. She was with an older graying gentleman in a black suit. "I'd like you to meet a very good friend of mine, this is Henry."

Friend. It was a word she often used to describe the men under her authority—it would've been frowned upon to announce in public that every man she was with wasn't her boyfriend or lover. I knew of him, but never met him formally. The times I encountered him, he was wearing ear plugs and blinded in some way.

"Very nice to meet you, young lady." Henry shook my hand. "Ms. Langston talks about you often. I see you take after her looks. I bet the men go wild over you. I have a young employee under me who would like to…"

*Not this…again.* I turned my ire toward my mother, adjusted at full throttle.

"Why are you doing this again?"

"It's not what you think." She held up her hand, blinding me with a rock that took up the entire space between her knuckle and joint. "We are ensuring you'll be set up when you come back to New York and have someone who will keep you safe. Officer Friendly would be a nice fling for the few days you have left in town. Don't get attached, you're leaving with me, and he has issues that keep him from being someone you could be with and...stable."

"Like?' I asked, raising a brow.

She floated around the room with her arms out on either side of her as though she was forced to navigate through high grass while maintaining demureness. "Henry has set up a room for you in his gorgeous penthouse in the Upper East Side. You'll love it."

It was fruitless to ask her to clarify about what she recently discovered of Mason. She'd likely had someone search for information on him and came back with things she didn't like, nor wanted to tell me. The woman often kept me in the dark. I didn't discover the identity of my father until I happened upon the information by accident. "And Sloane? Is she still with you in New York?"

"Sloane left a few weeks ago. She's in Miami with an old flame of hers." Waltzing up to me, she brushed her fingers into my hair. "She's fine," she reassured me, noting the concern I thought I hid from her. "Aren't you happy about this? I'm finally making good on my promise to you."

I gave her a fake smile, unable to expend the energy to give her a more genuine one. Needing her protection and asking her to be with me was a huge mistake. She hadn't changed at all, and if I allowed her back into my life, she would pull me back into the world that would eventually feast on my darkest parts until there was nothing left but a lightless ditch. "I have to make appearances at work."

"With all you've gone through, are you sure that's a good idea?" She looked at Henry, giving him a silent command.

He gingerly took her hand and kissed the back of it while bowing to her. With a nod, he disappeared into the hall.

"I know what you're thinking," she whispered to me. "Aesthetically, I could do so much better. But financially? He has more money than he knows what to do with. A widower with grown adult children. This won't be like any other time. This is real and for the long haul. He's one of the best submissives I've ever had." She threw her arms up, stressing her disgust at my choice of a living arrangement. "You can't be happy living this way. Don't you want to get out of this town and back into the life you deserve? The man I have for you? He's perfect. He's Nick…but better."

Her mention of Nick shut me down completely. Facts that I wanted to suppress came back to haunt me. I'd lost my mind and begun to destroy my own body while holding onto visions of Nick. There was a killer in this town toying with me at a time when my mind had begun to fracture.

My needs had changed. My future had changed. In a different set of circumstances, I would've easily jumped at the golden ticket she offered me. There wasn't a viable return path. Having made the descent into hell, there wasn't enough repentance in the world to bring me back into purgatory.

"Mom—"

"Don't shit on this opportunity." Her smile dropped and the authoritative tone made a speedy return. She hated the sound of the word mom, and she knew when I used it, it meant I was going to disobey her. "You're misunderstanding what I'm trying to say to you. The man I've chosen for you will someday be yours and take care of you in the manner you deserve. He's promised me. You're contracted to him. Money has been exchanged, and I can't exactly back out of it. I'm trying to keep you out of trouble." She flipped my hair over my shoulder. "I wish you would stop straightening your beautiful hair. You have such beautiful natural curls. Probably the only thing I can thank your father for contributing to."

Unable to look in the eye of the woman who essentially sold me to the highest bidder, I deeply regretted my decision. I wiggled out of her hold, wanting out of the house.

THE STARES THROWN IN my direction when I entered Wingettes couldn't be ignored. I no longer faded into the background. I was the girl the town condemned as being guilty of killing one of their golden boys despite evidence to the contrary. The court of public opinion had rendered a guilty verdict.

"Whitney, you're late," Baxter barked at me, showing no stitch of judgment or desire for me to be anywhere but there.

"Sorry, won't happen again." I tied the bar apron around my waist and washed my hands in the prep area.

I glanced over at Cinda, recalling that she worked at the gentleman's club part-time two counties over. With the hotel closure, and my termination from Alloy, I had nothing to ensure I could leave the town on my own for good. The need to earn my own money and leave town before I was forced to leave with my mother became my lone thought—especially armed with the knowledge my mother would never change, and my past would forever haunt me in increasingly harmful ways. Everything and everyone was a suspected thief in stealing my ability to adopt a new life.

"Cinda, are they hiring at the Red Pony?"

A blank look settled on her face prior to contorting into stun. "The Red Pony?" The words erupted from her lips like a dream she couldn't believe was real. "Not that I know of." She turned to me while waiting for the other wait staff in the prep area to leave. She grabbed my arm and brought me forward, whispering, "You know you can't talk about stuff like that around the people here. Especially with how your rep took a dive. Doesn't matter what the cops say. People think you did Blake in."

"You had something else you wanted to tell me," I urged her back on the path.

"Um…wait. I think a waitress quit since he started making them do lap dances. You're not thinking of applying are you?"

"The money is better there—that's what you always used to say."

"I don't think you'd fit in there, and do you really want to kill your reputation even more?" She eyed a staff member as they whizzed by us, throwing proverbial daggers in their direction until they left the area. "You're a shake of a tail away from the rabble rousers coming to your house and throwing rocks at your windows."

"It doesn't matter. I won't be here for much longer."

She leaned forward and spoke in hushed tone. "Are you okay with taking your top off in front of strangers? Or even grinding a stranger's lap?"

I swallowed hard.

"Oh, honey. What did you think we did there? Stood up there with our clothes on and danced? We aren't go-go dancers. We're strippers." She laughed. "You're pretty. You need to be sexy. I'm not talking about looks. The way you carry yourself. You carry yourself as awkward as you are."

"Are you done?" I asked with an edge.

"You wanted to know," she said in a sing-song voice as she carried her order off to her customers.

"Whitney, you've got customers." Baxter loomed in the doorway while keeping his eyes on his clipboard. "Get to your table."

"Yes, Baxter." I took my pad and whizzed over.

Every table I tended to was met with cutting glares, the hasty exit of the patrons, or requests for a different waitress. I expected nothing less when I reached the only table I had left. I repeated my script without looking up at the table until one of them slapped me on my ass.

"What's up, baby?" Mason gave me a wink and a smile.

He deserved a lot from me, things I wasn't able to give him. Today, I was able to ward off the woman he brought out of me for the woman I cloaked myself in every day. "If you do that again, I'll break your arm." My warning was gritted through my clenched teeth.

"Someone doesn't want a tip," the man Mason was with sang.

"Someone wants spit in their beer," I said wryly.

Mason stood and grabbed my arm. "Come with me."

I wiggled out of his hold. The anger I elicited on his face somehow sobered me. "I'm sorry I said that," I offered to him. "I just can't do this with you right now. I'm working, and I need all the tips I can get."

He softened completely and held my face in his hands. "Why didn't you say something to me?"

Mason's friend, obviously having several beers before he arrived, decided to try to touch me. He only made it inches from my body before Mason grabbed his arm, shoved the man's fist into the table in an awkward manner and elicited a grotesque cracking sound, followed by the man's screams.

I hadn't noticed Hayden was at the table until he swiftly slid out of the booth in a huff and headed elsewhere.

Fluttering my eyelashes, my attention was glued to the stranger's broken wrist in amazement. A shameful craving made my knees buckle.

"Hey." Mason grabbed my chin and turned me toward him. He was serenely calm as though nothing out of the ordinary occurred. "Talk to me."

"Later," I promised him, slipping out of his hold. "I'll get you a couple beers...unless you are taking your friend to the hospital." Whirling around, I headed toward the bar.

Hayden came to my end of the long, circular mahogany counter and leaned over while waving at me to flag my attention. "What's up with you?"

I had many accusations and questions whirling around my head for him. Deciding that Hayden was an asshole—and not the good kind—there was nothing more to expound on. I nixed the idea of probing him for responses to my unanswered questions. "Excuse me? Did you say something, sir? I'll be right back to your table with your beers, sir. Just give me a moment."

His eyes softened as he leaned closer...too close. "Can you tell me what I did?"

I had the sudden urge to check the dining area for Mason's location. He was watching me while standing in front of the table. For some reason or another, my interaction took priority over his need to take his friend to the hospital. While the patrons in the vicinity were eerily quiet, it seemed none of them felt inclined to pick up their phone and take action.

"Why would you care to know? It's clear your only concern is the person you see in the mirror."

He bit into his lip with a halfhearted smile. "You were serious that night...about me and you running off together?" He stifled a laugh "It was a cute plan, but why would I do that with you?"

"I know what you did," I hissed turning fully toward him while remaining conscious I was being watched. "The DVD with you, Marion, and Blake? You left it there for me to see, and I think you spread your own sex tape around town. I don't care what I might've wanted, right now, I want you to stay away from me."

His eyelids slanted downward as he tilted his chin up to look down at me. "I don't know what you're talking about."

"So you didn't release the tape of you? Or give me the recording?"

"To be completely honest with you, only one person had a copy of it: Blake. I had nothing to do with it. What you're doing right now—holding me accountable? Is this jealousy, Whitney?"

"Over what?"

"Right," he said with a smirk. "You had a chance." He glanced over at Mason. "And you chose him."

*A chance at what?* Unable to wrap any sense around it, I dismissed him with a wave of my hand. "Hayden? Fuck off."

Baxter cleared his throat, indicating he had been watching the whole time. "Whitney. Back room. Now."

Hayden tapped the bar, shooting a warning glance in Baxter's direction. "Don't fire her, Baxter. She's the best waitress you have. She didn't do anything wrong. It was just a little misunderstanding."

My eyes flourished, wondering the reason behind Hayden standing up for me. I didn't care to question or wait for the answer. I moved back to the prep table where Baxter stomped after me.

"You're lucky he vouched for you. You were seconds from getting fired," Baxter threatened me. "Between the customers complaining about you serving them and causing an altercation with an upstanding police officer... It's the kind of trouble I don't need."

My mouth fell open in complete awe over being accused of crimes I hadn't committed.

# Opaque Mirrors

"Get it together or I'll send you home."

# FIFTEEN

"OUR QUIET TOWN HAS been tainted by sin. Not only has the devil infiltrated our town's hotel, our homes, and our businesses, but it has squelched the lambs who've lost their way. Sexual deviancy has taken over our young people." The pastor slapped his Bible down on the podium, distressing his distaste for what he believed was the culprit for the disruption.

"I'm speaking to the young populace today. Remember Thessalonians: *'For this is the will of God, [even] your sanctification, that ye should abstain from fornication.'* Premarital sex is a sin. It is for you and the sanctity of marriage alone, and let's talk about some of the more deviant behavior we've all bore witness to. The debauchery of sadism, sodomy, multiple partners..." The pastor began to spit out his words in repugnance. His sweat-laden face turned ruddy with anger. He continued to berate the congregation, his wide and wild eyes sweeping over every person under thirty in the crowd.

I thought—and my mother agreed—that showing up to church would cull any severe retaliation from the town until I moved out. Her concern focused on my belongings making a safe transport out of town; I was concerned for my safety.

144

As the pastor spoke, I formulated ideas. The deaths could've possibly centered around religious morals. The drug addicts. The mother who had a child out of wedlock and was known to bed many men at her leisure. Blake, who indulged in fornication with a woman and a man outside of his marriage.

As I searched the pews for familiar faces, I found Penny in her Sunday best. I had tried calling her often, but eventually gave up when she wouldn't return my calls. No matter how sorry I was, and how compelled I felt to tell her the truth and have her believe it, it was a wound I'd never get the chance to heal.

A few rows behind her sat Mason. In a tailored suit and tie, it was near impossible to tear my eyes away from him. His arms were folded over the pew in front of him. He continuously thumbed his lips, the same thumb that made me come in his mouth two days ago. A suggestive wink and a grin was cast in my direction.

Feeling a heat ripple over my skin, I turned around, concerned for the sinful thoughts that crossed my mind, when I never would've cared.

AFTER SERVICE, HENRY PLAYED politics and networked with the churchgoers, pleading my innocence without directly referencing me. My mother played her part as she stood next to Henry. Dressed in a black jumpsuit that covered her from neck to ankle and a black turban, she resembled a movie star in the golden age of Hollywood.

A few women congregated several feet from where I stood and debated with one another: "All I'm saying is I agree with the pastor. There's nothing romantic about pain, being demeaned, or giving yourself to someone in any disgusting manner. It's sinful, like the pastor said. Love should be a romance between you and your husband. Any kind of relationship, consensual or not, where there's pain is unnatural and against God's law. Those people are messed up in the head and need prayers and blessings. It's abuse. It's abuse!

These women and men who put out such sinful temptations in movies, music, television, and books should be ashamed of themselves. They are promoting sin. I'm going to talk to the pastor about re-baptizing our young people and laying hands on the ones who need it the most." A curt look was shot in my direction by the three of them.

"You're very ill-informed," said my mother. "There's nothing sinful about a consensual relationship between two people. The world you're referring to is not about sex or deviant acts, it's about trusting someone and a power exchange. But let me make myself clear, if you think the person bowing on their knees to serve the one who has promised to provide and take care from them is powerless, not only are you misinformed, you're illiterate. The community you talk about with disgust has been around for a very long time and will continue to be. As for the fiction, let's remember it's fiction. You know what it says about people who can't separate fiction from reality?" With a sweep of her colorful scarf, she gave the women her back to view and sauntered toward me. "Are you ready to get out of this awful *fucking* town?"

The curse my mother overemphasized to rile the self-proclaimed social jury was met with gasps and glares.

"Give me two more days, Dreya," I pleaded, holding her off in hopes of avoiding the inevitable.

I scanned the parking lot for Mason but couldn't find him anywhere amongst the townspeople who filed into the parking lot.

I wandered off to Henry's rental car, trailing my mother. Halfway there, I was halted by something in my corner view. Hayden stood on the edge of the parking lot with something bundled underneath his shirt.

I held up a finger to my mother and plodded over to Hayden. "Are you here for someone else, or are you following me?"

"How do you know I wasn't in church repenting for my sins?"

"Because I didn't see you in there."

A dark brow curved over his eyes as a skewed smile contorted his mouth. "You were looking for me?"

"No. Where's Mason? He was there and disappeared."

146

"He had something to do." His brief explanation contained a razor sharp edge.

Something moved underneath his jacket.

"What's that?" I took several steps forward.

The head of a white kitten with a dash of black on her muzzle and eyes and piercing blue eyes peeked out of Hayden's suit jacket and meowed at me.

I took her in my arms, cradling her warm fuzzy body against my neck. I scratched her back as she purred under my neck and rubbed her face against my chin.

"You literally melted before my eyes. Am I correct to assume you forgive me for being a dick?"

I reluctantly tried to give her back. "If that's what this is for, no, I don't forgive you."

He jumped back with his arms raised.

"I can't keep her anyway. " I shot a forlorn glance in my mother's direction.

Her lips pursed in disapproval as she waved me over to the car.

"With it looking pretty likely I'll have no other option then to go to New York with Dreya, and she's allergic—"

He suddenly picked up his phone and quickly tapped a few keys on the screen. "If she's really going to have an issue with it, she can stay with the Babikovs. Garen loathes cats. You'll have to come by often and make sure he doesn't hurt her."

"Well played, Hayden. Would that second reason be you...or Mason?"

He moved his hand up toward me, thought better of it, and shoved it back down in his pockets. "Take a ride with me."

"Why would I do that?"

"Because I know you don't want to be around Dreya and the new submissive she's parading around." He leaned forward and whispered. "That's what he is? She's still in the lifestyle?"

"It's not really a lifestyle to Dreya. It's a part of who she is and not something she'll ever be able to stop for anyone." I rubbed my chin on the top of the soft kitten's head, less than willing to let her go.

He turned toward his car and opened the door. "Are you coming?"

PRIOR TO TRAVELING TO the Babikovs, we stopped by the local pet shop to get things for the kitten. With every interaction and every passing gaze from his hazel eyes, I tried to peel down the exterior and find an answer to my questions.

My sensors never detected anything from him; they constantly blared when Mason was near. He was a tightening and increasingly messy tangle that drew me to him despite the red signals forewarning of danger to come.

I WAS GLUED TO the floor of Hayden's bedroom. Between drinking the tea Garen reluctantly prepared for me at Hayden's request and playing with the kitten for hours, I was able to simply exist for a few moments.

I cracked my aching back, scared to move and wake the kitten. Hayden reached down to grab her. Wrapping my hand around his arm, I stopped him.

He put a finger to his lips and wrangled his wrists out of my hold. Being gentle, he cradled her in his arms and placed her on the bed with pillows. She stirred and settled in.

I bounded to my feet and continued to stretch. Feeling suddenly exhausted, I sat back down. "When I mentioned possibly moving back to New York with Dreya...you didn't say anything."

"Were you expecting me to?" Hayden's brows contracted. Behind his eyes laid a cold void.

Unsure of what I hoped to unearth by digging around his head, I rested my suddenly heavy body back on the plush cushions of the couch in his bedroom. A scratching sound underneath my feet alerted me. When it was followed by a soft and short squeak, I relaxed. "You should call the exterminator. I think you have a mice problem in the basement."

"Probably Garen doing some work down there," he quickly dismissed me.

The floor beneath me became my focal point as I waited to hear the sound again. "What kind of work does he keep down there?"

"Storage." Hayden's response was clipped and short, drawing my attention.

"Marion…was taken down there by Garen at the party weeks ago. Whatever she saw there, it scared her."

Hayden ho-hummed for a while and shook his head. Rubbing his hand down his face in a swift motion, he exhaled again. His gaze settled on me and teetered into a glower. "Garen is into extreme acts when it comes to sex. Leave it at that."

"From what I saw when she was with you, and what was on the tape with her—it seems like she's into some pretty heavy things, too."

"Leave it alone, Whitney." The grit in his command shook me and implanted a pit inside my gut.

I threw up my hands in defeat, submitting only because I knew I wouldn't get the answers I needed.

"You're not going back to New York with her, because it's evidently the last thing you want." The assuredness in his voice was alarming as he effortlessly shifted into another subject. "That's why I never said anything when you first addressed it."

"Oh? How do you know that? Short of getting a job at Red Pony, there's nothing else I can do in less than three days to get the money I need to leave before Dreya can corner me into returning with her."

Throwing his head back to the vaulted ceilings, his mouth gaped with his raucous laughter.

"What's so funny? You don't think a four can make enough cash as a stripper?"

"Come on." He dropped his chin to his chest and swirled his eyes around. "My number bothered you that much?"

"It didn't."

"It bothered you enough that you retained the number and remind me of it at every turn." He sauntered over to the chair in front of the couch and flopped down. Curving his spine, he rested his elbows on his thighs and maintained his cocksure smile. "You're better than a stripper at Red Pony. Those girls were rode hard and put up wet."

"I haven't the slightest idea what that means."

"Did you try out?" Suddenly no longer genial, he studied me with an unmovable concentration.

"I was debating it. I haven't taken the steps to get a position yet."

"You have to actually…dance and have physical contact with strange men. You're aware of that, correct? There's a difference between being beautiful and sexy. It's good to own your beauty and not try to be something you're not."

"A woman can't be both?" Catching onto what he said, I backtracked. "Wait…are you calling me beautiful?"

He cleared his throat again, visibly clamping down and proving I wouldn't ever get an answer. He moved to the stereo system and attached his phone. Scrolling through what I assumed to be his music playlist, he found a downtempo song with a heavy amount of bass. "So? Prove me differently."

"I don't think that's a good idea." I focused on the door, halfway expecting Mason to interrupt.

Snaking an arm around his back, he fished around in his back pocket. Opening the billfold, he pulled out a bill. He pinched it between his fingers and held it up toward me to show how much he thought my lap dance was worth. "Entertain me."

I approached the stereo and turned up the volume on the song, hoping it would be loud enough to silence my concerns. "I need more than a c-note if you really want me to entertain you."

He cut his eyes at me, taking everything out of his wallet. There was at least a thousand dollars there. A thousand dollars that I really needed.

150

"Good?"

"Where…do you and Mason get this cash?"

"Does it matter?"

I threw every inch of my accusations and questions at him with a steady stare. "It does."

"It's not from drugs, and it's not from our jobs."

"Is it illegal? Or does it have to do with the Babikovs owning Alloy LLC? Were you or Mason responsible for how easily I was able to get a job and get into my house?"

A spark of interest ignited in his eyes. It was quickly snuffed out. "Do you realize something, Whitney? You have yet to directly ask me if I somehow killed those people and staged it to look like a fetish gone awry. I believe you haven't asked me yet, because you don't really want to know the answer either way. You like the thrill of the bad. You ran to this town because you think you can hide from it, but it found you." Sighing, he lolled back on the couch. "Do you want the money or not, Whitney?"

Inhaling and exhaling at a delayed rate, I made an effort to regain my composure after the truth had robbed the air from my lungs. Trying to get into the music, I swayed and moved my arms.

He laughed at me.

"What am I doing wrong?" I flopped my arms down to my sides and slouched.

A shuddering slam sent an electric jolt to my body. On hyper alert, I turned toward the offending noise. Mason was at the door. His squared jaw ticked with anger. His fists were balled as though he was primed to swing at someone. His cutting attention darted from me to Hayden. Hayden, taking some sort of silent cue, stood to turn the music off.

"Don't. Sit back down, Hayden. Don't let me shit on the fun you two are having." Mason waltzed in, shoulders broad, stride long and slow. He whipped off his jacket and tie, throwing it in no specific direction while he ambled toward the armoire by the bed.

"You know what I was thinking a second ago?" He pulled out a few things indiscernible to my eye as he shoved them in his back pocket and with his free hand, unfastened a few buttons from his shirt. "I picked a bad fucking day to stop smoking."

Mason closed the armoire, sliding a leather glove into his front pocket. "Lighter?" He pointed to Hayden, who on command, fished in his pocket. Hayden held up a silver lighter and tossed it to Mason who caught it one-handed. Sauntering over to the seating area, he sat on the couch behind my standing position.

I faced Mason with the weight of heavy pangs of conscience sinking my posture. "I...looked for you at the church, and you weren't there."

Mason shot a brief look overflowing with menace at Hayden. "I was called away for some bullshit reason." The focus that made me feel as though I had been stripped of my skin returned to me. His hands moved up my legs. "I said, keep going."

The apprehension of being placed in his bright and burning spotlight left me without a clue as to what to do.

Mason leaned forward and grabbed my waist, pulling me toward him. "Come here, Whitney." His tone lowered in register and tightened the invisible lead he held on my submission.

I reluctantly straddled his lap while facing him.

Moving stray strands of my straightened hair away, he clasped the side of my face. "Show me what you were going to do to him."

"I wasn't—"

"Shh," he cooed, sliding his hands down the curves of my body. Gathering the hem of my skirt in both fists, he yanked it up until my panties were exposed.

Uneasy about Hayden seeing parts of me through my very sheer boy shorts, I tried to pull it down.

My hands were gathered and pinned behind my back. "Show me the sexy girl with a filthy, twisted mind, not the virgin you fucking pretend to be. Tease me like you're fucking me and won't let me come...and never take those pretty brown eyes off me. Make me hard. Make me want you so badly I can't think straight, baby."

I started to dance a little, swaying with awkward movements on his lap.

"Closer." With my waist in his hands, he pulled me closer until my breasts were mashed against his hard chest. "Move your hips...like you're riding my cock."

I undulated my hips in his lap, grinding against him.

"Slower...slower." He leaned back, relaxing from the state he appeared to be in only minutes ago. He watched me and I watched him. The exchange captured my attention and wouldn't release me. The woman I had adopted dissipated from the woman I once was and melded with the woman Mason made me become. She wanted one thing: to seduce the man in front of her and remind him he was hers, and she was his.

I pushed my crotch down against his groin and rolled my hips in slow, wide circles. My body took on a mind of its own, fueled by the palpable hunger in Mason's eyes. I arched my back, leaning all the way back down until my head touched the floor in the space between his legs. Using my abdominal strength, I delayed straightening my spine.

A throb puckered the crotch of his pants and rubbed against my slit through the thin lace material of my underwear.

I slipped the jacket down from my shoulders, revealing the low cut of my dress. I wrapped my hands around the side of his head, threading my fingers through the shortest hair and pulled his head down to get a closer view of my cleavage.

I deftly spun in my position while sitting astride his lap. Moving my skirt up to my waist, I rubbed my behind against his erection in tighter circles. Leaning my head back against him, I slid my hips back and forth.

His panting breaths skirted down my back. The grip he held on my hips began to burn, expressing his need. "Who are you pretending I am right now?" The deep, hoarse voice was barely audible, struggling to project between strained breaths. "Think about your answer before you speak. Think very, very hard."

My grin widened. The answer was easy. In this space, there was only

Mason and Whitney. "I'm not pretending you're anyone else." I slid down until my head rested against his chest. "Every time I close my eyes, you are the lead actor in all my dirty, fucked up fantasies."

His erratic heartbeat vibrated through the back of my head. I paused my actions to enjoy the moment.

A hand abruptly swallowed my neck. He spread his legs, making my thighs widen around him and wrapped his ankles around mine, trapping me in position with my legs spread.

"Put your hands behind your fucking back and leave them there." His voice dipped into the abyss, menacing and seductive.

My body screamed out, begging for him to make good on his threats while it perspired and trembled with an unrequited yearning. Alarms sounded, failing in their attempt to produce a negative stimulus that usually surfaced when a man touched me. The unmanageable and untamed reactions ruled by Mason silenced the aversions before they had a chance to build.

The echo of the reclining zipper at the back of my dress chilled my body. The straps slipped from my shoulders, falling to the crook of my elbows. A hand harshly tugged on the cup of my bra, exposing my left breast, and brutally pinched the sensitive dark pearl.

Footsteps echoed in the room, reminding me Hayden was in the room with us. He paced around the couch with an expression, I didn't expect—envy. I struggled, trying to wiggle out of Mason's hold.

Fingernails dug into my nipple as he pulled and rocked his fingers up and down. "Don't ever fucking fight me."

Wincing at the sting of pain pervading from my nipple, I put my hands behind my back and ceased movement. My body hummed with a stifling warmth.

Directing my neck, he pulled me fully toward his chest, securing my arms behind my back. He shoved his hand down my panties and wound the material at the crotch around his fists. With a tug and a pull, the material began to shred and expose me.

A rebuttal was on my lips, but I couldn't make it spill forth. Sense and carnal need battled for space, and the latter had won the fight.

Mason cupped my sex, pressed his fingers against my plump lips, and slowly spread me. "She has a very tasty pussy."

"I'm sure she does," Hayden answered, flopping down on the couch. "She's soaking wet."

"Soaking wet for *me*. I want you to remember that next time you pull a stunt like you did today. And if you need a reminder, I'm going to give her and you one." He adjusted beneath me to, I presumed, retrieve the items from his back pocket. The sounds of him hocking a spit lured my curiosity. The grip on my neck made sure I remained blinded to the actions behind me. "Push your hips up for me."

Struggling in the awkward position, I shifted my behind off his lap and inadvertently gave Hayden a view. A latex gloved hand slid up and down the center of my swollen lips, eliciting more moisture. He drove his fingers inside me, provoking a sharp groan from inside my throat. He withdrew and began to circle a lower hole.

Pushing his finger fully inside my behind, he wiggled it around. Waiting for me to relax, he shoved in another. He drew his hand up to grab something between us. The glimmer of a black, bell-shaped object caught my eye. A firm hand pushed in on my neck. Fingertips dug into the skin along my jaw, directing my jaw to face Mason. As Hayden bit into his lip, Mason slid the rubber plug inside my ass.

My lips quivered in protest when the thicker end widened me. Mason secured it fully in and twisted it. "That's not the only surprise I have for you."

In the corner of my view, Hayden rose from the opposite side and stood at the edge of the coffee table facing me.

"Keep your hands behind your back," Mason warned again. He held something out in my view; a chain attached to the cursive metal letters—the name Mason. Multitasking, he slid the leather glove on his right hand. "The necklace is a gag gift that finally has a use." With his arms partially surrounding me, he ignited the lighter and brought it across the letters in the chain. "Do you remember what I said about getting you ready for me?"

My eyes widened at the answer formulating in my head. I slid my body down to get away.

Mason's ungloved hand jammed into my hair and forced me to bend over the table in front of him. He pressed his body against my back and lifted my skirt a little more. Leaning down he kissed the left side of the swell of my ass. "In case you ever fucking forget again, I'm gifting you with a permanent reminder."

My skin sizzled. Hot and prickly pain ran roughshod through my nerves and attacked my pain sensors. I lost the will to hold myself upright on the table and collapsed forward, quivering at the pulsing torment.

Mason pressed the hot metal to my ass until he was satisfied—until involuntary tears spilled from my eyes.

A hand clamped around my throat, another slid down my body, discovering my sex.

Mason lifted the excess skin on the hood and pinched the tiny nub, sending a sharp tinge of pain in my abdomen. "Did you think you could keep teasing me and it would all be okay? That I wouldn't take out my payment on your pussy? Did you?" Mason's breath and deeply erotic words danced across my ear.

"No." My voice was lost in surprising sensations: the throb on my raw and burned behind. The cutting pain in my sex. A moan slipped through my lips as he circled my nub with the pads of all four of his fingers, rubbing against my increasingly wet lips and soaking my bundle of nerves, aching for more contact. My hips began to oscillate against his hand. Mason stopped his manipulation and pinched my clit hard, digging his nails into the overly sensitive flesh.

My mouth opened to scream.

"Shh." He pressed a warm gloved hand over my mouth. "You wanted this. Take it." He held my nerve center in a vice grip for several agonizing seconds.

I quaked, fending off revulsion while crying out through his hand.

Mason released me and shoved me to the ground. My knees and the palms of my hands hit the floor simultaneously.

The music flooding the room was quieted.

"Lessons over," Mason intoned and plodded toward the sound system. His back heaved, flexing and stretching his black tailored button-up, showing every defined striation of his lean back. He turned to me and removed his glove, dropping it to the floor. He licked his fingers as though he'd polished off a decadent meal. The mask of darkness and his hand dropped simultaneously. "Did you get the fucking message?"

I couldn't have been sure if he was speaking to me or Hayden.

Hayden nodded and replied, "I know when to fold. You're always the one who had the best luck in life. Past and present."

"It's never luck. Me and Whitney are *not* about luck." Mason glanced over at the kitten. "Did you think of a name for the kitten I bought you?"

The movie scene had changed, and no one told the main actress how she should behave.

Mason masqueraded as a shallow creek when in truth he was an ocean so deep, if I ever gathered the courage to take a dive, I would fall into the endless void, pulled to the darkest depths by a strong current. But my lack of courage mattered little. I had plunged into the unknown some time ago.

The last thing I wanted to do was show Mason he had full control of my hollow spaces and had filled it with opaque water. From the look on Mason's face, he knew my act to deny and elude had been rewritten to follow his script.

Hayden cast a chilling look my way and exited the room, muttering to himself.

Aware my clothes were disheveled, I fixed them and stood tall. Pretending my clit wasn't wailing in agony and that the burn on my backside didn't scream in defiance, I tried to walk and failed. The plug inside me and the pain left me stumbling for balance. Electric waves sliced through the picture of my surroundings.

Mason was there to catch me and guide me. "Drank a little too much, baby?"

"I didn't have anything to drink," I slurred.

"You're staying here for the night."

The thought of spending the night with two men who made it known they were fucking with me—one whom I couldn't control my budding and insatiable need around—was one of the worst ideas I could've fathomed. My choice was rendered an illusion as my eyelids betrayed me and held my vision hostage.

# SIXTEEN

THROUGH THE BLACKNESS BEHIND *my eyelids, his presence is a prickling sensation on my skin. He's returned. I don't want to wake up. I don't want to feel the torment of being pulled in opposing directions, telling me I want this and don't want this in equal measure.*

*Another woman takes over and fucks my vacant spaces. She whispers to me and makes me believe I want this.*

*"Hurt me. Kill me," she says as I feel the cold jagged end of a sharp piece of metal pinch my throat. The pressure of his naked body lays against me, pinning me against the soft mattress. I open my eyes to see him hovering over me—Nick.*

*No longer in a uniform, he's completely nude, but dressed in his never-ending tattoos. His eyes are unshielded and contain dark brown wells that magnetize me.*

*"You dirty fucking whore. You gave him what belonged to me?"*

*I can't answer; any small movement in my throat presses what I know to be a knife further into my flesh. The trickle of liquid tickles my skin. My brown eyes implore him and tell him no.*

*The undercurrent of Nick's need for revenge never changes.*

*He lifts up the knife and rakes the pointed end down my body. Every trail feels more painful than the last. He reaches my pelvis and pushes down until I wince. The knife stops at my clit.*

*I don't beg. I don't plead. I don't struggle. I want it despite everything in me revolting against it in silence.*

*He flicks the knife back and forth across my slit. The sharp sting makes me squirm.*

*"Don't move again, or I'll cut the lips of your pussy off and jam this knife inside your cunt—just like Kylie." He slides down my body and tastes me.*

*A moan is uncontrolled. Dark eyes dart up to mine, warning me to be quiet by glancing at Mason, peacefully sleeping on his back away from me. Screams that this should be Mason in my dreams destroying me permeate my thoughts until I hear nothing else. In the firm, king-size bed, Mason's too far out of my arm's reach*

*Sharp teeth sink into my clit and yank.*

*Unfettered tears stream from my eyes.*

*He doesn't stop. He bites the lips of my sex and pulls, sinking his teeth into the flesh until I feel a burn. My body begins to shake as he places his entire mouth on me, clenching my swelling nub between his teeth and stroking up and down between the assaulting sharpness, leaving me sore and bruised.*

*He pulls up, steadying on one of his arms and rakes the knife up the middle of my body, sliding it around my belly button. He turns the handle around while sitting on the back of his heels. Snaking an arm around my leg he adjusts me until my bottom rests on his lap. Gripping the sharp blade so severely his hands begin to bleed, he removes the plug Mason left inside my ass and tosses it aside. He shoves the hilt of the knife inside the opening of my ass.*

*I want to protest against the stinging pain. But instead, it warms me. The pain...fills me with a sick brand of euphoria.*

*"Take it, you dirty bitch." He pumps the cold, rigid metal handle inside me repeatedly at faster intervals. Watching my every reaction, his wells begin to deepen.*

*An explosion rips through me, and I soar. He withdraws the knife, covered in blood from both of us and turns it around, rocking it back and forth outside of my*

*slit. The look in his eyes tell me his intentions; he wants to shove the sharp edge*
*inside me...*

"Mason!" my own scream awakened me. Disoriented, I grappled to find level ground. The cold hardwood floor greeted my underdressed body. A T-shirt, not belonging to me adorned my body and was ripped in random places. The white material was saturated in carmine liquid and clung to my skin. Something cold and sharp was planted inside my fist—a knife. Roaming my empty hand around my body, I tried to find a wound. The knife wielding hand was decorated in fresh calluses. The amount of blood staining the knife and on my shirt indicated that someone died tonight. My attention followed the trail of dried, bloody footprints that only lead one way—toward my position.

The blockage, preventing me from hearing anything around me, cleared when my eyes settled on a shocked Mason, standing several feet away from me. His bed-head hair and slightly red-streaked eyes suggested I had awoken him from a deep slumber. Dressed for bed, he scratched at his chest from underneath his worn T-shirt.

He gaped at me, to the trail of blood leading down the door. "What the actual fuck, Whitney? What did you do?"

"I—I didn't do anything," I denied my unknown crime with conviction, imploring him to believe me.

He shoved his hands in his hair. His shirt creeped up in a way to reveal his defined abdomen. In his dismay, I could almost pry a modicum of innocence in his features.

I glanced from the knife back to the trail of blood. A startling revelation, pulled my steps forward.

"Stop!" Mason moved quickly to stand in front of me and held his arms out. His light brown eyes were wild as though a million things were running through his head and had no idea how to proceed. For the first time, I'd witnessed Mason's less assured side. He wouldn't tear his eyes from the sight of the knife and the calluses on my right hand.

"I have to see. I have to know what *he* did." Either shock or confusion delayed him from stopping me. I followed the track of my bloody footsteps toward where they led.

The door to a room I'd never visited was cracked open. I pushed the door ajar with my bloodstained hands and the scene before me pulled an incoherent wail from my chest.

Garen laid in a bed stained in his blood. His eyes were closed as though he never had a chance to awaken from his sleep. A gaping wound opened across his neck to reveal the layers of flesh. The blood on his chest indicated there were possible stab wounds on his body.

"What's with the screaming?" A yawning and tired Hayden appeared in the hall, blinking away his sleep. He hadn't opened his eyes fully to see the evidence of a crime. When he did, he staggered.

My mouth moved in opposition with my brain and spoke the truths I couldn't avoid. "I didn't do this. You have to believe me. He did. I was supposed to kill him, but I didn't. I thought I did, but I couldn't have." *It's not my mind playing tricks on me. It's not me. Nick's making me think things that aren't real, and he's killing people to torment me for not killing him.* "He's been trying to make me pay. He's killing people. He won't stop until everyone is dead—"

"Slow down." Mason grabbed my shoulders and spun me toward him. "What are you talking about, baby? Who is *he*?"

It was hard to digest the look in Mason's eyes. It was uncharacteristic of him. As though he didn't know whether or not to trust me, or commit me.

The look pained me so deeply it zapped the strength in my posture. "Nick. Nick Kent. He was a torture porn actor, but he did other things—illegal things, I think. I killed him. I was supposed to. He said he was a killer, and he wouldn't stop killing people, so I did what he asked. I thought I did, but I didn't because he's back and he's going to make me pay."

I couldn't take the look on Mason's face. He thought I was crazy. He exchanged a look with Hayden and they seemed to agree with one another.

I backed away, holding firm to the knife. "I won't go to jail for something I didn't do."

Mason sighed, closing his eyes for a moment before landing his soft and tired brandy-hued eyes on me. "I believe you, baby," Mason said, his voice not sounding like his own.

"What?!" Hayden plodded toward me, keeping a fair distance. "How can you? She's covered in proof. I know you see the calluses on her hands. The bitch is fucking insane."

"First of all, don't fucking disrespect her like that. If anyone gets to call her a bitch or a whore it's me when I'm fucking her." Mason inhaled a wavering breath and folded his shoulders, diving into a calm. "You really think she could've done this? Had the strength to pull this off? You know Garen, and you know he could and has kicked both our asses."

"Explain to me how she's covered in blood, has offensive wounds, and is holding what she probably used to kill him? She probably did it in her sleep. Stop thinking with your cock and see the real picture. She needs to go to prison."

"I didn't do this," I proclaimed my innocence through quavering lips. The sensation between my thighs solidified what I knew. Nick was alive, and he was tormenting me. "Nick Kent did this. I could never kill anyone."

"Right, because you didn't kill him before?" Hayden chortled in indignation. "The man who used to live here, who used to be Aksyna's adoptive son, who went off and did porn, then disappeared? He miraculously came back to town to kill people, to what? Torment you?" Hayden shook his head in contempt. "If you won't arrest her, Mason, I'm calling the sheriff."

Mason threw his ire at Hayden with a slight nod of his head and the slant of his eyes. He quickly took off his shirt and neared me. "Take it off and put this on. Wrap the knife in your shirt and give it to me." He shoved his shirt into my hand. "Take my jacket hanging by the front door. The keys to my car are on the hook by the dash. I want you to drive, and keep driving until you're almost out of gas."

I peeled out of the T-shirt, sliding my arms across my breasts, stained in sticky blood, and wrapped it around the knife, handing it to him. I quickly slid into his T-shirt using one hand.

Mason disappeared from the room. During Mason's departure, Hayden silently gave me long periods of his silent disapproval.

Mason returned within minutes and stuck a phone in my hands. "When you get to a gas station, call Hayden's number. It's in my phone. When I pick up only give me the address, don't say anything else. Stay put. I'll come find you."

"What am I supposed to do?" I held out his phone, unsure of what to do with it.

"There's no way out of this. We're going to have to run, baby."

I glanced back at Hayden.

Mason encased my head in his hands and leaned into my ear. "Don't worry, I'll take care of Hayden. Now go."

# SEVENTEEN

My DIRECTION TOOK ME toward my house. I parked a block away and watched the sun dawn on the roof. A rental car remained parked curbside, indicating my mother was there, waiting for me. Holding my hands up, I eyed the shoddy job I did in trying to wipe the blood away. Every time I looked at my hands, shards of a nightmare slashed my mind to pieces with their horrid visions:

*The knife is in my hands. I straddle Garen's body. He's sleeping so soundly he doesn't feel me on top of him. I hold the knife to his throat, and with all my might, slice clean through the flesh intending to reach so deep, I sever his spine. He gurgles blood in his sleep and dark crimson fluid flows out of his yellow and red flesh.*

They were daymares. Not real. Only my guilt formulating a scene that didn't happen.

*I didn't do this. I wouldn't kill someone.* It was a belief I strongly held. What I thought had happened with Nick never truly did—it was the only explanation. I must've only suppressed his breathing long enough to make him fall unconscious. My true crime was taking money I didn't earn. A crime I shielded myself away from believing because in a warped sense of self-preservation, keeping my word to commit an immoral act was easier to deal with than being a thief. It had to be true. I had failed to kill him, and this was my penance.

I pulled the car into drive and continued on my way, putting my blind faith into Mason and kept driving.

THE GAS IN MASON'S car ran out about twenty miles from Charlotte, conveniently next to a gas station wedged between a diner and a dive of a hotel. I sent a text to Hayden's phone with an address. I couldn't bear to speak to him or Mason. The ordeal was surreally painted in bleak and lightless hues. The blood of another was on my body. My ass was acutely sore from being branded as belonging to Mason. The twinges of pain between my thighs and the sore throb of my nipples reminded me that my nightmares had become real.

Fastening Mason's police jacket as it swallowed my body, I headed to the diner next door.

The hostess seated me and offered me a menu.

I shook my head at her, denying her attempt to hand me a menu. "Just tea please."

"Sweet or unsweet?"

"H-hot tea, please."

She made a face and with a nod then turned on the heels of her orthopedic shoes and disappeared around the bend.

"Are you okay, hun?" the waitress awakened me out of my involuntary nap.

Pulling myself together, I eyed the mug placed in front of me as she poured a cup of coffee, instead of the tea I requested. My former self had left me marooned in uncharted territory, and I was in no position to speak up.

Every instance of the bells jingling over the entry door, watered my fear. I hoped the next arrival would be Mason, but dread made me believe it would be only a matter of time before a police officer arrived to arrest me.

From the time displayed on the analog clock above the prep area, four hours had passed since the incident. The trip only should've took one.

I was near to giving up, until the familiar scent filled my senses and his warmth surrounded my left side.

"I didn't hear you come in," I said, eager to sink into the comfort of Mason's eyes. They were genial, belaying a little of my apprehension.

"You can barely keep your eyes open." He lifted my chin over his closed right fist and slid the coffee away from me with his left hand. "Coffee is the last thing you need. Get something to eat, then we'll hit the road."

"Where are we going?"

He flagged the waitress down and asked for menus. "Wherever you want to go." Shortly after contemplating the menu selections while the waitress patiently waited, he ordered two breakfast platters to go and shot a pointed look at me. "And for you?"

"I'm not hungry."

"Order something and eat it later."

The large window beside me held a prime view of the parking lot. The car Mason had loaned me was no longer in the space I had left it in. It stood idle in the turnabout for the hotel. Hayden sat in the passenger seat.

I tore my glance away and settled it back on Mason.

"We'll talk about it when we get out of here."

I fidgeted with my dirty hands underneath the table, hiding them from the impatient waitress. "The bacon sandwich and fries," I told the waitress.

She took our menus and disappeared.

"Will we be on the road for long?"

A comforting grip surrounded my trembling hand. He pulled it toward his mouth and placed a kiss on my clenched fist, successfully dosing me with an opiate drug.

Exchanging nothing in the way of verbal communication, our gazes were locked. I couldn't uncover anything in his expression to completely suppress my sense of consternation coiling inside my abdomen.

"We won't be on the run forever." Mason broke the silence. "Don't ask any more questions about it. If you need something more, you'll never have anything to worry about."

"I have so much to worry about."

Dropping his hold on my hand, he leaned closer to me. "Not when you're with me. Not when you are *ever* with me."

"You can't fight the demon following me, he'll hurt you."

His eyes darkened and his features firmed. He ever so slightly leaned forward and had issues with taming his smirk. "No one has ever fucked with me and won."

A shiver worked up my spine, and it wasn't the comforting kind. Having no idea what to say, I chewed on my bottom lip. "Why? What did I do to get you on my side?"

"I don't do the romance shit, Whit. What I've done for you should be enough."

I touched the edge of the burn on my behind, feeling the bumpy ridges of the scar of Mason's name through the material of the T-shirt. The biting subtle pain reminded me of my fears. "They aren't. Especially not with who's waiting in that car. You need to give me something to make me think I'm not stupid to trust you."

"My actions aren't enough? Okay." He sank back in his seat, taking my hand with him. "I'm trying to figure out what the fuck you did to me...because I think about you more than I want to. I can't think of a time when I'm not... thinking about you. I noticed you before you noticed me. If you want to know if I had something to do with your job and the house, then yeah. I did. I wanted you to stay in Bebletown, and I'm not apologizing for the strings I pulled to get you to stay.

"After what you said to me the night of the storm, I had to have you. Be with you. Own you. Give you everything you needed and some things you didn't know you needed." He slowly grinned. "Are we good now?"

*Worse.* "I don't know…and I don't know if I can blame you for some of the things that have happened to me, because I don't know what's real and what isn't anymore." I put my elbow on the table and nervously rocked my top leg over my bottom. "I don't know why I said that."

He slid from my side to sit across the table from me; my gaze landed everywhere but on him. "Why can't you ever *really* look at me, Whitney? I catch your eye for maybe seconds, and when I do…you aren't really looking at me. You're somewhere else."

"I just…can't. Maybe I'm not ready to face the reason why." I rubbed the ache behind my eyebrows, but it did little to subdue the increasingly painful throb. "Where are we going to go?"

He lolled back on the red fake leather booth, setting his attention out the window. "Hayden mentioned something about you wanting to go to west. We'll start heading there and see where it goes."

I sat back, felt the discomfort in my slowly healing body, and sat up straight. I discreetly pointed to the car from the window. "Is *he* going to be with us the whole time?"

"He doesn't have a choice. And neither do you."

"What guarantee will I have you won't ditch me on the road or turn me over to…"

"I would've done it by now. Besides…" His eyes drifted out of the window. "…you'll never be anywhere else other than with me."

# EIGHTEEN

AT THE CAR, HAYDEN slipped in to the backseat, conceding the passenger seat over to me. Mason handed the take out containers to Hayden while I adjusted my seatbelt. "One is for Whitney, so keep your fucking paws off it."

Mason pulled out and headed for the highway going southwest. I thought I was subtle in my glances toward Hayden, but his dramatic foray into annoyance indicated otherwise.

"Whitney?" Hayden snarled with indignation. "Because of you, I haven't gotten much sleep. If you have something to say, say it."

"I thought you were convinced I was a criminal," I replied, turning back toward the road. "Why are you here, helping me get away?"

"I was *convinced* otherwise." With a few muttered and indiscernible words, he popped open the takeout container, filling the car with the scent of fried eggs and bacon.

The scenery whizzed by, swiftly putting distance between us and the horrible scene we left behind.

Too many questions lacked answers because my mind was no longer a reliable resource. I hoped the two men—who helped me escape a grizzly scene staged at the childhood home of the man who haunted my nightmares and my fantasies—would help me find a sense of reason.

"I probably wasn't clear with the way I rambled on yesterday after..." I cringed at the memory of my unhinged state. Nothing I said probably made sense to them. "There's a lot of things you don't know about me. I think you saw how unsafe it is to be around me. You could die like everyone else. I don't blame you if you want to make this the end of the road."

"An explanation for your rambling would be nice," Hayden stated while Mason remained suspiciously quiet.

"You're going to think I'm crazy."

"You're late on that assumption, Whitney. I thought you were psychotic the second we crossed paths," Hayden said, taunting me.

Taking my time to make things perfectly clear, I told them the truth about my past and nature of the things I did for the men who paid to spend time with me. Through the retelling, Mason appeared ready to rip the steering wheel column apart with the grip he maintained on the wheel.

I spoke in more detail about what happened to Nick—or rather, what I fooled myself into believing had occurred. "Something went wrong, because he's alive and he's taunting me by murdering people around me. I don't know why he hasn't attacked Dreya or the two of you yet. He's waiting for something. It won't stop until he's caught."

Mason shot Hayden a look in the rearview mirror. If I felt any stitch of comfort, it was no longer the case. I stared at Mason until he would speak.

"It's a really fucked up situation," Mason remarked, his voice strangled with exhaustion. "Aksyna raised Nick and has been looking for him. His disappearing act is the reason Hayden and I came here—to help her out with the businesses she owns in and outside of Bebletown. Telling me you tried to kill him and didn't—that he might be killing people in town to screw with you?" Shaking his head, he shuttered his eyes for a split second longer than normal. His broad chest inflated and receded in his apparent attempts to diffuse. "First you were in my bed, and then, sometime in the night, you wound up on the floor. I was so out of it after we fucked, I guess I slept through it. When I woke up...you were covered in blood and thrashing around on the floor. No one else was in the room but you and me, baby. I would've heard them."

I swallowed the tidbits of new information he provided, leaving me with a bitter taste on my tongue: Aksyna owned several companies in Bebletown—two of which I became involved with in different ways. Nick was raised in Bebletown. Hayden and Mason gave up their lives to help Aksyna. Above all this, I happened upon a postcard to entice me to visit the town? This wasn't a coincidence. This was Nick's doing, and I wasn't sure of his most desired outcome.

"We...had sex?" I asked, unable to hide my shock as I tackled the issue that perturbed me the most.

Mason did a double-take and the tell-tale sign of his anger began to manifest in his wide jaw. "Are you fucking kidding me right now? As much as you begged me to fuck you and screamed your head off every time I made you soak my dick, you don't remember? I made my marks and left you sore. I can tell I did every time I see that little wince on your face when you sit down or walk that you feel it. Are you...fucking with me right now?"

"Too much information," Hayden barked.

"You've already been warned on the way here." Mason snapped his neck to regard Hayden for a few moments. "Don't make me remind you again."

"I remember. I was just...confused." The huge lie was unstable on my lips. Why else would I have been wearing his shirt or felt sore between my thighs? *But the dreams...* "I didn't kill Garen," I said quietly. "I could never kill anyone. Nick is setting me up to hurt me."

"Not that I'm surprised, but what you're proposing doesn't make sense," Hayden piped in. "Why kill Garen and leave Dreya alive? If the situation were in my hands, and I wanted revenge on you, I'd kill her first."

"I—I don't know why he hasn't." I rubbed at the throbbing ache in my head.

"Hey." Mason reached out to brush his hand down the side of my face. "Why don't you try to get some sleep?" He glanced back at Hayden. "Give her the blanket."

Hayden threw it toward the front, calling a chastising glance from Mason.

"Don't worry about the asshole in the back. He's a sore ass over your decision to be with me." His brandy-hued eyes projecting a calming kindness alighted on me. "Get some sleep."

AN ABRUPT AND URGENT sound pulled my eyes open. Hayden was at the wheel persistently clearing his throat.

In the backseat, Mason was sprawled out, laying as flat as he could on his back. His baseball cap was pulled partially over his eyes. An arm was casually folded behind his head while the other rested against a slow rise and fall of his chest. In the unsteady streaks of light, rolling over his form, the imprint of his body underneath his T-shirt was visible. My hands closed into little balls, wishing they could run along his square jawline and touch the light decoration of stubble. Despite myself, I couldn't help but smile.

The stroke of sadness was thick and unrelenting. I returned to my forward facing position with a frown staining my face. "When I went to sleep it was morning. Now it's dark. Why did you wake me up?"

He snorted and swayed his head. "Funny how you never have this smart mouth around Mason."

"He makes me feel differently."

"Different how?"

I folded my arms over my grumbling stomach, protesting my inability to fill it with anything. The lingering smell of my untouched breakfast no longer filled the small space. "Did you want to talk about something?"

"I need to take a detour before we get to wherever we are going, and I need you to keep your mouth shut about where it is to him." His chin angled in Mason's direction.

"A detour where?"

"My grandmother. She lives in Dallas. It's on the way if we take I-10. Since you're not in a rush…"

"I don't know if I'm in a rush, because the both of you won't tell me what happened back in Bebletown."

"Nothing of note," he admitted with a shrug. "We spent hours cleaning up the mess. His experience as a cop came in handy. We didn't call anyone, packed very little, and left town."

"So…we're all wanted?"

"If there's no body, and no evidence of a murder, there's no crime."

"But the disappearance, they could question—"

He shushed my intoning volume as it dipped into panic and shot daggers at the reflection in the rearview mirror.

Taking my eyes off the road, I stared down at my lap. "I won't say anything as long as it's not something that'll upset him."

"At first it will, but it's for his own good."

"If I'm going to keep things from him, you need to explain. Is this…his grandmother, too? Mason said you two were raised together for a while and adopted apart. I figured it could mean a lot of things. I didn't want to assume."

"We share the same father, but not the same mother."

"I share the same mother but not the same father with my sister. I might have more siblings. I don't know them." I changed my tone upon realizing we were having a civil chat about our lives.

"Earlier, you said you have issues keeping things from Mason. Aren't you keeping things from him now?"

My head shook with vehemence. "I've told him everything, including the dirty truth."

He looked at my hands, taking note of the way they trembled prior to my need to shove them underneath me. "I'm unsure of what happened back at the Babikovs' house. Not sure I'll ever wrap my head around it, but Mason thinks you are innocent. I'll support him. You aren't being completely forthright with him. I can't be sure of what you're holding back, but it's something."

I fiddled with my fingers, stretching and itching them from underneath me and accidentally grazed against my burn. I subtly rocked in my seat to soothe away the ache between my legs and emanating from my behind. "There isn't anything."

He shrugged it off and flipped on the radio, keeping the volume low.

I changed the channel to something less pop oriented. "You haven't given me a reason to hide your detour from Mason."

Hayden adjusted in his seat, leaning away from me and designated one hand to control the steering wheel. "Our father wasn't mentally well. The things you claim your stalker, Nick, does to you, pale in comparison to what our father has allegedly done to others. We both know the eyes of a killer. Our father looked into our eyes daily for our most formative years and still managed to do the things he allegedly did."

I glanced back at Mason feeling more solemn than I already did. "Why wouldn't Mason have told me this?"

"He cut ties with both his father's and his mother's family once he was adopted. He was lucky in who he was homed with. They are good people, who love him and gave him opportunities to make something of himself. Bringing him to our grandmother will remind of all the things he doesn't want to remember. It's why you can't tell him where we're going. But my grandmother isn't doing well, and I'd like to see her since we're headed that way."

I touched my aching heart and glanced back at Mason. The misguided courage to keep myself from him and to deny what was branded on my skin fell apart. "I don't feel right about keeping it from him." But I knew it was important he connected with that side of his life and said his goodbyes. Amends can't be made with the dead, and regrets could last a lifetime. "I don't know where we're going and why. That's all I can give you."

He gave me a slighted nod. "That's all I'll request."

Reclining the seat, I tried to close my eyes. After nearly half an hour of trying to find comfort in the black leather and lacking the ability, I sat up. "Can we take one more detour?"

Hayden raised a brow at me, glancing briefly at me before turning back to the road.

"Miami. I have to check up on someone."

"A family member?" he asked with a curl of his dark brow.

My sentiment about making amends with the dead rang clear for me in a stark way. "Maybe. I owe her a goodbye."

"A goodbye? What do you mean by that?"

"I'm tired," I whispered, snuggling up against the window and pulling the blanket up to my neck.

# NINETEEN

HAYDEN DROVE FOR TEN hours straight, only stopping for gas when needed and to get food to ensure we arrived in Miami expeditiously. At a gas station, Mason bought me a new set of clothes to wear and pain medication. I cleaned up in one of the bathrooms prior to changing into the new outfit. In the middle of changing, I caught sight of superficial and linear marks on my abdomen. The lack of profuse bleeding from my sex indicated that pieces of my nightmare with Nick and the knife might've been real, but many others were not.

What worried me the most was my lack of mental acuity to determine which pieces were nonfictional.

AN HOUR MORE INTO our travels, we stopped at a barbecue place in Boca Raton.

Paranoia over the possibility of being a wanted woman sent shockwaves through my nerves. I vibrated in place while eyeing the patrons, wondering if the police had caught on to the disappearance of Garen Babikov and were conducting a nationwide search for the three of us.

"Baby, eat something. I don't want you to lose your curves." Mason nodded to me as he finished his plate of ribs. For his body to be dramatically sculpted, he surely knew how to put it away.

I picked up my fork and pushed around my mashed potatoes.

Hayden leaned back and stretched, satiated by the meal he'd devoured. I couldn't understand how the both of them could be so at ease. It was as if questionable murders occurred around them daily. Sense told me not to look too closely at the fact they helped me, but I could barely help myself. The belief they simply cleaned up and disposed of my mess and went on with their way continued to be a truth difficult to swallow.

I trusted Mason, but I didn't hold very much confidence in Hayden. The pin inside my gut that cursed me to lash out at him when he took things too far stayed ever present. It was there for a reason, and it was because the man who was adamant in hiding things from his brother had likely kept more secrets from him.

"Is someone going to tell me why we're headed to Miami?" Mason kept his eye on the task of removing the barbecue from his hands with the moist wipes we were provided.

With a little over one hour to Miami, I was becoming anxious. Since my phone was left in Bebletown, I used Mason's to call my sister a few times. She never responded. It may very well have been a waste of time to visit her—it was possible my mother lied to me about Sloane's return to the city she loved more than life with her family.

"My...sister, Sloane, might be there."

I had both men's attention at once.

"Sister?"

"Might?"

Their questions layered over one another.

178

"Miami's a nice place." The fork began to tap against my plate as my hand persistently shook. "If she's not there, maybe we could do something else?"

Mason slipped out from the opposite side of the booth to sit next to me and grabbed my chin. "Stop averting your eyes and look the fuck at me."

As the wells of moisture threatened to spill my secret—that I was scared—I did as he demanded.

"Nothing is going to happen to you. I told you I would take care of it and you, and I meant it."

My fate wasn't my only concern. I swiped the moisture from my cheeks and acknowledged that I understood to alleviate the worry pinching his features.

"Why are we going to see your sister? Is she a safe place to go? Does she know you're coming?"

I knew Mason wasn't asking if it was physically safe, but rather, if my sister could be trusted—she couldn't. It mattered little in the dire circumstances. I had to see her. "She doesn't know I'm in the state."

He chewed on the corner of his smile and swayed his head from left to right. He dropped his hold on my chin. "You're very bad with the whole planning thing."

"It doesn't matter how well-organized you are, things always go off path," I countered.

A crooked smile appeared on Mason's face. "Unlike you, I plan shit out, and it never goes off path."

"What about me?" My question was whispered with innocence and anticipation. "Did you plan for me?"

"I planned to have you, and despite whatever the fuck I have to do to make sure you stay with me, my plan will never be screwed over. Ever. You? The jealous fuck cutting his eyes at me right this moment from across the table?" He quickly tipped his head toward Hayden. "Nothing will ruin my plans."

The inky well didn't need any more accessories to seduce me into its grasp. Mason managed to make it more alluring in the moments we spent together. He'd be the end of my beginning someday soon. Hiding anything from him cut me to the core, and I no longer had the intention of agreeing to Hayden's idea. "I need to tell you something…"

Hayden cleared his throat loudly and reined in my guilty conscience from threatening to tell Mason the truth.

"Well?" Mason questioned, raising a brow.

"Thank you." I gave him a sullen smile, gently kissed his lips, and turned back to my meal. Stuffing a piece of a corn muffin in my mouth, I easily influenced him to veer off the path toward the truth.

I tossed my last rib bone in my plastic basket. I held my stomach, thinking I shouldn't have ordered the three meat sampler. My phone rang in the midst of Mason settling the check. I plucked up Mason's phone from his lap and grinned immediately at the name blaring across the screen. Sloane. Finally.

Mason and Hayden were locked in a stare exchanging many words that couldn't be heard. I tapped Mason's shoulder and nodded toward the entrance. He reluctantly let me out of the booth.

I removed myself from the table and made a speedy exit to gain some semblance of privacy outside.

"I'll pay you back," Sloane spoke through slurred words.

Falling silent for a minute with my smile fading, I waded through her admission. I could only assume she was referring to the fact my mother had shared a great deal of the cash Nick had given me with my sister. It explained how she could afford to move back to a city she claimed was too expensive for her. "It's not why I'm calling."

"Then, what's up?"

"I wanted to make sure you were okay. You just up and left."

She started to laugh. "You mean the way you up and left me and Dreya? Whatever." She sighed heavily through the phone, rattling my eardrums. "Me and Dreya got into it. I went to stay with my father in Augusta for a while. Met some guy who was headed to Miami and here I am."

"I'm in Boca Raton, and I wanted to come see you."

"W-what? Why?" Her shrill volume rang painfully in my ear.

"I know you can't pay me back." I was apologetic over things I hadn't done wrong, nor needed to apologize for. "That isn't why I want to see you. Give me your address."

"I'm house-sitting for someone right now. You can't stay here, but you can visit for a few hours. If you're not coming after me for the money, I'm at 4111 Collins Street. Apartment 2020."

"I'll be there tomorrow. See you then, okay?"

She ended the call.

"How'd your sister get beach front property?" Mason asked as he stood on the sidewalk with me.

"You've been to Miami?"

"Now you know that I have." He shoved his hands in the pockets of his slim fit jeans, making his shoulders broader than they already were. His lids halfway obstructed the view of his eyes, reflecting glimmering bits of amber from the direct light of the sun.

"She claimed she was house-sitting."

"Right," he drawled.

WE CHECKED INTO A hotel across the street from the barbecue restaurant. Having been on the road for several hours, I was ready to take a full shower and get into a warm bed. I assumed Mason was the one in charge of the money; Hayden had to convince Mason to get a double to save on cash. There was something about the way Mason scrutinized his brother. It held so much more beyond his simple concession.

My position and ability to argue didn't exist. Left alone in a hotel with my unreliable mind fell far from my ideal situation. It had been proven that being with Mason didn't keep me from my nightmares, but he somehow was able to stop the worst from happening. The false sense of safety fueled me with the belief he could erase them altogether by being the man in my fantasies.

Locking the door, I indulged in what I had ached to do for twelve hours; I took a long, soothing bath and changed into a pair of fleece pants and a T-shirt Mason had bought me at a gas station.

"You took forever." An exasperated Hayden sprawled on the bed closest to the bathroom.

"I had to…shave." I slipped into bed next to Mason, who rested on top of the duvet cover, and cuddled up into the crook of his arm, resting my head on his bicep. Placing my hand on the bumpy and firm ridges of his torso through his T-shirt while he rested on his back, I kissed his cheek and elicited his grin.

"Nothing sexual between you two." Hayden stopped midway to the bathroom to point at me. "I would rather not sleep to the sounds of groaning and screaming."

"Not promising you shit." Mason's deep voice vibrated through his chest and sent pleasurable tingles to my ear.

The television hummed in the background, set on a nature channel, and threatened to pull me into slumber.

Mason's fingers in my wet and curly hair were a soothing mechanism. If I stepped back from the actuality of the situation, we were two people enamored with one another who decided to take a road trip to strengthen our relationship. I inventoried my thoughts to uncover how it had happened. The crimes that occurred at the Babikov house had brought us closer. I had no place to run but to him.

He shifted, pushing me on my back. The weight of his lower body pressed me fully into the mattress. His face was only inches from mine. The soft breaths of his exhale kissed my face. The caresses from his soft ample lips tore my head in two. His tongue urged its way between my lips.

Abject dread overtook the need to succumb to him. I pressed my hand against his chest and shook my head. "Can I be honest? I don't remember the night we had sex. I really, really want to, but all I remember was a nightmare, and you were sleeping in that dream. I think…" I thought about the tea Garen made for me. It wasn't the brand I'd normally drink but it was still the same type: matcha. The tea was difficult to find in the small town. I was left to ponder how Hayden knew it was my drink of choice—unless Mason told him for a reason beyond my grasp. "I think someone drugged my tea that night. If there was no one else there, like you said, maybe it was Hayden? Maybe Garen?"

Mason leaned his upper half apart from me by the strength of his arms. Staring down at me with question and moderate shock, he condemned me with a discrediting shake of his head. "Why the fuck would they do something like that?"

"I don't know." Running my fingers along the dusting of hair on his jaw, I traced the definitive lines in his face. "I don't trust Hayden."

His eyes wandered away, as though he was searching for a ghost. The increasing tension in his sharp bone structure revealed he didn't find it. He turned back to me with eyes so cold, a frigid chill swarmed my body. "Did he give you a reason not to?"

"The way he blamed me at the house—"

Mason ejected from the mattress to stand opposite the foot of the bed.

Sitting upright, I tucked my legs underneath me, careful not to agitate my slow-healing burn or my sore sex. "I'm not trying to point him out as the culprit, but it all feels really weird to me. He was the one who drugged my tea—he had to have been. The things he's said to me while maybe knowing how I felt about you, and you about me? No." I bolted from the bed to stand before him, resisting the marks of pain from showing on my face. "I'm sorry. I don't trust him."

"Look…" He leaned back and away to rest his lower half against the dresser. Turning his hands inward, he gripped it with a pigment stealing grasp. "You've had a crazy few days and it probably fucked with your head."

"Do you believe him, then? Do you really think I did it? You think I killed Garen?" Incredulity marked my words, leaving it standing between statements and questions.

His long thick eyelashes receded over his eyes, leaving only peaks of his brandy hues visible. They warned me and demanded I listen. He pointed to the bed and then to me.

Defiant, I folded my arms across my chest and shook my head.

"I'm not saying another fucking word until you sit the hell down and listen. Read between the lines, Whitney."

An ache that hadn't been cured wanted to disregard him and have him speak with his body instead of his words. Tonight wasn't the night to push him. I took my time and complied.

"Don't ever fucking question me like that. I said I believed you, and I meant it. After what I saw, I had every damn reason to believe you did it and arrest you. Be grateful I put my trust in you."

My posture sank as I stared at the floor. "I am. You know I am. It's why I give you things I haven't given anyone else—have never given anyone else."

"Like?"

I gestured around my position on the bed. "Control of me."

He ran his hands through is hair, messing up the already messy style. "Let's not talk about this anymore." His cadence was quiet and earnest. "Get some sleep. I need to get out of here. I'll go find that tea you like. It calms you down, right?"

My back straightened so quickly, the dull ache transformed into a pulsating series of stitches. "Don't leave me alone with him."

He took one large step forward. The return of the menacing reservoir trickled into his eyes. "What did I say, Whitney?"

I had no recourse, and I felt trapped. Underneath the colorless abyss, he was an officer of the law. He knew how to wipe evidence away, and he knew how to make it reappear. Pissing him off was the last thing I wanted to do.

"Okay," I gave in.

He kissed my forehead and tangled his hands in my hair. "Don't think I didn't catch what you owned up to." Releasing me and turning on his heels, he grabbed his keys and headed out of the door.

Minutes later, Hayden popped out of the shower with only a towel around his waist. The tattoo of a monster with half a face, the other half a grotesque skull that took over his entire chest, iced me to my bones.

"Like it? Mason designed it." Hayden flexed in front of me, appearing proud of the design.

"I didn't know he was such a good artist." I receded to the head of the bed and hugged my knees to my chest.

"He's designed many tattoos for many people. Even as kids he was a talented artist. I thought maybe he'd be a tattoo artist. He would've been amazing at it."

I hadn't the slightest idea. I'd seen pretty much every part of him and never noticed any tattoos. "How did you know who he designed for when you two, I guess, weren't in each other's lives?"

"Doesn't mean I couldn't keep myself informed about what happened in his life. He's my brother, I'd never leave his side, even if I'm there without his knowledge. He wanted a different life and I let him have that, until I couldn't anymore." He flopped back on the bed with his arm propped behind his head.

Hayden had just been caught in a lie.

"He never could stick with anything for very long. He gets bored easily. With women, too."

"Why are you such an asshole?" I asked, snarling at him. "From what I've heard, you were given the same opportunities as Mason, maybe more. You had a chance at a football career and ruined it. I have every reason to believe it was you who needed Mason's help and not the other way around. Why does it seem like you don't like it when your brother is doing well...without you?"

"You might be right." A wolfish grin spread across his face, deepening his dimples. "Possible that you shouldn't believe a word I say. What if...neither Mason or me could be trusted? What if we're playing a game with you?"

"For what?"

"Entertainment."

"Why do you think you have to be this way to avoid getting hurt—or to deflect whatever it is you're upset with me about? You know I didn't do anything to Garen. Someone set it up to look that way."

"I think you're capable of many things, Whitney. Murder…is just a drop in the bucket."

My entire body tensed to the point of aching. It would be the second of many lies Hayden had admitted to. "Why did you come along, then?"

"Mason had his way of convincing me, and that's all I'll ever disclose to you."

The conversation would go nowhere. "Goodnight, Hayden." I snuggled under the covers and rolled over to face the opposite side of the room.

"This is going to drive me mad, Whitney."

"The fact that I'm not drooling over you, letting you have your way with me, because you're irresistible?" I asked. "That was sarcasm, by the way. I don't do it well. Thought I'd put it out there in case you didn't get it." The silence he threw at me, convinced me to turn around.

He managed to smile while he sucked his bottom lip. "Aren't you curious about us? What it would be like if we fucked? When we're done, I'll get back in my bed and we can pretend like it never happened. Or…Mason might surprise you and share you. Haven't you fantasized about it? Two men fucking your tight holes at once?"

"Don't speak to me that way," I snapped, shooting up in bed.

"Why? The show I put on in your house? You're aware it was for you, aren't you? Are you going to pretend you didn't like it?" He adjusted his legs and released the erection he had hid. It bowed the towel and began to throb.

The oxygen was sucked out of the room, leaving me gasping for air. My heart thumped dramatically, straining me of my normal abilities. I immediately flopped around and gave Hayden my back.

"Whit," Hayden cooed, "when you danced for me…and he put you on display, I could see it in your eyes. You were begging me to join in. Be patient, wishes sometimes come true."

My eyes brightened and I sat up in bed as though I were a windup toy primed to surprise.

186

"What? What?" He stood up searching the floor erratically.

"Did you... Did you perform in that sex tape with Marion and Blake to impress me?"

He rolled his eyes. "The world doesn't revolve around you."

"You admitted to fucking the waitress to catch my eye. Why is this so different? When was it recorded?"

"Does it matter?" He guiltily averted his eyes.

"I don't know whether I should be flattered or put off."

"I wouldn't be flattered if I was you. I told you, it's a game."

I immediately frowned, moving my attention elsewhere. "For you, and only for you—because it's about culling your ego: I know I'm not supposed to want Mason and what he offers. I'm supposed to want a man who makes love to me, buys me flowers, and treats me like a queen. It's boring. Colorless. I want a man who degrades me with a sick, twisted form of love. I want Mason.

"When I imagine him demeaning me physically, mentally, or verbally, it makes me feel stronger. It's like my body is teeming with a surge of power. It's erotic, transformative, and addictive.

"I know he's messed up...but so am I. He's real. I believe in him. I don't believe in you, and I don't believe you mean me well." I slanted my eyes at him and wore a frown so severe I could feel its weight on my face.

"You only further proved how deeply separated you are from your own mind," he replied, his confession thick with stillness. "It was a valiant shot and misdirection but you failed. I think you're the killer who disrupted Bebletown, but I can't act on my belief. Mason has completely lost his senses over you. I won't turn you in for his sake, but that doesn't say that I won't fuck you when the opportunity presents itself." He slipped in the bed and turned on the television. "You might want to know one more thing: Mason was responsible for a lot of Nick's tattoos." He turned up the television, ending the discussion.

I didn't sleep until Mason returned, and I never questioned him about how well he knew Nick. Denial fed my need to grasp the one thing serving as my calm center—Mason.

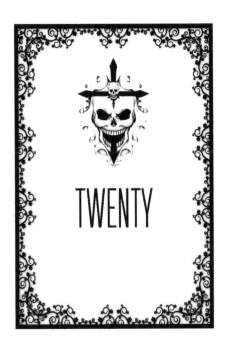

# TWENTY

MASON LEFT HIS CAR in a parking garage two blocks from my sister's condo. The busy street full of men and women dressed for the beach brushed past us in the opposition direction to head toward the restaurants or the shore. A man cast a look in my direction and triggered Mason's response; he put his arm around me and brought me close, keeping me at his side the remainder of the walk toward my sister's place.

Hayden's habit of muttering indiscernible things under his breath was never more recurrent.

Two residential towers faced the shore. A garden with a colorful array of flowers split the wide walkway. In the lobby, white porcelain floors padded my steps. The guard manning the station took our names and alerted my sister to her new arrivals.

The three of us took the elevator up to the twentieth floor.

The door was ajar when I approached the entrance to Sloane's condo. A white bikini top and sarong stood in a beautiful stark contrast to sun-kissed brown skin. A placid smile puffed her cheeks. Despite her tepid welcome, she appeared to have none of the stress she carried in her face while living with our mother.

Her cold smile warmed at the sight of the two men on either side of me. "Come inside." She waved me in.

Polished marble abounded the hallway. Custom boudoir portraits of Sloane lined the gold damask wallpapered walls.

I followed her down the long corridor to the living area. Mason and Hayden trailed me.

A breeze carrying the scent of the salty ocean blew in from the open sliding patio doors and swirled my T-shirt around my hips.

Sloane's glamorous appearance would've made Dreya proud; it made me acutely aware of how homely I looked in a T-shirt and sweats and my hair in desperate need of better products. It was silly to focus on the vapid when too many horrid thoughts and memories disfigured my landscape.

Without ceremony, I introduced Sloane to Mason and Hayden.

"Drink?" She sashayed to the fully stocked bar and glanced back at my companions.

"Driving," Mason gave her a simple answer, walking around the place with disinterest and finding a chair to plop his tired body into.

"Who owns this place?" I questioned her, eying the gorgeous view of the surreally green palm trees lining the drive along the beach, pale tan sands, and turquoise waters from the open glass doors, leading to her sizable terrace.

"A friend." She flipped her sunglasses on top of her head to reveal her dark brown eyes, complemented with bronze shadows and lined in heavy black kohl. She plucked up a box from a lower shelf at the bar and set it down on the glass top surface. Leaning forward, she squeezed her arms together to rummage through the box full of packets of green herb. The overt display of her cleavage didn't escape Hayden's notice.

She fiddled with the herb and sprinkled it over a small white, thin sheet of paper. "I hate rolling. Can I get some help?"

My mouth fell open to protest and signal her to the cop in her presence. A cop who easily protected me, going against his sworn duty, when all facts pointed to me being a murderer I never could have been.

I immediately closed my mouth.

"I can do that for you," Hayden offered and rounded the bar.

She looked him over with a smile and he exchanged a flirtatious one with her.

"Your sister is a definite ten." Hayden ogled my sister's body, and she lapped up the attention with greed.

Mason reached out for my hand while I stood by him, bringing me close to sit on his lap. "Don't let that fucker bother you."

"He doesn't," I confirmed.

The pads of his fingers dug into my waist as he pulled me closer. "He better not." His heated words brushed at my ear, reminding me underneath the endearing could be a remarkably formidable man.

"I was on my way down to the pool." Sloane mindlessly rubbed Hayden's shoulders as he busied himself with the task my sister set out for him. She picked up her phone, focusing on her screen. "It shouldn't be too busy at this time. Why don't you go in my room, Whit? I have a swimsuit in there with the tags still on it." She perused over my body with a deepening scowl. "And some clothes you should borrow."

I embraced the back of Mason's head and gave his enticing lips a short peck. "I'll be right back."

He reluctantly released me.

I grabbed my sister's hand along the way, dragging her with me. "We need to talk."

She stumbled in her high stilettos before finding her stride. I hurried down the hall and found the bedroom I assumed was hers. Sloane's favorite color was maroon and the room was loaded in the varying shades of the same color. I gently closed the door and spun around to face her. "Did you take the money I left with Dreya?"

Exhaling a dramatic one-minute breath, she threw her hands on her hips and rolled her eyes to the ceiling. "You said this wasn't about money."

"I said that I wouldn't ask you to return it." I flopped down on the edge of the bed. It was too much to hope for. I had no idea why I wanted it back. An offering to the revived dead to coax him into leaving me alone? I doubt Nick cared much about money, he was out for blood and there was no rhyme or reason to whom he would strike at next. "It's pointless now. If I called all the money you owe me due, you wouldn't be able to live in this condo."

"It's not mine. It's a friend's." She dismissed me with a flourish of her hand and turned her back on me to roam in her walk in closet. Taking different clothes with tags still attached from their hangers, she tossed them at me. "You look like shit. With all the pretty women willing to take your man with the bat of an eyelash, you might want to actually put some effort toward reminding him why he's with you and not them."

"He met me as I look right now."

She robotically turned her head toward me. "Since when did you stop giving a fuck? That client Dreya gave you fucked your head up, huh?"

I fingered the luxurious materials of the clothing on my lap. "What do you know about him—Nick?"

"Not much." She said with an easy dismissal. "Dreya claimed he would set you up for life—scratch that." She pointed in the air and scrunched up her nose. "It would set *us* up for life was what she said." She hooked her thumbs into the waistband of her sarong. "Funny how that money didn't satisfy her. She has a sick fucking addiction to screwing men up the ass with her heels for cash."

"Your friend," I effortlessly changed the subject as I grew concerned about her ending up in the same state my mother plucked her out of, "is he an athlete or a pimp?"

"Aren't you the smart one?" Swaying her hips with a theatrical movement, she sauntered toward the bed and sat next to me. Coconut-scented perfume wafted around my nose. "Athlete. Let me guess, you thought I'd go down that road again? I'm much smarter than you or Dreya give me credit for."

My mother and Sloane hardly got along. Their fights were numerous, and Sloane would often leave with no word and come back beaten, bruised, and strung out on a new drug. The last time she was found, my mother threw her into rehab. My mother wouldn't allow Sloane to work for her as I did, and I believed it was the source of her resentfulness. I had yet to understand why.

My mother made sure Sloane was cared for and never asked anything of her.

She leaned back on the bed, propping up on her elbows and chuckled. "Put on the black bathing suit I gave you. We'll talk at the pool while I entertain the men and get blitzed." She nudged me with one of her long legs. "You ever make an Eiffel tower with those two?"

I put the clothes down beside me and plucked myself off the bed. "This isn't a vacation for me. I just wanted to see you, and…I'm not even sure what I wanted anymore. I guess I wanted us to be on better terms by the time I left."

"I didn't know we had issues." Her posture became ramrod straight, the permanent grin she carried since resting her eyes on Mason and Hayden disappeared. "Come on, put on the fucking bathing suit and take a swim with me. I know you don't want to leave that fine man you were hanging on alone in this place. There are a lot of thirsty hoes and bored mistresses in this building looking for a fuck buddy. Take a shower and do something with yourself. Since I've been in this Miami sun, I think we're about the same shade now."

"I think I might be losing my mind, Sloane," I admitted more to myself than to her. "Nick—"

"Don't say any more," she snapped at me and turned in time to the door creaking open. Swiveling back around to face me, she plastered on a fake smile. "Well, if you're not here to enjoy Miami, what the hell did you come here for?"

Hayden cackled to himself and sidled into the room. "She never plans for anything." He mocked me while leaning back on the wall beside the door.

Sloane touched her nose and pointed to me. "It's crazy, isn't it? She can be so smart at some things, and so dumb at others."

*And leaving my money with my mother to allow you to take it was obviously one of my many dumb decisions.*

Hayden extended the joint he rolled to my sister. "She's not too terrible at all avenues of critical thinking."

"You're supposed to be on my side." She slipped the joint from his fingers and examined it. "I was going to share this with you, but I'm not sharing now."

"I barely know you. I can't smoke anyway. My brother wouldn't let me hear the end of it." Hayden shot a look in my direction. "And if I were you, I wouldn't touch it, either. He's in a mood."

"He was fine before. What did you say to him?" My accusatory eyes sliced through his smugness.

"Whit can't smoke anyway," my sister said with a laugh and apparently was unable to keep her hands away from Hayden. "She has enough delusions running around that crazy head of hers." She lit the paper with a lighter she retrieved from the tie wrap of her sarong.

I searched Hayden's exterior to determine if he caught Sloane's little slip up about my mind running away from me. I received no confirmation nor a denial.

After she took a toke, she stared at me. "Go. Get on a bathing suit. Then, we'll chat about whatever it is you really came here for. In the time you take to put some makeup on that face and look like you belong to someone, you'll remember."

As I looked at the bathing suit she spoke of, a black one-piece with strategic cut outs in the torso and a plunging halter style neckline, I questioned if I could pull it off. I plucked the suit up from the bed and headed into her bathroom.

This wasn't a leisure trip for me, but I had to play things Sloane's way to obtain one goal; to accomplish what I wanted for more years than I cared to count in only one day.


*"When you look better, you feel better."* It was one of my mother's many words of wisdom in sculpting me into the person she wanted me to be. For the day, I followed her advice. Holding on to what occurred in Bebletown while trying to spend time with my sister put a damper on the occasion. She wasn't faultless, neither was I. There had to be some way we could leave things on good terms. Pushing aside the dark cloud that permanently remained over my head was the only way it could've been accomplished.

Using some of her makeup, I spruced up my face, leaving it falling somewhere between the woman I used to be and the one who stared me down in the mirror at the present. I slipped into the bathing suit and styled my curls into a neater bun.

Once complete, I stepped out in the living room.

Hayden, bringing a tumbler a quarter full of amber liquid to his lips, choked during his swallow.

Searching the room for Mason, I found him out on the balcony, having a conversation with someone on his phone in quiet.

"Nice. Lose the sneakers, though." Sloane kicked off her flat gold sandals and pushed them over to me with her big toe. Hayden's persistent coughing lured the attention of the both of us.

"Hayden…really?" I gestured over what I was wearing. "Is it that bad?"

"He's hard," my sister stage-whispered to me.

"What did I say?" Hayden struggled through is urge to crouch to chide my sister. "Eyes away from the area. You've already been caught once."

"I get it," she taunted him. "You're a one-woman man."

"We aren't…together," I remarked with a modicum of distaste.

Sloane started laughing. "So clueless. Why Dreya loves you more, I don't know. I would've been the better protégé." She sashayed away, brushing against me as she did.

"Let's go," she barked over her shoulder.

Moving upright, Hayden directed his hands over his crotch in an awkward way. "I'll come down in a few moments. I need to change into something… else."

I held up my hand to Sloane to ask for a moment and walked out onto the balcony. Hushed words in what I assumed were Russian streamed from Mason's mouth. Catching a glimpse of me, he said, "Excuse me" to whomever he was speaking to.

"Are you coming down to the pool?"

"Not yet, baby. Something you needed?"

He barely looked at what I was wearing and seemed agitated and impatient for me to leave.

"Is everything…okay?" I shook my head at my inane question and switched gears. "I know that's silly to ask, but—"

In one long stride, he was in front of me and I was in his arms. His soft lips brushed against my mouth, a prelude to a different kiss that knocked the strength out of my legs. Filled with lust and desire, his lips intended to send me a message.

Message received.

He delayed in pulling his lips from mine. "Feel better now," he said, because it was unnecessary to pose it as a question. "I'll join later." His lids fell halfway down his eyes while he regarded the bathing suit. "Sooner, rather than later."

THE MIDDAY HOUR RENDERED the pool as nearly deserted. A handful of women were sunbathing in the lounge chairs in lieu of taking a dive in the cool water. The scent of chlorine commingled with the fragrance of the ocean and the greenery.

"I'm not going back, if that's why you're here." Sitting next to me underneath one of the umbrella lounges, Sloane liberally applied sunscreen to her legs. "I know you want me to come back because you feel all guilty about leaving Dreya alone."

"I haven't really left her alone." I faced her, slouching over my lap. "What did Dreya tell you about my last job?"

Her brown eyes drifted over the top of her sunglasses to quiz me.

"Nick didn't—I didn't do what I was paid to do. And now he's following me." I shifted in discomfort and perused the immediate area before continuing, "He's killing people."

She swung her legs around to face me and slammed her sunglasses on the top of her head. "And you came to me?"

"He hasn't hurt anyone close to me, and I don't think he'd hurt you. I don't know how to make it stop."

"Yes, you do." She rested back on the lounge draping her arm above her head and resting her other arm on the side. The sun kissed the diamond manicure on her toes, sending a prism of light to decorate the roof of her umbrella. "That's why you're here."

"It's not about returning the money," I reiterated.

"Seems like you blew through whatever you took anyhow."

With an inquisitive tilt of my head, I questioned how she came to the conclusion. I tried to avoid speculating the worst scenario, but I couldn't help myself. "Sloane, did you use mom's credentials and empty my bank account?"

"What if I did?"

Shocked, I was unable to formulate a perfect reply to her indifferent admission. "Why would you do something like that?"

"Because you were never going to use it, and for the record, Dreya only gave me a small amount of that money. When I asked for more, she wouldn't give it to me."

"I never took any of the money Nick gave me when I left. That money wasn't from Nick, and it was all I had. Why would you do something like that?"

"Seems you didn't need it. You've got two Mr. Moneybags paying your way." She shot a glance of accusation in my direction. "You'll be Dreya Jr. before you know it."

"It's not like that...at all."

"So they're not paying your way?"

"You took what money I had left, and I had to leave town after...Nick. Nick..."

"Stop talking." She held her hand toward my face. "You were always good at spinning your crazy delusions. How do I know you didn't really kill Nick and these are nothing more than made-up stories?"

Lost in a dark sea of nothing that had any reason, my mind was jumbled and infiltrated by an imploding bomb.

"I was right about him. I knew he had a hot body underneath those clothes." She gestured across the way toward Hayden. "He's trying to make you jealous."

Hayden had made himself comfortable with the two women who loitered by the pool.

"What he does, doesn't matter to me." The words slipped through my lips with a detached distance.

"It does. You like him. You're being greedy with those men. Take one and leave the other for someone else."

In acts of transparency, Hayden flirted with the two women, and I was almost sure numbers were exchanged.

I continued to visually search the area for Mason. *Where the hell was he?* "I don't know why I came here." My thoughts had finally returned to a more manageable place. "I hoped things between us would change. But they won't." They never would. She would perpetually play the victim and grasp beyond her reach to paint me as the worse one of the two of us.

"Don't try that act with me." In anger, she wrestled with her own body in an effort to find her footing. She stood over me, pointing her finger in my face. "Don't you dare try to feed me some bullshit like you're better than me. I know what Dreya used to schedule you to do for her clients who were fucked in the head. I know you enjoyed it. You're going to judge me because I'm working men the right way? Really? Dreya should've committed you to a home. You're off your rocker and a murderer."

I jolted up from the lounge, no longer seeking peace between us. "I came here to make sure you were okay, and not in a gutter with your face beat in and a bruised vagina. I came here to say goodbye because my life is in danger, and I didn't know if I'd see you again. Excuse me for ever caring for you. I'm not going to take your abuse because you're upset Dreya played favorites and you were never hers."

She arched her back, tilting her head away from me as though I dared to breathe offensive air in her direction. "As you can see, I'm perfectly fucking fine. I'm not like you. I can function in the real world. I'm smart enough to know how and when to manipulate to get my way. I'll be fine. It's your life, and the disaster it's going full force into becoming, that you should be worried about. I'd put money on the fact you will be dead or in an insane asylum before you know it."

I lurched forward, deleting the space between us.

My vision hazed over in red: *A rope tangles around her neck, syphoning the life from her eyes.* It was a want so severe and alive it manifested before my very eyes.

My hands surrounded her neck. Her thrashing body pinned underneath me. Her arms waved about, scratching at my skin as she gagged and struggled to breathe. Long, black strands whirled around my face, having fallen from my bun from the violence of my movements. My screams flooded her ears with accusations: "You've stolen money that doesn't belong to you, treated me like shit for years, and now that gives you the right to be a bitch to me? You had no right to take money you were too lazy to earn. You did nothing but sit around the house with your mercurial moods and took what didn't belong to you."

*Die you fucking bitch,* whispered a voice that wasn't my own. It was... Nick's.

A strong forearm wrapped itself around my waist and pulled me from my sister. When I wouldn't release her neck, I was painfully forced to by a pinching, biting grip on my wrists. "Not here." Mason's words were quiet but carried enough force and authority to dump a bucket of frigid water over my heated anger.

Cognizant of my surroundings, I noticed the women loitering by the pool were watching us; one had her phone in hand. The word police contorted her lips.

Hayden stood on the other side of the pool, wearing a smirk with such a sinister nature, it submersed me into desolation.

My sister struggled to stand and brushed her windswept dark long hair from her face. "Oh, you're so much better than me, huh? You're in-fucking-sane. I can't wait until your delusions get the best of you, and you do the world a favor and take one more psychopath out of this world. Kill yourself—"

"That's enough!" Mason released me to stand between her and me. "Get the fuck out of here."

She didn't need a second warning. Her face completely sank, making way for reaction unfamiliar to her—fear. She yanked up her belongings and with a twirl, left the poolside.

"We need to get the fuck out of here... Now!" Mason eyed the scene before us and clutched my elbow.

I stared at my trembling hands, remembering the strong pull inside me. I began to think my sister was right. What if Nick was a figment of my imagination? What if I had killed those people?

"I almost killed my sister. I almost..." I could barely breathe as I felt my throat close in. My skin burned and itched. My vision became cloudy.

"Breathe, baby. Fucking breathe." Arms enveloped me in comfort, but my body received it as though Mason had pushed me down underneath the dense water.

# TWENTY-ONE

"HAYDEN WANTS TO STOP off somewhere when he takes over driving." Mason informed me upon noticing I had roused awake.

The speed and sight of cars whizzing by in the opposing direction on the four-lane highway left me feeling slightly ill.

Mason clutched a bottle of water from the center console and extended it to me.

I bobbed my head in appreciation as I twisted off the cap and took a sip of the water. The sweatshirt covering my body was new. The uncomfortable bathing suit underneath it reminded me of what I longed to erase from memory.

"Tell me something, baby." His eyes darted from the road to me.

"I have no idea what to say."

Hayden lightly snored in the back. Beyond reason, he was able to rest comfortably in the back seat.

I had many things to say, but feared Hayden might've overheard my confessions and used it as an instrument to torment me. I wanted an escape from Hayden, the events in Bebletown, and Miami. I wanted an escape from myself.

"She was wrong about you," Mason urged, replacing the water bottle back in the center console and sliding his hand into mine.

I leaned against the passenger side door, wishing I wasn't afraid to fall asleep for more than an hour. "You don't know that." The hoarseness in my voice made my words quiet. "I wanted to kill her, Mason. I would've done it if you hadn't stopped me."

His silence was a reply that left me without any hope of receiving a raft to lead me out of the heavy current.

"What if my red dreams are my way with dealing with the things I've done?"

"Red…dreams?"

"I have these dreams of Nick hurting me…tormenting me. The things he does to me are so wrong, but I like them. I want them. I wanted them with you. But what if the dreams are something else? What if the dreams are my way of hiding all the wrong things I've done? What if Nick *is* dead, and I'm the one who murdered all those people? You're not safe around me."

Flipping the turn signal, he changed lanes and pulled over the side of the road. The inertial force from his abrupt stop threw my body forward. He removed his seatbelt and exited the car in a whirlwind.

He stood in front of the hood pacing while staring at oncoming traffic. A random driver honked his horn at him as though it was the correct thing to do. Without looking at me, Mason signaled at me to join him.

Checking Hayden in the back and discovering he slept through Mason's erratic driving, left me baffled. He had to have been faking it.

I slipped out of the car, slamming the door behind me.

Skeptical over what he could've wanted, I stuffed my hands in the pockets of the sweatshirt and took small steps toward him. In a rush, my head was in his hands and he forced me to stare up into the storm brewing in his eyes.

"You're not a killer, baby. You never were."

"You don't know that. Stop saying—"

He firmed his hold on my cheeks. His jaw turned hard, his eyes cold. "You...are...not...a...killer. Do you understand what I'm getting at?"

"It doesn't make sense. No, I don't understand."

"Then fuck understanding and believe what the hell I'm telling you."

I needed an explanation. I searched through his volatile light brown hues to find one but came up empty. I needed answers to make sense of what I assumed: his and Hayden's connection to Aksyna and the reason he remained in the house, yet never clued me into their affiliation with Nick. The phone call on the terrace of my sister's condo. Wrapping my mind around the idea he came to Bebletown to help a real estate investor didn't make sense. What of the people who elicited fear strongly, Penny left the party held at the Babikovs' home? What about what Marion witnessed in the basement that filled her with dread when she was no stranger to pain through sex?

Something...wasn't...right.

"If you know anything that will bring sanity to my insanity, please tell me, Mason. I'm losing it."

"Are we going to get going or what?" Hayden stretched as he stood merely a few feet away from us. "Give me the keys." He extended his arms and gesticulated with his hands. "It's my turn to drive."

Mason gave me a kiss laced with a whisper, "Trust me, baby."

FARMLAND STRETCHED BEYOND MY visual perception. The brick ranch standing in the middle of the expansive area was a decent size, surrounded by a wrought-iron fence. The entrance gate had fallen off the hinges, permitting easy access to the house. Up along the gravel drive that led to the house, thirty Yorkshire Terriers frolicked and barked at the new intruders from their fenced enclosures.

Mason was eerily silent during the ride to a town on the outskirts of Dallas. He didn't protest our destination. It was unnecessary for Mason to stress his discontent; the waves of anger couldn't be denied. I endured the brunt of the heat strongly as it boiled my skin with its temperature.

"She's a breeder." Hayden offered an explanation for the sight in front of us as he drove up to the house, pulling the car into park.

Mason and I equaled in our sluggish exit from the car.

Hayden's steps were alive with a new sense of purpose, rushing him to the front door. He pressed an index finger along a doorbell that didn't emit a sound. He rolled his shoulders, tempering his genial attitude and knocked on the door.

It could've been minutes or seconds. The air between the three of us had changed dramatically, rendering every second of silence as agony inducing.

The state of the porch forewarned of the condition inside the home. Trash and pet supplies littered the area.

A gray-haired woman dressed in a blue floral muumuu answered the door. Her red, high-powered, large square glasses obscured half her face and magnified her eyes in a cartoonish manner. The smell from inside the house wafted around the porch, tickling my nose with irritants.

"Boston? Is that you?" She squinted at Hayden, her cadence was thick with a Russian accent.

"No, Grandma. It's me, Hayden."

"Boston? Get in here." She reached up and grabbed Hayden's shoulders, drawing him toward her for a hug. "I haven't seen you in forever." She patted his back repeatedly and lovingly pushed him away to get a better look at him. My presence drew her stare. "Ashley?"

"This is Whitney Tyler." Hayden glanced to his brother. "And you remember Mason, don't you?"

"Well, come in." She ignored Mason's presence completely. "Come in. I was making supper."

Stepping inside the house was the equivalent of walking into a live episode of *Hoarders*. The smell assaulted my nose and stung my eyes with tears. I tried to be discreet, but there was no way around it. I used the sleeve of my sweatshirt to cover my nose.

Every piece of carpet that may have been white, was now stained brown—a few places were sunshine yellow. Piles of dog excrement dotted the carpet. Stacks of old papers and boxes abounded and impeded our ability to easily travel inside the home. Newspapers taped up across the windows with duct tape left the space dimly lit.

At least a dozen Yorkies encircled our steps, inquisitive or downright hostile. I tried to make friends with one of the quieter ones, but the two beside him or her snapped at me. As I examined the pup with patches of hair missing, it appeared to be swarming with flees.

The kitchen was the only semi-decent space. A baby gate kept the numerous amount of Yorkies away from the area.

The snag inside my heart was tugged by an unseen force. The conditions of the animals and the conditions of the woman, who obviously wasn't well, shattered my heart. I stared at the back of Hayden's head as if it would fill in the holes or provide me with some sort of reason for why she was left this way for such a long time. He was likely a puzzle I would never solve.

The back patio doors were open and I immediately went over to them. An RV sat in the middle of almond-colored grass with several flat tires.

Hayden and Mason's grandmother traveled toward the stove and prepared a plate of food for one. Hayden politely sat at the small kitchen table with metal legs and a yellow linoleum surface. They spoke to one another, but it was difficult to hear with the dogs beyond the baby gate whining and barking.

"How are you, Boston? I haven't seen you since you were itty bitty." An expression I couldn't quite label as a smile crossed her face.

"I'm Hayden, Grandma." Hayden took on a new face. He was mannerly; a doting grandson who loved his grandmother in a peculiar way.

I'd never witnessed Mason so stone-cold silent in his anger. I was sure at any moment he'd explode and disclose the reason behind the visit and the truth Hayden wouldn't reveal.

Her eyes twitched at Hayden's reminder and remained distant as though she didn't understand. "How long are you staying? Don't forget to visit your grandfather upstairs. I know he can't talk, but he'd be so glad to see you."

The break I anticipated in Mason went down with a slam of the back door. I moved to follow, but Hayden grabbed my hand and shook his head. "Let him cool off," he whispered underneath his grandmother's ramblings about Boston's wife Ashley—how they never had kids and how she disagreed with them marrying so young. "Our grandfather died when we were toddlers."

"I don't want to be here with you." I yanked my hand from his hold.

"How badly do you want your answers, Whitney?" His hazel eyes glittered with allusions to the unsaid.

His grandmother abruptly took my hands and glanced me over. "I don't remember your wife looking like this, Boston." She reached up and stroked my hair, tied in a bun. "You remind me of me when I was your age. Men would break their necks to have a look at me."

"Why don't you go get the pictures and show her?" Hayden suggested.

The grandmother muttered something in Russian and went in search of the pictures.

Hayden sported a grin reminiscent of a caricature. "We won't stay in the house tonight if that's your concern."

*That is the least of my concerns.*

"Did I tell you the story of how I met my husband, Boston? Your grandfather?" The grandmother returned, clutching a photo album. She set the book down on the kitchen table. She flipped through the pages, containing black and white photos, showing her slimmer figure and a headful of thick, black, curly hair. She paused on a picture of a man standing next to her. "He looks just like Boston, doesn't he? They say it skips generations."

A ghostly sensation ran through me and pinned me to the chair. I couldn't move. I couldn't speak. The sensors telling me to run were no longer prevalent. I fooled myself into believing it was a coincidence. Everyone in the world had a doppelgänger completely unrelated to them, didn't they?

The man standing next to her in the picture was the splitting image of Nick.

The heavy pressure of Hayden's smug gaze elicited uncontrollable reactions; my palms sweated, the sweatshirt felt too heavy and warm on my body.

"Wasn't he a stunner?" she asked no one in particular. "We all lose it when we get older."

"You're kidding. You haven't lost it at all," I told her, my dry throat adding a croak to my words. Smiling despite everything, I played along for my own safety.

"You're sweet, Ashley. I knew not to pay any mind to what *he* said about you being a hassle."

My dramatic swallow seemed to carry off the walls. "How long have you been breeding dogs?" I fought to maintain my smile and appear unflappable.

Hayden slid from his seat to stand in the doorway of my only way to the exit. I had no way out other than to use my brain to slink out of the situation.

She began to count in her native language and dipped into expressions I couldn't understand. There was an audible pause as sadness draped her face. "...but they just keep breeding." She looked down at the floor and dotted the tears from her eyes with the end of her dress, flashing the slip she had worn underneath. "Can't let go of my babies."

Something continuously attacked my bare legs, making me smack them. It was then I saw the floor had a few hop happy flees.

The grandmother wandered toward the refrigerator, mumbling something about kartoshka cake.

I glanced down at one of her dogs who had jumped over the baby gate. His back hunched as he struggled to relieve himself in the middle of the kitchen. Satisfied, it walked bowlegged over to Hayden's grandmother.

"Um...Grandma." I nodded to the mess. "Do you want me to clean it up for you?"

She looked wild-eyed at the mess. "No. No. Don't touch that. That's weapons of mass destruction. I'll have to label that or the government will label me a terrorist and put me in jail. Boston, find my paintbrush."

It was the most inappropriate moment to do so, but I couldn't hide my laughter. I couldn't make sense of myself other than to assume I'd entered a state of delirium. Hayden glared me down like he would hurt me if I didn't stop.

I excused myself and ventured outside. The second the door swung closed behind me, I was grabbed and pushed harshly against the brick exterior of the house.

Mason's wild and untamed eyes stared me down. "Now that you know the truth, do you want to run? Because if you do, I have to warn you, baby, you won't get far."

"I don't know what I know, and I'm not going to run."

He studied my trembling shoulders with a frown and glanced back at the house as Hayden joined us in the back yard.

"Since Mason isn't going to fill in the blanks for you," Hayden shoved his hands in his pants, sporting his newly ever present grin, "allow me."

"Don't you think you've done enough?" Mason's hold on me pinched to the point of making me whimper.

"This is revenge over Nick?" I asked. "You both lured me to Bebletown and made sure I'd stay?" I curved my neck and stood on my tiptoes to near Mason's face. "Why? To make me pay?"

Hayden rounded our position, his shoulders broad, his demeanor sure. "You surprised us, Whitney. We had no idea you were as fucked up as you turned out to be. We did give you a little shove to get you to this point— desperate and willing to access the money Nick wrongly gave you. You've taken too long to lead us to it. We want what Nick stole, leaving his brothers indebted to people we'd rather not be associated with."

The money? This was all over the money Nick gave me? "Ask Nick, he's still alive."

"I can't pretend I'm not a pissed off Hayden folded early," Mason spoke. "But this is where we are." Sighing in what I could've been fooled into believing was regret, Mason lowered his eyes. "Nick is dead. We have his ashes to prove it."

"No." I shook my head emphatically. "He's not dead."

"Think, baby. The red dreams you told me about? You were right about them. It was you who committed all those murders. What do you think would've happened if I didn't jump in and stop you from making your sister another victim? Face it. You're a killer, exactly like our brother Boston Babikov. You knew him as Nick Kent."

A coiling pinch in my stomach bent me forward. I slipped against Mason's body, weakened by the pain. "No," I mumbled. "I didn't. I didn't do it. I didn't kill those people. If Nick isn't alive, then…the both of you committed those murders."

"You're beyond the realm of psychosis," Hayden muttered with a shake of his head. "We're going to finish this road trip and do what we planned." Hayden nudged his brother's arm as he stood next to him. "Are you going to let me tell her the bulk of our story, or are you going to push my patience and keep looping her around? Let's end this."

"It can wait." Mason wouldn't take his eyes off me as they stripped me raw. "I need your fucking word that you will never run."

I had been lied to and had been lying to myself at such extremes nothing made sense anymore. "I'm not going to run," I promised the both of them.

Mason released me, and his gaze threw threats, forewarning of repercussions if I didn't keep my word.

It took some convincing, but the grandmother caved and respected Hayden's wishes to stay elsewhere. In the remote area, the nearest hotel was many miles from us. She reluctantly gave us the keys to the RV instead.

Mason and Hayden walked on either side of me as we headed for our place to sleep for the night.

"I appreciate you not bitching about the temporary living situation." Mason draped his arm over my shoulder and kissed my forehead as though none of what I stumbled upon had mattered.

"You're probably wondering why we'd leave our grandmother in these sorts of conditions," Hayden uttered. "She lost her mind when my father was executed in prison. We didn't know of her—because we were too young to remember her—until our brother Boston went missing several months ago. Mason and I discussed moving her somewhere else. The people in this town

208

remember what our father did to the teenagers he kidnapped, and they tormented her for years. They drove through that gate and had she not been armed—well, we won't discuss the what ifs." With a relaxed sigh, he opened the door to the trailer. He went in for one second and came right back out wrenching and coughing. "Something died in there...probably forty years ago. We can sleep in the car."

"No. Tonight, we'll sleep outside." Mason cast his eyes to the sky. The clear night gave a view of the stars unobstructed by the city lights. Any other time, I would've reveled in it. At this moment I was on hyper alert.

"I'll get the blankets from the car," Hayden volunteered.

"Baby." Mason darted out his arm to the ladder and bowed.

Leary in my movements, I climbed up the step ladder to the roof and sat as far away as I could from Mason. Clearly, he wouldn't allow me the space to think. He grabbed my legs and dragged me back to our previous position. Settling himself down, he cradled me in his arms as I sat between his open legs.

Hayden returned with the blankets. "Grandmother's gotten worse. We can't continue to leave her this way."

"I'll do something about it in the morning. I can't get a signal for shit here." Mason leaned in my ear and whispered, "Consider that a little warning in case you had any ideas about breaking your promise to me."

Like a woman possessed, I persistently scratched at the flee bites on my legs. Mason reached around to touch me, and I jerked up out of his hold with an abruptness that stole my balance.

With swift movements, Mason was up and caught me before I fell off the edge.

I quickly sat down, scooting away from him.

"Shit, is it that serious?" Mason asked with a soft laugh.

"You two are fucking crazy," I snarled as I hugged my knees.

They both looked at each other and exchanged varying grins.

"Glad you're not mad at me anymore," Hayden said, punching his brother on the shoulder.

"I am. So don't fucking push the line you already shat on." The lightness in Mason's face was gone for a cautionary message.

I fought against letting the facts affect me, but all I felt was that my death was near. What else did they want to do with me, other than torment me and kill me when they received the money they wanted?

"Hey." Mason softened at the sight of my tears and approached me. Subduing my struggle, he wrapped me in his embrace. "You have no reason to be upset. Trust me."

"A-are you going to kill me?"

"Shhh," Mason whispered against my lips. "Sleep. We've all had a shit day. We'll talk about it in the morning."

TANGLED IN MASON'S ARMS as he went fast asleep, I kept my eye on Hayden who never showed any signs of turning in for the night.

"I don't sleep much anymore." He stared up at the sky with a big supercilious grin. "I pretend to when I need to." He dropped his chin, coasting his eyes in my direction. "He's sleeping now. Would you like to hear the story?"

Whether I could withstand hearing the truth or not, a part of me wanted answers, and made me nod my head.

"Boston, Mason, and I have different mothers but the same father. Our mothers were our father's victims. We were all born in my father's basement. Our mothers were co-stars in my father's films, commissioned and sold to people too powerful to name. He got caught because he was sloppy with the death of Boston's mother. I think she was the only one he really loved. He saved her for last. We were taken in by the Babikovs when we were kids. Aksyna is my aunt. Garen is—was her son. He was a sick son-of-a bitch as a kid, and the town being the way it was, someone alerted the officials to our treatment. They split us up, but Boston wasn't agreeable. He ran away and returned to Aksyna to work for her, performing in the films that sparked your interest—and a lot more. The son commits the sins of the father. Ashley was Boston's *co-star*"—the inflection of the word co-star was clearly a mislabel for a woman who was a victim—"whom he married, and later murdered. It was her death that probably explained his need to end it all—to find you and have you kill him."

"I didn't kill him," I protested my innocence through gritted teeth. "I didn't kill anyone."

"Are you in denial because you don't want to take the blame for killing all those people in Bebletown? You have an addiction. You tried to overcome it and it got the best of you." He leaned forward, glancing from Mason to me. "Why do you do it, Whitney? Is it the power? Did killing Nick start a habit?"

I turned away from him, because I didn't want his skewed version of the truth. I wasn't the killer.

With a tilt of his head, he climbed down off the top of the RV to pace around the back yard.

Mason's eyes were open and he was staring at me. "Can you trust me?" he asked so low I wasn't sure I heard him correctly.

"How can I trust someone who lied to me, keeps lying to me, and wants to kill me?"

He pulled the blanket over my body while taking my hand. I felt the pressure and slight warmth. It was unsettling and made me feel annoying pricks. He ducked his head down, calling for my eye contact.

Pressing his weight fully on top of me, he slid his fingers down my arm, fingering the red mark of the cigarette burn on my hand. Moving toward my hips, he slipped his hand underneath me to finger the brand of his name through my jogging pants. "Do you remember what these are?"

I got lost in his eyes for a moment, forgetting things I shouldn't. I slipped my fingers into his hand, wanting to know none of it and slip deeper into the oblivion. Preparation and a lesson: the purpose of the marks he left on me. I blamed my muddled mind for lacking the wits to make sense of what he told me then, and tried to tell me now.

"Trust me," he insisted, kissing my forehead.

# TWENTY-TWO

I CAN HEAR HIS *mocking laughter all around me, but I'm unable to see beyond the red thick fog. I feel the pain he leaves me with between my thighs and the ache inside my throat. I can't remember how it happened—how he was able to fuck me again, but I know he's been at it for hours. His arousal fills all of my holes and leaks out of me.*

*There's no light to guide me in the sky. The stars are removed from the darkest of night. The dry and sharp grass serves as my bed.*

*Visions that double as memories slide across my view like strips of film…*

*The homeless man is too drunk to realize what I'm doing to him. I tie the belt wrapped around his neck to the faucet. He fights but he's too drunk to best me. I hold on to his body to bring him down, careful not to pull too hard and pull the showerhead from the wall.*

*The second homeless man is in a drug induced state. Strangling him is easy. He sleeps through the entire ordeal.*

*Kylie screams and begs for me to stop. She doesn't understand what she's done wrong. She doesn't understand why I hate her and want to hurt her. She lays before me, mutilated and tied to a bed in a location unknown. It's dark and dank there. The musky smell of rust-tainted water fills my senses. The water tank, no longer in use, sits in view of the only window in the place—a warehouse.*

*Flashes of fucking Mason into exhaustion fill my head. I wait until he's sound asleep and exit the room.*

*Blood pulsates from Garen's wounds. A sick smile of satisfaction spreads and tightens across my lips. In a daze, I walk out of the room and fall asleep on the floor of Mason's bedroom. The murder knife is held tightly to my chest; it comforts me.*

THE SUN BEAMED DOWN on my skin, and the erratic barking of the dogs woke me up. Inwardly, I remembered my dreams and they tore me apart, filling me with despair and guilt. My panties were saturated with moisture and clung to me, leaving me feeling filthy. A persisting sensation, similar to a hangover, slowed my movement.

I needed help—a way out of the madness and an exit door out of the tight confines of men whose intentions weren't easily deciphered. I peeked over from the roof of the RV, watching Hayden throw a few ratty footballs into the field. Mason was sleeping next to me.

I climbed down from the ladder, hugging myself from the cold.

"We really need to find you new clothes," Hayden said of my T-shirt.

I hadn't the slightest idea where my jogging pants had disappeared to. "It's the last thing on my list of priorities." The fatigue cracked and mangled my words.

"Found these in the attic when I tried to take a shower." He tossed the pigskin football into the air and caught it on the way down. "I fell asleep for two hours." He cut his eyes at me. "You fulfilled your promise not to run, but I wonder how long it will last." He threw the football, sending it flying low into the air. "My father wasn't the monster many painted him out to be. He was good to his sons, and the law took him away from us."

He quickly cleared his throat and changed his posture. "I remember him teaching me to throw footballs around the yard. He'd always say to me, 'Since I couldn't make it to the pros, you should.'

"I was doing well for four years. My stats were incredible. My future looked better than I could've ever imagined. I wanted to wait until I had a degree under my belt before I went up for the draft. It wasn't my sexuality that killed my future. It was the death of my brother.

"Mason is better at pretending not to feel and get things done no matter what. He did what he said he was going to do and became a cop. Nick…the Babikovs pimped him out every chance they had. He became tangled in their very secretive and private business offshore. Of the three of us, Nick's sickness was the most severe. My father's less savory traits were amplified when it came to Nick."

"You act like he was the victim," I muttered, "but from what Nick told me, he did those things of his free will. And his death? He begged me for it. He paid for—"

Hayden was before me, glaring me down with a silent threat. "And what have you been doing, Whitney? Playing the victim so hard your mind fucked you into thinking someone else held responsibility for the deaths you caused. Even now, you want to blame Nick for the things *you* have done."

Turning slightly from me, he threw his arm, sending the football soaring across the field. I caught sight of something affixed to the palm of his hand. He quickly gave me his back and flexed the tension out of his shoulders, denying my ability to figure out what I had seen. "We only want the money. Your sister's accounts were empty, and we couldn't get to Dreya without using you. The woman has a plethora of protection around her. Invisible, but there. She… doesn't have the money, either."

If that was true, what had she done with it? The idea that my mother had done away with the money concerned me. She never would've parted with it unless for a life-threatening reason. "And Blake? Did you stage a crime scene in my house to tip the cops off and make me bring her to Bebletown?"

"You killed Blake. The only thing I did was call the cops to bring you in."

"I didn't kill Blake, and I don't play the victim," I said quietly. "I don't trust what's in my head that tells me things I know aren't true, but I know I didn't kill those people."

"You haven't tasted near enough of what your punishment should be for taking our brother away from us," Hayden spat at me. "I hope someday you will. You're lucky Mason has a soft heart. I couldn't care less about the money, but with Garen dead, I don't exactly have a leg to stand on. Aksyna wants her money, or I'll be short another brother. You're going to lead us to it."

"Do you think that's why I'm going west? Do you think I hid it somewhere, and I'm taking you to it? I left it with Dreya. You're never going to get it back."

The barking dogs increased in volume; they sounded panicked.

He glanced over to the house. "Is it me or are the dogs a little more obnoxious that usual?" Swiveling around, he regarded the house for a few silent moments.

As though a signal gun had been fired, Hayden began running and pulled me along with him. I stumbled a few times, unable to keep up with his pace. He released me once we were inside the home and stumbled through the crowd of dogs and trash to reach the landing of the stairs.

In the upstairs hall, a pair of feet hung outside of a room. Keeping my distance from Hayden, I followed him to the door. Grandmother Babikov lay on the ground halfway between her bedroom and the hall. Her dogs stood around her, protecting her. It took Hayden quite a bit of maneuvering to get past them.

My steps were delayed as I watched Hayden frantically work to try to revive her. From around the bend of the doorframe, I viewed enough to know there wasn't a way; no one could've saved her. The blood had begun to coagulate as it pooled around her head in a peculiar pattern. Her brown eyes were now gray, and her mouth was frozen in a slightly ajar state. The cramped room was hard to get around. A short statue wasn't far from her head—a statue that belonged outside as a garden ornament and was sprinkled with dark red blood and chunks of an unknown substance. A man's belt was wrapped around her neck in a loose fashion.

"Hayden, she's gone."

216

He spun around to stare me down from his towering position. His red-streaked eyes and balled hands indicated he meant to end my suffering within seconds and that he somehow had blamed me.

A prickle at the back of my neck made me turn around. I was halted halfway through the motion when Mason enfolded me in his strong arms.

"Can't drag this out any more." Hayden shook with anger, the brunt of which he threw at me. "She killed her."

"Did you see her do it?" Mason maintained an eerie calm.

"I fell asleep for two hours," Hayden countered, "and I know in those two hours that bitch you're protecting did this to *our* grandmother."

"Do you have proof?" Mason pressed, spacing out the words and enunciated each vowel.

Hayden looked down at his lifeless grandmother and conceded with a shake of his head.

Mason tightened his hold on me. "We can't leave the dogs like this in their own shit and piss. We'll have to get rid of her body and leave an anonymous tip."

Hayden brushed past me, sending a curt glance in my direction.

I turned to face Mason, exchanging wordless communication.

The stone mask fell from Mason's face as he smiled down at me. Reaching me, he brushed a thumb across my bottom lip. "That woman was the only one he really cared about in this world. I'm not mad at you for doing this. You put her out of her misery."

If Hayden could love his grandmother as he said he did and abandon her until the state of her mind resembled her house, I held no hope toward either brother showing me mercy.

My silly heart and dull brain couldn't release Mason. If I was to die by his hand in a way that resembled my fantasies, I couldn't have thought of a better way to end the madness.

HOURS AFTER THE GRANDMOTHER had passed, I was handcuffed to the steering wheel of the car while they busied themselves with getting rid of their grandmother's body.

Hayden and Mason stood on either side of me as we remained hidden in a thicket, looking on as the authorities descended onto their grandmother's home.

The dirt driveway was littered with vehicles. If the men standing next to me didn't contribute to my nerves, the probability of the tragedies that occurred by my hand continuously pulled me underneath the sinking colorless sand.

A part of me just wanted it over. I'd been haunted long before they came into my life. Carrying the weight on my back had exhausted me to the point of depletion. I could no longer fight to win over my insanity and proclaim my innocence—psychosis had gained a foothold and threatened to win the battle by a landslide.

"What do you think will happen to her dogs?" The distance and disconnection in my voice was palpable.

"Don't know," Hayden said, his voice floating dreamily in the wind.

"What did you do to the kitten?" I asked, my voice barely audible.

"I gave her to Marion," Hayden replied, his tone deepening in the austere.

It was a simple answer that bothered me for reasons beyond comprehension.

# TWENTY-THREE

I MENTALLY CHECKED OUT the morning of Irina Babikov's funeral. It was a lonely affair with only three people in attendance and a fresh grave in the middle of nowhere.

A fraud stood between the two brothers, one visibly grieving while the other remained emotionless. A dress and shoes Mason had brought for me were my chosen attire for the solemn occasion. The previous night, Mason asked for a list of things I needed and traveled to the store while Hayden stood watch over me at a hotel thirty miles from Irina's home. He retrieved most of it. The razors I asked for were replaced by an electric shaver.

The view of newly disturbed ground, burying Irina in a deep grave, proved too much. Every second my eyes landed on her final resting place, I replayed the scene—reality or fake?—of choking Irina with a belt, failing, and instead pushing her into the statue to kill her.

Directly after the burial ceremony, we traveled on the road, heading west to nowhere.

MASON LEFT ONE HAND at the wheel and reached in his pocket to toss his phone onto my lap.

He loosened his tie and blew out a breath as though the air had turned into his cigarette. "Put your father's address into the nav."

I blinked in incredulity and clutched the phone to my chest, wondering how I could call my mother to tell her a goodbye I had long avoided.

"I don't know where he is," I claimed my innocence. "I've never met him. Don't make me find him. I swear, he doesn't have the money."

"Make me ask you again, Whitney." The bark bit into my defiance with a vicious bloodlust.

Solemnly, I did as he said, conducting a search for Pastor Jessie Tyler. I found the address of his church and through a reverse search, his home address.

Mason practiced skill in multitasking, keeping his eyes on the road while making sure I did exactly as he asked.

"You know what I don't get? The woman was the picture of fucking health," Hayden cut in, his voice soft and low. "You know the last conversation we had? I went back into the house to hit the head. She mistook me as someone else. She thought I was our father. She said I took her life away, that I never should've killed those girls. She said she took care of them and they would've never turned our father in or escaped had he allowed her to nurture them. We would've been the family she always wanted."

A forlorn sigh reverberated in the small space. "I was fucking tired of her—and the bathroom? The toilet had been clogged for weeks. I allowed it to affect me and I snapped. I blamed her for the life she led after our father... I made her cry. I could..." His voice broke. "I could hear her sobs outside the door. And I left. Left her that way instead of fixing what was broken. Is that how she'll always remember me? I know it will be the last memory I ever hold of my grandmother. I can never be okay with that."

From over my shoulder, I caught sight of him as he bit his quivering lip and cast a look of hatred in my direction. Draping his hand across his eyes, he receded into the seat. His heavy sobs filled the dead air, killing what was left of my desire to live.

Hayden slept through the remainder of the drive toward the Texas border. Mason ignored the southern route and kept north while avoiding the major highways, evading the border patrol stations down south altogether. Beautiful rocky scenery, hued in brick red, surrounded our travels. The little things became big things as I pondered my fate.

In a little town two hours from Santa Fe at three o' clock in the morning, Mason decided to stop at a hotel.

Hayden concluded he couldn't bunk with us any longer and made reservations for his own room.

"I have to call my father before we get there," I told Mason as he came out from his shower after me. "He doesn't know I'm—we're coming."

He handed me his phone. His stance indicated he hadn't planned on allowing me to have a private conversation. I dialed one number, but let it slip and called my mother, hoping Mason wouldn't see the slight of hand. As it rang, I turned down the speaker volume to prevent him from overhearing.

"Hello," the voice of my mother rang out from the other end.

"Hi, Dad." My voice trembled and the pain I pinned down to make it through the torture decided to unfurl.

The sound of her hard swallow was audible to my ears. Seconds passed of her saying nothing at all. "You're in trouble? Tell me where you are."

I couldn't speak; the emotion clouded my voice.

Mason crouched down in front of me and clutched my knee.

"I'm in Santa Fe on my way to see you—" I mewled as Mason's grip bit into my skin. I held up my finger and shook my head at him, proclaiming my innocence before he condemned me and took the phone away.

Following Mason's eyes, I spread my legs to call his attention away from my face.

He took the bait and allowed his attention to linger underneath my towel.

I turned down the phone's volume to a barely audible level

With a curled lip smile, Mason promised, "After you get off the phone."

"Henry is making arrangements as we speak. Tell me the name of your hotel, and I'll get you out of there. Bebletown has...we'll speak about it when I get to you. Stay the strong woman I know you are, and bide your time. Do whatever they want you to do until I can get there with help."

The negation of her calling the cops made me feel very uneasy. She painted herself as the one at fault for what happened to the money. There was no other reason I could discern for why she wouldn't involve the local authorities.

The tears streamed down my cheeks in the midst of my battle to swallow it down. I was trapped between a life sentence with Mason while battling with mania or death at Hayden's vengeful hand, offering eternal peace. I couldn't determine which one was the better option.

"It's nothing," I said to her, carrying on with the fake conversation. "I know this is odd timing, but I think it's time we met the entire family."

"We?" My mother questioned. "Who's with you? Is it the woman who's currently wanted for...many crimes I can't even name them all? Is it Aksyna?"

I dropped my chin to my chest to keep Mason from spotting my astonishment. He immediately snatched the phone from my hands and roughly spoke a "hello" into the phone. Puzzled, he stared at the *end call* on the screen. He called the number and put it on speaker. A busy signal resounded.

Inwardly, I sighed in relief at my mother's stroke of genius.

The second Mason touched me, I whimpered. "Now about the fuck you wanted…"

# TWENTY-FOUR

DARK SHADOWS FILLED A room unfamiliar to me; a hotel room I'd never visited. Half awake and unable to determine if my reality melded with a dream, I searched around for something familiar. The double beds were unoccupied and the silence kidnapped my strength, unleashing me into terror. The acid bubbling in my throat had a familiar taste—my matcha tea—tea I couldn't recall drinking before I turned in for the night. The last thoughts I was able to grasp, were of Mason's promise to fuck me.

A shadow swayed in front of the entrance door. The fog lifted, revealing the features of the man who had come for me...Nick.

He had returned to star in my private movie featuring my debauched fantasies—to punish me with pleasure wrapped in insanity and suffering. Tonight may be the night he granted my greatest wish and relieved me of my sickness for good.

Tonight may be the night I would die by his hand.

I wouldn't fight it; I wanted him to kill me.

Every long stride of his legs compacted the walls around me, squeezing the life from me.

Closing my eyes, I tried to gain control of my thoughts and erase the woman who pined for the sweet silence of death. I fought to take command of my nightmare by branding it with a context; it was a drug-induced hallucination, elicited from a drug Mason or Hayden slipped into the tea—I couldn't recall drinking—that swirled inside my abdomen. *I'm dreaming. I have to be dreaming.*

The room was shrouded in a tightening clear plastic overlay. The air was snuffed from my lungs. A plastic bag sank against my face the more I struggled to breathe. Tight and thick leather wound around my neck. I struggled to get free and was thrown down on the bed.

Nick stood over me in the aviator shades reflecting streams of red light. His jaw hardened and tensed, his hair hidden under his cop cap, casting a daunting shadow over his face. With a biting grip, he secured my arms, tying them to the rails of the bed with twine. He moved down my body, running his gloved hands down my legs and secured my ankles to the bed posts. "Did you think this was over, bitch?" His dimples appeared with the imprint of his sinister leer. "Your mind, your heart, your body, your nightmares, and your life belongs to me."

He squatted between my legs and slowly rose to stand above me. "I have a surprise for you." A modulated tone registering lower than possible shocked my spine with an icy chill. "I'm going to ruin your cunt tonight. You know what you deserve. You're a very sick whore who needs her medicine."

Shallow breaths were barely manageable. The lack of oxygen in the plastic bag surrounding my head gave me very little leeway. Dots of white spotted my vision, threatening to obstruct what Nick had presented to me when he unzipped his pants and reached down to pull out his cock. It was sheathed in a black leather sleeve. Petite barbed wire wrapped around the leather.

He dropped down to his knees and ran his fingers up my naked waist to painfully clutch my breasts. The other hand worked to rip my panties away from my crotch.

*This is it,* was whispered in my thoughts by the woman taking residence in my void. She filled me, relishing in the precursor of pain and death. She wanted to drown in the poisonous and lightless pool. She consumed what was left of me, possessing me. A sense of calm washed over me, holding to one thought: it would finally end. This would be the moment I'd finally die.

Nick flexed his hips, pushing inside me. The ripping spikes made me painfully aware. Shredded nerves cried out as tinges of torment shot straight from my core. The excruciating pain throbbed inside my sensors and weakened me. Tears stung my eyes. Panting breaths stole what little air was left in the bag.

"Please." A portion of the bag entered into my mouth only to be blown away by a weak breath.

He slowly slid out. His soft actions pained me deeper, to a place intangible and untouchable.

"Punish me…" I whispered as my eyes drew heavy. "Kill me."

SCREAMS OF PERIL AWAKENED me. Reality slammed into my sights, taunting me with a descent into lunacy. A cold body was positioned underneath me in a frigid room. I blinked through the fog and felt the tightness of leather wound around my hands.

Motionless, his eyes glassy and devoid of vitality, Hayden lay naked beneath me. A belt was wrapped around his neck, the other end wrapped around my hand. I released it immediately but it was of no use. He was covered in thick blood from the neck down, his skin and any wounds he might've carried were indiscernible. His chest ceased to rise and fall. I unwound my hand from the belt to check for his pulse.

"Whitney?" Mason called out on the other end of the room from my nightmare—or reality.

My hand halted its intended purpose as it began to tremble.

When I didn't answer, Mason's knocks become room-quaking thumps. "Open the fucking door." The deadbolt rattled with each brutal force. Sunlight emerged through the curtains, announcing the arrival of dawn.

Shocks of pain between my thighs made me whimper. The fullness made me guiltily aware that Hayden was inside of me. The soreness between my legs stung and ached at my attempt to move. Riddled with anguish, my body revolted and began to shiver. I wanted him out of me. I wanted away from the scene. I screamed through the stitches of pain and rolled my hips back. His cock fell out of me, sheathed in a soft barbed silicone sleeve with a pliable pin, extending possibly one and a half inches, that I assumed was meant to pierce my cervix for maximum pain. Trickles of blood coated his lap, sliding out of my sex.

I slithered off him, falling to the floor, immobilized from the shredding of my pain sensors.

"I-I can't." I shouted to the other side. Sitting or standing, nothing was possible. Dried blood tightened around my thighs, peeling and flaking when I touched it. The copious amounts of blood coating Hayden and the bed hadn't come from me, and I was unable to find his wound from a brief sweep of my eyes.

Fighting from the rifling edge of inner and outer torment, I limped to the door, while wrapping a sheet around my naked body. I collapsed the second the lock slipped from my hands.

The door burst open. Mason rushed in, taking in the scene. The sight of his brother created tension in every feature of Mason's face. He quickly ushered into the room, closing and locking the door. In reverie, he perused over my body and plodded over to the bed. He reached out to touch his brother, but thought better of it and withdrew his hand.

"I didn't do this. Please. You have to believe me." My body trembled violently, revolting from the twinges riddling my sex.

Exhaling brusquely, he sank on the blood-stained bed and put his head in his hands. "What the fuck am I supposed to do here?"

"I swear, I didn't do this. I didn't—"

He held out his hand and shook his head at me. "Don't speak. Don't say another fucking word."

"No. No. I won't be quiet. You...you've been drugging me. The tea—you've been drugging my tea. You set me up."

He marched toward me and placed a hand over my mouth to shut me up. He pressed down hard and pushed my body back toward the opposite bed. "The next time I tell you to shut up, do it. I'm so fucking close to ending your pitiful fucking life, Whitney. You're very goddamn lucky I..." He sank his teeth into his lip and stole the rosy pigment from his ample lips. "Don't speak again." He released me with a slam and turned his back on me. Fishing in his back pocket, he picked up his phone and began to speak to someone in Russian.

The only word I caught was the name Aksyna.

I lost it. Nothing that bled from my mouth had sense or purpose. My pain was ignored for my screams. I had begun to think I was no longer a passenger to my own mind, I was in the backseat of a vehicle filled with unstable demons.

I was in Mason's arms and too riddled with the aches pervading throughout my body to protest. The concern in his eyes shocked me to the core. "What are you talking about, baby? Where do you think we are?"

What had I said? I swallowed it back and blinked blankly at him. The hotel wasn't the same, but I couldn't fathom how I would've completely slept through another round of travel. "We're in...New Mexico."

His brandy colored eyes widened a tad. A look of confusion was cast to his brother. "We're twenty miles from the Alabama border. You fell asleep after you saw your sister in Miami and we had that talk, remember?" He continued without waiting for an answer, "I didn't want to wake you so I brought you here. You were so tired, you slept through it all. I put you to bed..." He glanced over his shoulder at his dead brother and winced. "Alone."

"No. NO." I balled my fists and weakly pounded his chest, shaking my head with a frenetic motion. "We went to Texas to see your grandmother."

"Baby, look at me." He held my head. "I don't have a living grandmother. The one I knew of died years ago."

"That's not true." I tried to push him away. My feeble state was no match for his strong embrace. "You're fucking with my head. You and him..." The mere act of lifting my arm to point to Hayden was too much.

Worry creased Mason's brows and tensed his forehead. "Answer this, why would I protect you the way I have? Why wouldn't I have killed you when I had plenty fucking chances?"

I had no answer for him. "But the red dreams…"

"You had another?"

I nodded, and then shook my head. "Yes. No. It was different."

Closing his eyes, he exhaled a wavering stream of air and cursed. He chanted his pet name for me repeatedly—each instance of the word held with more concern than the last. He released me to fall to the floor and moved over to the end table between the two double beds and plucked up a brochure to hand to me.

The address was as he said. We were in a hotel in Brent, Florida.

"I…need the date."

He slipped his cell phone from the back pocket of his jeans and held it up to me. It was the day after I visited my sister in Miami.

"B-but I called my…" I nearly slipped up and said mother. "Called my father."

"Call him again." He offered his phone to me.

I dialed my old disconnected number and put it on speaker. Thankfully, no one had taken the number. I received a recorded message: "This number is no longer in service."

The phone call mattered little in the situation. My head was stuck between three worlds—reality, dreams, and the spaces in between—and couldn't remove itself from one.

"I…don't know what's happening to me."

The look Mason shot toward me painted me in the dusky brush of insanity and possibly hatred. The last brush stroke mangled my insides and stole what little was left of my vitality.

"Why Hayden?" A curt glance at the horrid scene of his brother on the bed haunted me. "I was on your fucking side. I ignored what I thought you did—knew you did—and this is how you show me you're grateful? You took Nick, and I could almost forgive it because…he was fucked in the head, and I wouldn't put a shit of anything past him to ask for it to end. Call me fucked up, but what's burning me up the most is the fact you fucked Hayden. Why would you do this to me after all I've done for you?"

Unable to look at him, I set my gaze to the peeling wallpaper.

"Fuck it. We have to get out of here. I'll figure out what to do with you later." Swift in his movements, blowing the air around him, he headed to the bathroom. The water ran in the tub, filling the room with much-needed noise.

Returning to me, he scooped me in his arms and settled me in the tub. With his pants rolled up to his knees, he sat on the edge with his feet dipped in the water and took the now soaked bed sheet away from me. He grabbed a rag and began to bathe me, washing my face first. In silence, words beyond any comprehension were exchanged between us.

In spite of his dissent, I could feel it manifest deep under my skin. Mason's feelings for me were still there. The stretch of concrete, paving the road to nowhere, had run out of miles. But for now, Mason would be the eye in my storm.

# TWENTY-FIVE

THE HOTEL IN FLAGSTAFF, Arizona was beautiful in its rustic architecture. It resembled an expansive lodge with a two-story lobby, the dim lighting and the heavy use of dark natural wood in the floors, ceilings, and support beams.

We resembled walking catatonics as we ascended the elevator to our room. Mason hadn't spoken to me since the death of his brother. I hadn't garnered the courage to ask questions about the state we left Hayden in. I further contained my questions when a new car, instead of Mason's sports car, was parked on the curb, waiting to take us west.

If Aksyna ruled over Nick and controlled his actions, there was nothing beyond the woman's capabilities in extending her help to Mason.

Mason dropped our bags in the middle of our suite. It could've been any hotel room in any city; it didn't mesh with the scenery in the lobby or with the exterior. The walls were cream-colored and the oak queen bed clogged most of the space.

The scenery of the red mountainous terrain surrounding the hotel pulled my consideration the strongest. My minutes of living to take another breath were numbered. Any stitch of beauty presented to me was quietly reveled and revered.

Mason's phone buzzed with an alert. Whatever he saw, induced contradictory and abrupt changes in his light brown eyes. "You need to know something." Shaking his head, he dropped his phone on the bed. He shoved his hands into his hair and brought them down to brush across his eyes and scratch against the dusting of dark blond hair decorating his jaw. "In Miami, I found out where the money was. I never told my brother I knew. Can't tell you why right now. It was in an account—your account—under the name Sumi Tyler."

I swayed my head from left to right in a drunken manner. "I don't remember opening the account."

"Well, you did, and every cent of the money Nick stole from Aksyna is in the account."

"It must've been Dreya. I gave her the money."

"If I fucking believed you," he muttered underneath his breath.

"I'm going to take a bath." My voice was stuck in the same dream as my thoughts.

I slipped out of my clothes, leaving them on the ground as I dragged my naked and sore body into the bathroom and locked the door. I filled the bath with water, caring little for the temperature. Once the bath was full, I slid into the water, keeping my head just above the full level in the garden tub.

*"You will die tonight."* Nick's voice rang in my head. A pressure against my cheek fooled me into believing he was there, touching me.

"I know," I whispered into the poorly lit bathroom. The time had come to silence my chaotic mind, warring against reality and fiction while losing a battle between deciphering which to live in.

I sank down in the tepid water. My hair swarmed around me, forming pretty dark swirls in the water. Releasing the last tiny morsel of strength, I allowed my body to sink fully under the water and closed my eyes.

Copious amounts of water spurted from my mouth and onto the soft white terry cloth towel beneath me. Bubbles of water were caught in my throat coaxing me to gag up the liquid clogging my lungs. Hands gripped my shoulders, steadying me. Tearing at the towel, I tried to cover up my naked body as I screamed for death.

"Whitney, open your fucking eyes." Mason's brusque voice slammed into my head and halted my struggle.

The disappointment over waking to my living hell dissolved my will to go on. "Why didn't you let me die?"

Mason held my head, bringing me closer to him, clasping his forehead against mine. "You're not as crazy as you think. I'm the fucking crazy one."

Water coated my eyelashes clumping them together. I blinked it away to look into the strong pull of his warm brown eyes. "You might be right. Because you keep saving me."

He snaked his arms around me and grabbed my ass, evoking a wince. He directed me to straddle his lap. He sat on the floor with his knees bent and his legs tucked underneath him. Picking strands of my coiled hair away from my face, he held me strongly with one arm, enforcing our eye contact with the sheer intensity of his gaze.

The door opened behind us. A cold tingle touched my spine, eliciting a shudder from my body. I struggled to look behind me, and when I did, I caught a glimpse of Hayden.

"Oh my god," I mumbled, my lips quivering. Tears showered my cheeks.

Hayden's tan tone had taken on a pale hue. His eyes were sunken in and marred by dark shadows. Glimpses of his tattoo were underneath the collar of his open shirt. He tore at his clothes and stood inches behind me. Mason struggled to make me turn back around, but I fought to watch my personal hell unfold.

"He's here…" I whispered.

Mason painfully clutched my head, forcing me to face him. "He who?"

The only person reflected in Mason's eyes was me. I flooded the brandy hues, leaving nothing else in their reflection. His eyes pulled me from straddling the lie by forcing me to sink into the truth. It was too late for me; my mind was gone.

"Hayden." Fright took a hold of my voice and made it squeak.

"Baby?" Mason shook his head in scorn. "Hayden is"—his voice cracked —"dead."

Hayden pressed against me, his cock throbbed against my back through his pants. His tepid breath brushed against the fine hairs along my neck. "Stand up."

Obeying Hayden, I rose to my feet off Mason's lap, but Mason wouldn't let me go. "Who do you see, Whit? Say it out loud."

"Hay—"

"No." Mason's booming voice reverberated off the walls and shuddered down my spine. "Answer me again: Who do you see?"

I tried to ignore Hayden as he touched me, probing me in sore places I didn't want him to explore. "You," I forced forth. "I only see you."

Mason picked me up and threw me on the bed. The men were side by side for a moment, but neither noticed the other. Mason crawled on the bed, blocking my view of Hayden. He removed his belt from the loops of his jeans. "Who do you belong to? Whose name is branded on your ass?"

"You."

"My name, baby. Say it."

"Mason." I chanted his name repeatedly until my voice gave way. I continued to repeat it through his actions to secure the belt around my neck and loop it through the metal. With one yank, he tightened it.

"Louder. Say my name until he goes away."

I did as instructed, closing my eyes through the sound of Mason's clothing being removed. When I opened my eyes again, Mason was the only person in the room.

"What are you doing?" I perused over Mason's naked and perfect body, quivering from pain and the lasting effects rattling my nerves.

"I think it's time you stopped fucking around and gave me details about your nightmares and your fantasies."

"Why?"

The well usually hidden in his eyes by a shallow shield had revealed itself to me. It was never more deep and dark than it was in that moment. "If I have to enter your nightmares, make them your fantasies come true, and kill your demons for you, I'll do that."

"But what about—"

"Who do you see and who owns you?" he pressed again, tightening the grip he held on his belt.

"You."

Swallowing hard, I disclosed to him all my fantasies, daymares, and nightmares, leaving out no sordid detail.

Inscrutable in his response, he listened to my retelling of the things that haunted me.

He brushed his fingers across my lips, opening them, and swayed his lips inside my open mouth. "Are you ready?" he mumbled against my parted lips. He rested on one elbow and squeezed a hand down between our mashed together bodies to find my sex. His fingers slid between the sore, swollen lips. "You feel ready." Finding a sopping place, he used the wetness coating his fingers to lift the hood hiding my clit and gently pinched it between his fingers. His grip rocked up and down coaxing my clit to swell between his grip.

"Mmm." The soothing sensation seduced my impulses out of hiding and intertwined with the excruciating pain.

Heavy with pleasure and desire, his lids rendered his eyes barely slits. "Whitney." The cooing of my name was a gentle urge, giving me permission to let go and to feel what Mason dug out of me.

Underneath him, I vibrated, torn between persisting aches and a pulse of ardent pleasure.

I released my hold on everything I tried to hide away. "Mason," I gasped, shuddering with the thrill of pleasure overcoming my aches. The feeling softly staked its claim, leaving me at a place just underneath a plateau. My eyelids fluttered open to rest on Mason's face.

I placed my palms on his bare shoulders, pulling him closer. I moved my lips to speak but he covered my mouth and shook his head vehemently.

He shifted, reaching down to grab himself and guide it inside me.

The lacerations inside me opened immediately, sending me into a debilitated state underneath him. I sucked my breath as the tears of pain tickled the corners of my eyes.

"You're my bitch, and will take everything I give you. I don't give a shit if you cry. I'm going to tear up your pussy and your ass." He pressed his mouth down on mine and moved faster, pushing the full extent inside of me, ripping my mending core back open again.

"Don't move. Don't do anything." He undulated with increasingly violent movements. "Take this and show me how much it hurts you."

The full stretch made me shiver. Tears spilled from the corners of my eyes and trickled down my hairline. A soft sob resounded.

"That's it, you crazy fucking whore. Cry like the weak bitch you are." His hips slammed into mine. The skin to skin contact slapped with violence, echoing into the room.

My body's reactions were his source of power. He quickly grabbed my legs up and pushed them down until my legs were spread widely and my knees were mashed against my breasts. He probed deeper; I was stuck underneath him unable to do much more than to give him what he wanted. The tearing sensation garnered a hold of my body and claimed me, leaving me pining for more.

I wanted him to wreck me completely and make me want to live through the punishment instead of wishing it would be the end of me.

The friction and the fullness elicited an electric surge through my nerve endings. He rode me harder. The headboard knocked against the wall with an offbeat rhythm. His panting and grunting over my whimpers and moans flowed in a chaotic symphony over the squeaking springs of the mattress. He fucked me like he intended to break me in half, and it tore me apart in a dirty and exquisite way.

I threw my head back against the pillow, arching my spine. Mason crashed into me, breaking me into pieces, and let the tingling rush swallow me whole. I whimpered and convulsed as it swept through me.

He pulled out of me without ceremony and tossed me over on my stomach. I clung to the sheets, bracing for what I knew would come next: The sound of him hocking up a spit. The slimy sensation of his saliva glided down my ass.

With a shove and a series of tears, he was inside my neglected entry. He slammed into me hard, ripping me apart.

"You like being fucked in the ass because you're a dirty fucking whore." He reached around and grabbed my face, turning my head to my right side. With the back of his hand, he slapped my cheek hard enough to make it throb.

He rocked in a hard, violent sway, fully withdrawing and plunging deeply inside to remind me he wielded my pain. Snaking his hand around my neck, he wrapped the end of the belt around his hand. The leather strained around my neck, sucking the air from my lungs.

A violent need empowered the thrust of his hips, pushing him deeper inside me.

I revolted, involuntarily scratching at the sheets. The swelling in my eyes began to throb. He pulled harder, the tension of the belt distorted the color from his hands.

As he thrust into me, he leaned down sinking his teeth into the skin on the nape of my neck until he elicited a burn. Warm liquid drizzled from my open skin and wrapped around my neck.

The belt tightened further around my neck as my body rocked with his brutal pace.

I expected him to let go.

He didn't.

Blotches of black assaulted my vision. My lungs were filled with prickly sensations, unable to work properly. He leaned forward, increasing the tension of the belt as I thrashed in response to his unrelentingly harsh thrusts.

"Always mine," he reminded me in a low, guttural voice, straining through his exertion to obliterate me. "Always will be no matter what fucked-up things you do to me. Here. The afterlife. My fucking name is imprinted on your goddamn soul. My whore. My bitch. My slut. All for me. I love you, baby. Sleep. I'll see you on the other side."

Black botches widened and thickened into a fog. My limbs were loaded with ten ton bricks. Nothing would move. The world around me was snuffed out in a haze of dense dark. My lungs recoiled in pain, dying in deprivation of the thing they needed most to thrive. They were stolen from their purpose.

*This is dying.*

*This is silence.*

# TWENTY-SIX

MASON

THE LEATHER FUCKED UP my hand, cutting into my skin. I didn't let go until her body stopped shaking and her chest stopped moving. I ran a hand down the skin on back, so fucking soft and perfect—my beautiful doll. Her warmth disappeared under my touch. Gone.

Her face and naked body were relentless in keeping my attention. I kept staring at her, wanting to touch her, kiss her, and fuck her again.

She was mine for fucking eternity. Always would be, and no one—not even the afterworld—would stand in the way of that.

I kissed her back and pumped my cock inside her bleeding ass two more times until my balls tensed up and I exploded inside her. I fell on top of her, breathing hard and fast. No time to enjoy the moment, I shot out of bed and picked up my phone to send a text:

**I know you're still here. Come back. She's dead.**

I picked up my clothes from the floor, shoving them on and walked over to the air conditioning unit, putting it on full blast. It took him ten minutes.

Hayden charged into the room obviously in such a fucking rush he forgot to remove his makeup properly. "I thought we'd fuck her together. What happened there?" He tried to approach the bed, but I put a stop to it, holding out my hand and told him to fuck off without a word. No one would ever get to touch her but me. Unconscious. Dead. Alive. No one other than me would ever touch her again.

"That wasn't a plan you cleared with me." I hated the way he looked at her. I hated the way he always fucking looked at her. I untucked the comforter and pulled it over her body, covering her from head to toe.

"Cut me a break, Mason," he complained, "Besides being drenched in pigs' blood for more hours than I care to count, I've been on a plane for an hour too long."

I jerked my head toward the door and shoved him on his way. We walked down the hall and took the elevator down to the lobby. I made him wait by the door and did an about face to check in with the desk attendant and make sure she followed my directions down to the goddamn letter.

Grabbing my brother on the way out, we left the hotel.

"WHAT ARE YOU GOING to do with her body? Did you call Aksyna and tell her she wasn't getting another girl?" Always the yappy young puppy who didn't know when to shut up, my brother shot a stream of questions at me as I drove away from the hotel. The last thing I wanted to do was talk.

"I made a deal with Aksyna," I said to Hayden. "Whitney's body is mine. Death doesn't make my claim on her disappear."

"That's a beyond me type of sick, Mason."

It was like a psychopathic killer telling a sociopathic killer he wasn't on his level—asinine. I kept quiet and pulled onto the highway, heading toward the desert. No civilization meant no witnesses for the very last thing I would ever do for Aksyna Babikov.

"Question." Hayden tapped his chin like something was bothering him. "I understand I took you by surprise, but I didn't care for how you edged me out of the picture. I thought you wanted to break her mind completely and release her to Aksyna. Now I know that isn't the case, but why kill her? From the belt, and what I saw coming from her ass... I'm going to guess you decided to have a little fun? How are we going to cover up her death as a suicide with your marks all over her?"

"No one is ever going to find a body, what the hell does it matter?" I wrapped my fingers around the wheel tightly. It could've doubled as his neck. "I can't believe you're questioning me about this. I got the money. The bitch who killed our brother is dead. Our debt is paid."

"You should bury her, Mason."

"You...of all people?"

He raised his right hand, revealing the bandage I caught on his palm the night he staged his death that he still hadn't removed. I had no idea where it fit in until Whitney told me about her dreams.

His eyes snapped on me. "What the fuck do you mean?"

"You tell me." *Take the bait, you deceitful fuck.*

"This is about what she talked about on the road? The things she saw when she was under the influence of the tea we dosed?" He blew out a spat of air and slouched his seat. "Whitney lost her mind in thinking Nick was alive. Why am I explaining this to you? She killed our brother and stole money that never belonged to him. We got it back. You decided to kill her. End of everything, correct?"

"She told me about the hallucinations. She called them red dreams and told me everything that happened in them. Was it you fucking her all those times?"

He was in the hot seat, and it showed. "I had to make sure the tea and the cameras were working correctly, so I slipped into her house a while back—before you and she were whatever you think you were. When she called me Nick, I saw an opportunity. It was about us and our goal, and I continued to do it.

"It doesn't matter if I fucked her more than you have. It definitely doesn't matter that I fucked her on the floor shortly after you had her while you were sleeping the night Garen died and again in his bed while he was bleeding out. It doesn't matter that I fucked her for hours on the ground by the RV while you were, again, sleeping. None of it matters because she's dead and we've finally paid off a debt that never belonged to us. We can move on and be the brothers we never were. This drew us closer. Can move on and be who we are supposed to be? Brothers who look out for one another?"

He took the bait and admitted to more than I thought he would. I pulled onto a side road, taking us off the highway and deeper into the desert. "We're supposed to be real with each other about this. One goes off plan and it could fuck up everything. Whitney was only supposed to hallucinate and let her mind fuck her with guilt. The stunt you pulled in Brent wasn't a part of the plan. Fucking her *definitely* wasn't a part of the plan." I tapped the steering wheel, lost in a thought. "The homeless guys at the hotel? The sex tapes? You're lucky I caught the movie you sent her before one of my fellow officers got to it. Do you know what would've happened if they did?"

"I wasn't expecting Whitney to develop a conscience. But we would've been safe either way. She thought it was Nick on the tape, and I'm not sure how you knew it was me. I was wearing a mask and temporary tattoos. The drug did its job, like I knew it would—because I tested its effects firsthand. What does it matter if I went off plan? I knew what I was doing, exactly as you've gone off our plan and were able to reach the same goal."

"Blake. Kylie. Garen. Our grandmother. That all part of your plan, too?"

"They deserved to die," he bellowed. "I had to raise the stakes a little. Your plan wouldn't have been enough. A woman like Whitney needed more than the blood of Nick on her hands." He sighed and folded his arms, pouting. "What's the problem? Why are you upset with me? You're the one who killed her."

242

"I have a problem with why you did it."

He shoved at the air. "It was entertainment for me, nothing more. My only regret is I wasn't able to fuck her one last time. She was...really sweet." Hazel eyes tried and failed to poke holes in my armor. "How was it?"

"How was what?"

"Killing her."

"What do you want to know? Did I fuck her first and come after she died? Did she struggle? What the fuck is it you want to know?" I pulled off on the side of the road, slamming on the brakes to jerk his body forward and back. "It's been a long fucking road to get here. Lay off. I'm not going to jump around like a little girl who was asked to prom." I turned my back on him and got out of the car.

I spent my life running away from my two brothers who were everything my father aspired to be. I tried to live in my new life and forget about the family of criminals, criminally insane, and downright sick in the head. Being a cop was the only way I could apologize to the world for the damage my family had done to innocents. The mother I barely remembered drove me to be a better person.

She was fifteen when she was stolen, raped, and kept inside my father's basement. She was sixteen when she had me. He killed her before she turned twenty-one. I remembered pieces I tried to forget of living with my father. One thing I remembered really well...living with the Babikovs when my father went to prison.

My brothers never knew I was the one who called child services and had us separated and sent to foster care. The way forward wasn't the way back. If I had stayed in that town, I would've been made into a worse version of my father—a clone of my brothers. I had a chance to be someone different from the crazy family who reared me.

In different ways, Nick and Hayden held me back. I thought being able to escape the psychotic gene would've kept me safe. I didn't factor in one detail; my brothers would never let me go.

Nick had his issues and got caught up with my aunt and her illegal businesses. She sucked him into a world that fed his demons a buffet. But his demons weren't satisfied and took over control. For some reason, Nick thought it'd be a good idea to steal from the woman who made him her bitch and use the money to have someone else end his life. His idea put Whitney on the Babikovs' radar.

Aksyna had deep connections. Too many connections. She sent her son, Garen, to bribe my brother Hayden into finding the money. When Hayden told him to fuck off, the video of him fucking his teammate made the rounds at school, added with the news of Nick's death by way of autopsy picture. Instead of being resilient and staying strong, Hayden folded and begged me to help him fix the mess.

I came back into town to make peace and wound up a prisoner in Aksyna's house in Bebletown. They used my brother against me, making me have feelings I didn't think I had for him. They used my brother to replace Nick. They profited off his growing sickness by having him act in their fucking movies for rich elitist who wanted to direct their fucked up fantasy. And when that wasn't enough, Garen'd threaten to put my brother into a coma.

I was glad Hayden killed the bastard. For me, my brother murdering a man that would've sent a ripple of vengeance to steal one more person from our family was worth the risk. But it made a debt come due sooner than expected.

I never planned to give Whitney to the Babikovs. I loved her too fucking much to do that to her. I'd rather she died in her fantasy with me playing the role of her monster, sending her to the hell in style, than to break her mind and have Aksyna go forward with her plan to take her, and send her to a sick fuck to do whatever he wanted with her.

Hayden became a setback to my strategy.

The scene I walked in on, with him playing dead once we doubled back to Florida, wasn't how things were supposed to go. He diverted from the scheme, and he's lucky Whitney didn't really kill him. He's lucky she didn't have an evil bone in her body. I may have had my doubts before, but I knew it now; she would never kill anyone.

Nick never should've used me as his contact to clean up after he did what he paid her to do; I would always be the black sheep in the family. I followed Whitney to the hotel, and I watched her from the hidden camera. When she didn't have the strength to kill him and left in a hurry with the money, I slipped into the room and finished the job. Nick's directions were the opposite; I was supposed to kill her if she failed and let Nick find another woman to fulfill his request.

I would always be Whitney's anti-hero. I had one last time to do right by her and become the villain.

"Is it her? Are you upset over killing her?" Hayden walked alongside me, never asking questions about where we were going.

I held up the duffel bag, he probably thought was the cash to clear our debt.

"I have someone more your speed," he kept talking. "I trained Marion for you. In fact, she's waiting for us in a safe location. After we're done, we can visit her for a little time to play."

"You think we're free now that we have the money?" I turned my head to glare him down from over my shoulder. "I can't blame Aksyna for feeding your monster, you did that all on your own. I had hope for you—that you wouldn't turn into Nick. I was very fucking wrong. How many people have you killed to get us here? And Garen? Whatever I felt about that fucker, his death is going to come down on your head."

"Two million dollars." He propped out his hands and made a rectangle with his fingers. "I needed to state that to remind you of the bigger picture."

I did an about face and dropped the bag full of clothes—not money—on the ground. "I always had my eye on the bigger picture. It never included you."

The rude-awakening sank his entire face. "What do you mean?"

"Why did you really kill them? Was it about you giving up on fighting the demons our father cursed us with, or was it a tribute to Whitney? Did you think you'd catch her eye and she'd fall for you? What? What the fuck was the plan?"

His forehead frowned and he tried to deny it. "I didn't feel anything for her." A nervous smile spread across his lips. "Where's this going?"

"You did it for her, didn't you? You thought you'd drug her, treat her body like it was an all-you-could fuck buffet, and eventually win the girl in the end, didn't you? You were pissed she chose me, so you took it out on her when you were fucking her behind my back."

"Where are you going with this?"

"Did you think I'd put up with you since you turned into our father for the rest of our lives? Did you think we'd ride off into the sunset and live happily ever after? Aksyna already has the money. The problem is, she wants payback for Garen." I lurched forward with my hands behind my back. "The debt? It will be paid back. And then, I can begin my life without you or Nick standing in the way of my view of the goddamn sun."

"Even as a cop you couldn't take a life," he rasped. "You want me to think you suddenly have the balls because you killed her? I'm your brother. The only person you have left in this world who loves you. You need me."

I grabbed him by the back of the neck and pulled him in close. "I *loved* you. You had a chance to be better than our father, and you fucked it up. After all the things you've done? The things I know you'll do, it's time to let you go." My training in law enforcement pulled me through and made sure I was able to best my brother before he could fend me off.

My arm crushed his throat in a choke hold as he struggled. I said goodbye to what held me back for years. "You are the final payment. Go to fucking hell, and when you're there, make sure you tell Nick I sent you. You two will have a lot to chat about, because I'm the one who sent him there." As I could feel him fight to breathe, I wanted to send him down to the fiery beyond with one thought on his mind. "Whitney isn't dead. I never killed her. After you die, and I bury you in this fucking desert, I'm going to be with her. You lost." I shoved my hand on his jaw and gripped his shoulder, with one strategic and brutal move, I broke his neck.

THE END

IT WAS AS THOUGH I had walked out of a tunnel that imprisoned me for twenty-seven years. The horizon was within my reach, showing me a beautiful scene I'd been deprived of for too long. A light and airy feeling filled me with hope. For the first time in a very long time, I was sweetly lulled out of a beautiful dream.

Well-rested, my lids easily slid open to reveal the scene of the lush hotel room. Fluffy white linens stained with his scent make me smile. On a pillow next to me is a note:

**Will be back later. Wait for me.**

An aspirin was placed next to the note. Feeling the strain in my neck and the throb of soreness between my legs, I debated dulling the pain, but I forewent the idea altogether. Torment by Mason's hand was something I wanted to have stay with me for a while.

The demons whispering disparaging words, intending to unglue me from mental acuity weren't gone, but for now, they were silent. It would be a constant battle, but the cleansing sensation, removing the dirtiness from my hands cleared the way for renewed strength and resilience.

A soft knock on the door echoed into the bedroom. I slipped into one of Mason's T-shirts set on top of his open duffel bag, acutely aware of the pain in every part of my body. Without looking at the peephole, I swung the door open to greet him. "Did you forget your—" My sore throat made my voice raspy and the volume was stolen in response to the woman who stared me down. "Dreya?"

"We need to have a discussion." She slid her sunglasses up on top of her head and wrestled something from her large shoulder bag.

It was my preferred box of tea. As I clutched it in my hands and checked the expiration date, I knew she'd taken it from my home. "Why do you have this?"

"It's laced with a drug. I had no way of testing it, but when I received an ominous message last night from whom I assumed to be Hayden Pierce, the man currently wanted for murdering countless people, some of which were in Bebletown, I was more than skeptical. Then, I drank a cup of tea using that powder." She waved her hands in a dismissive manner. "Don't ever say I've never put myself on the line for you. The things I saw under that drug were worse than any coke or acid I tripped on when I was still an adult film star. I could've sworn they were real, and if you had taken them, I can't begin to guess what you might've seen. You need to let me in."

I slid back from the door, allowing her entry.

She waltzed around the hotel, checking for what I could only guess was a recording device. Shivering and closing her leather jacket, she shut down the air conditioning unit. She turned to me, her face stone serious. "It's time I told you what I knew: the Babikovs had their hand in everything. I had a few interactions with Aksyna when I was performing in movies in L.A. Rumors swirled around that they did some shadier—seedier shit. She asked me to star in a few torture porn films, but I declined. No one can prove it, it's just a myth in the industry; offshore, they film movies without the makeup and CG for the highest bidder. That last part I didn't find out until after your friend tried to charm the pants off me. I have a detector for bullshit, and my alarms were quite loud with him."

She paused to take a breath and sat on the bed. "Did you hear about the serial killer in Texas? He kidnapped girls barely into puberty and kept them in the basement? It was said the place was supposed to be a stopover before they were sent overseas to do the Babikovs' movies. Some of them became pregnant, and I don't believe it was a fluke. That deranged man wanted to keep those girls. None of the women survived. Well, Hayden and Mason called that certifiably deranged man their father.

"The evil running through that family is genetic, because now that Bebletown has state police involved, evidence was found, bodies were exhumed, and a case has been brought against Hayden Pierce. That's not all. The basement of the Babikovs' house? Evidence of people being kept down there and possibly killed were found. They found Kylie's blood and several other unnamed victims in the basement. One of them was a waitress you probably worked with in that god-awful fattening restaurant."

"Marion?" I asked, my mind reeling from what she had revealed. What I was fooled into believing to be a hallucination, was proved otherwise.

"Yes, that's it." My mother wagged her finger at me.

"Can I…see your phone?"

Puzzled, she extended her phone to me.

The date on her phone was four days later than the date it was supposed to have been.

"They were so lucky they found her in time. She said Garen kidnapped her and was going to send her off to god knows where. She also said some awful things about Hayden and what he forced her to do."

My nails had been bitten down to the skin. Blood began to appear, reminding me I was close to descending off the edge again. "I-is she okay?"

"She will be." She arched her neck and squinted at me. "What's wrong with your voice?"

I fixed my hair to further hide my neck from the purple marks left by the belt. "Coming down with something," I told her quickly.

"Anyway, I was concerned when you were sent to jail. I had to think fast, and I thought that family was fucking with mine. I opened an account under the name Sumi Tyler and put what I had left of the money from your deal with Nick into the account. I was able to match what I spent thanks to a man who will soon be taking care of you.

"When I arrived in Bebletown, I contacted the Babikovs and made arrangements to settle the debt. I had no idea Nick had stolen the money he gave you from them. I thought it was the end of it, but then you disappeared."

Everything I was told by Mason as being a lie was the truth. And the truths were all lies. I couldn't make sense of why he would do any of the things he had unless he wanted me to kill myself in an effort to escape my mind...but then he saved me.

"You have to come home with me," my mother pleaded.

"That would be the normal thing to do," I stated underneath a heavy breath. It would've been, but I had no inclination to leave. My feet had dug into the space beside Mason. There were things I knew all along and it pulled me to Mason. I endured through the worst because I knew the outcome would be worth the scars. Mason had become more than just the recipient of my lust. He was the ultimate at wielding my deterioration.

"I..." I ticked my neck and slid my hand between my thighs. The exquisite pain made me smile. "I love him. I...love Mason."

My mother jerked upright with her face scrunched in horror. "W-what?"

"It wouldn't make sense to you even if I tried to explain it. But I'm happy here. He took me on a ride to nowhere, and along the way, I found me. I found me again." My smile broadened.

"Whitney...this..." Unable to continue, she brought a trembling hand to her forehead. "What can I say to make you leave?"

"Nothing." I shook my head at her, genial in spite of the look of horror she presented to me. "But you can leave."

"Excuse me?"

250

"Don't you see it? The reason I'm here? You did this. You set me up with Nick while you knew about his connections. You did it because you chose money over me—like you always do. And then, you tried to sell me off to another man to replenish what wasn't yours from the start." I touched my sore neck, struggling to make my words audible through the rawness of my throat. "Mason chose me over his brother. He chose me over his family. He chose me when no one ever does. And you question why I would leave him? He's my fucked up dreams made reality."

She shook her head in awe. "If you want a master, Whitney, I can arrange it for you. It makes me sick to my stomach at the thought of you being someone else's submissive, but it can be arranged. Because this?" She circled a finger around the room. "There's nothing sane about this."

"I don't want a master. I wanted a mother, but instead I got you."

At the cusp of her sucking in a sharp breath, I staggered to the door and opened it for her to leave.

"I'm going." She broadened her shoulders, maintaining her signature emotionless expression. "I would rather not be here when the man you claim to love returns. You have my number, and I hope to fucking hell you come to your senses, Whitney."

THE DOOR LATCHED, ALERTING me to Mason's arrival. My legs were perpendicular to the floor and made quick strides toward him. I wrapped my arms around him, giving him a kiss, urging his lips to open with my tongue.

It immediately disarmed him, and whatever weighted his expression before lifted away. I combed my fingers down the back of his head and bit into his lip. He slammed the door behind him closed.

With a groan, his hands moved down my back to touch the brand. Cupping my ass, he gave it a tight squeeze until I whimpered. Lifting my thighs, he forced my legs to tangle around his body and took me down to the bed.

"What's this about?" A tame grin crossed his beautiful face.

I slid my hands down his chest and unfastened his belt. Sliding it off him, I placed it around my neck as though it was a necklace without an end. "I want to fuck you. Hard."

His eyes smiled in unison with his lips.

Wrapping myself around him, I rolled, changing our position to have him underneath me. Working kisses down his body, I unzipped his jeans and slid them off his legs, revealing one of my many favored portions.

I snaked my hand into his boxer briefs to wrestle his cock from the pouch. Before he could say a word, I wrapped my lips around him, swirling my tongue around the tip.

"Ah, fuck yeah, baby," he urged me on with a sensual cadence.

I slid my mouth down as far as it could go, getting him wet with my saliva and hard enough to ride.

I sat astride him. The belt still ominously hung around my neck. He made a point to show me he noticed but remained silent about it.

I swallowed him inside my sore sex, slowly working my core down the length of him and bounced hard and fast. It was more than he could stand, and he fell under a spell beneath me.

The tears inside me opened again. As I looked down, my blood coated his thickness. The sensation otherworldly, I shivered at the erotic purging of my senses. His eyes closed tightly shut. A groan emanated from deep inside his throat.

I quickly slipped the belt from around my neck and wrapped it around his. The undulations of my hips never wavered. I slipped the leather into the metal fastener and pulled. The jerking action called Mason to open his eyes.

I waited for a protest, but there was none. I pulled until his face transformed into a different hue. In his struggle to breathe, I felt numb. The sensation I once derived from the act was palpably missing.

"Why aren't you fighting me back?" I panted through the exertion and rode him harder. "Don't you know what I've done? I've killed people. I could kill you."

"You're not a killer, baby," he wheezed. "You never were."

"No matter how much you and your brother twisted my mind," I paused to express my pleasure, "I do know one thing. Nick isn't alive like I thought he was. He's dead because I *did* kill him." I rocked harder, waiting for him to open the door and show me that there would be no more lies between us. That this would be a new start, and we would be a two headed monster destined to live as one.

"You never killed him, baby. I did."

The belt immediately loosened in my hands and I halted all movement. "Why? How?"

"You thought you were alone with Nick in the hotel? You weren't. He called me to make sure you did what you were supposed to do. He tracked me down and brought the worst shit into my life." He grabbed my hips, forcing me to slowly grind against him. "I sent Hayden on a one-way trip to hell for what he did to you. The red dreams? It was him doing those things to you. Not Nick. Not your own fucking head."

I couldn't move anymore, no matter how much his hands dug into my hips.

That bastard…that bastard took what didn't belong to him.

I swayed my hips to push Mason out of me.

He grasped my hips and slammed me down hard on his erection. "No," he pressed with a guttural, low register and sat up to hold me closer to his form. "He won't ruin this." Sliding his hands up my body he found my jaw and swiped my tears away. "Tell me, who do you see?"

"You," I said though quivering lips. "I only see you."

"And I am all you will ever see." He kissed my lips gently.

I swallowed it back, blinking away the moisture. "W-why tell me the truth now, when you lied before and made me believe I was crazy?"

He leaned back on his elbows, swallowing hard. "It *was* the plan….it changed."

"What changed?"

He wouldn't engage in eye contact with me. No matter how much I rocked with him inside me to elicit a reaction or grabbed his chin with my eyes boring into his, he denied me what I needed.

He jerked up and rolled me over on my back. Grabbing my bottom firmly, he dug his fingertips into the brand on my sensitive flesh. "I was supposed to believe you were a cold hearted bitch who killed my brother to steal his money. I had to believe it to make Hayden believe it—to make people more dangerous than Nick believe it, until Hayden dug his own fucking ditch." He dropped his eyes from me. "I never in a million fucking years expected him to do the things he did, and I *never* expected him to take advantage of you in that way. I planned and set things in motion before you even knew I existed, and I had to see them to the end." His eyes flickered erratically under half closed eyelids. "I'm not going to tell you more until you face the facts."

"What fact?"

He clasped the side of my head. The piece that should've slapped him, hit him, screamed at him didn't exist. In losing him, I would've lost what was left of me. I couldn't kill him even if it meant he'd kill me.

"Did you see how I didn't struggle?" He glanced down at the belt around his neck. "If you wanted to kill me, I'd let you do it. I'd rather die by you than to live without you." A sullen and subtle grin contorted his soft lips. "You know what it is. You've done it so many times. You've looked at other people and couldn't see yourself in them. You couldn't connect with them because there's this thick wall between you and them. When I look at you, Whitney, I finally see my reflection. You think I'd ever let anyone destroy something like that? Not revenge for Nick. Not for Hayden. Not for anyone in this world. No one will take that away from us.

"If you want to make me think the idea of you being fucked over didn't get you off, I'm not going to buy it. You wanted me to destroy you. You got exactly what you begged me for, baby."

Mason had taken my secret fantasies, the world I lived through in my staged movies, and made it reality. He was my dream and my living nightmare. I asked for him subconsciously, and he was gifted to me.

The lines between reality and fiction were no longer bleeding. The crimson liquid had run dry and the line had disintegrated into a dark blend of pain and debasement.

Sanity didn't exist in this world—our world—because it was always a version of fiction toted as reality.

"I think you turned my fantasies around and made them more depraved. Even though you and your brother nearly ruined me, I enjoyed it. What does that say about me and what you did to me? I should be ashamed." I immediately pulled the belt from around his neck, releasing the strangled hold I had on myself. "But I'm not." I rested my forehead against his and sighed, "I love you, but I don't forgive you for lying to me."

"I have the rest of our lives to make it up to you. Don't think I won't use every fucking second I have to make you forgive me."

"What are we going to do, Mason? About us? What are we going to do with each other?"

With a broad smile, he held my head and whispered, "Be who we really are."

A sudden shot of euphoria coursed through my veins, leaving my skin tingling with a sensual high. "This? This is falling. This is what it's like to die."

# END CREDITS

V, D & J, thank you for being my foundation.

Mavens of Mischief, I can never accurately express how grateful I am to each and every one of you. Your amazing support of me keeps me motivated. I'm so lucky to have each and every one of you to help me through the craziness.

K. Swiss, you are truly one of the kindest and most genuine people I "know". You've helped me at my lowest of points, and someday I will pay you back for all that you've done.

Silla, thank you for always making time for me, and having such incredible things to say about my writing. I appreciate you.

Jamie "The Hammer" Buchanan, I'm so glad you bulldozed into my life to keep me together. Where would I be without you? Rocking myself to sleep in a corner while starving, that's where.

Jettie Woodruff, as is my tradition, thank you! I'll never forget how you supported me early on. You have a huge heart and I'll constantly root for you. May all your dreams continue to come true.

My beta-readers, Annmarie, Felicia, Tara and Jamie, your feedback made this book stronger. Thank you for taking time out to critique and chat about this book (and thank you for hitting me over the head with the truth when I wanted to scrap certain scenes).

To the bloggers who are always there with their undying support:

# Opaque Mirrors

Rachel from Bound By Books, Ebbie from Author Groupies, Di Covey from Twisted Sisters', Diana from Bookaholic Confessions, Tanya from Tasty Wordgasms, Catherine from The Cat's Meow Book Stop, Aliana from Fallen for Books, Karen from Kazza's Book Blog and Reviews, Agnese from Agnese Share Book, and so many more. I know it can be a tough and often times unappreciative job. Your dedication, support, and encouragement are very much appreciated.

Mavens at the "Corner", I'm so happy to be able to communicate with all of you. Your camaraderie is refreshing and something I often look forward to.

A special thank you to the team of advanced readers who read and review my work time and time again.

To all the authors who share my posts, review my work, and are always so kind to me, thank you so much.

Readers, thank you for the messages, recommending my books to others, taking the time to leave reviews, and your constant support. I am forever grateful.

If I've forgotten anyone, please forgive the oversight of my mind and not my heart.

**other titles  from Courtney Lane**

Delusive

## THE BREAKING INSANITY SERIES

The Sordid Promise (Breaking Insanity #1)
The Starkest Truth (Breaking Insanity #2)
The Darkest Descension (Breaking Insanity #3)


## Punk Shock Love Society(The StrangeHer love Trilogy)

Punk (book 1)
Shock (book 2)
Love Society (book 3)


## Wicked Trinity series

The Sect (book 1)
The Rebirth of Sin (Book 2)

coming soon in the series
Seducing Virtue (book 3)
Cult of wrath (Book 4)

Courtney Lane has been creating her own little world since she was very young.

While many of her works touch several different genres, she has an archetype when it comes to the female protagonists in her stories — they have to have certain brand of strength, be deeply flawed, and harbor layered personalities. In her books you will find themes that reflect the darker side of life with a tremendous amount of depth and complexity. She also has an affinity for characters that aren't necessarily the girl or boy next door, or the people you'd encounter in everyday life. In other words, she prefers to explore characters who aren't easy to fall in love with.

Currently, Courtney can be found either working on her next book, playing the latest role-playing game on her X-Box (preferably a game by BioWare), or spending time with her family.

@AuthorLane

https://www.facebook.com/CourtneyLaneAuthor

http://www.facebook.com/AuthorCourtneyLane

Reader Group: https://www.facebook.com/groups/359454797555300/

Street Team: https://www.facebook.com/ groups/1507321302831545/

authorcourtneylane@gmail.com

Made in the USA
Middletown, DE
16 July 2022

69540523R00149